WALK
WI
MURDER

An absolutely gripping cozy mystery novel

JEAN G. GOODHIND

A Honey Driver Murder Mystery Book 3

Originally published as
Walking with Ghosts

JOFFE BOOKS

Revised edition 2022
Joffe Books, London
www.joffebooks.com

First world edition published by Severn House Publishers Ltd in Great Britain and the USA as *Walking with Ghosts* in 2008

Cover art by Dee Dee Book Covers

ISBN: 978-1-80405-271-6

CHAPTER ONE

Honey Driver was very aware of her own mortality; she knew sure as eggs were eggs that one day she would die. Up until tonight, however, she hadn't anticipated falling off her perch for a few years yet. Weren't the mid-forties the new late twenties? But Mary Jane had had the bright idea of going on a ghost walk.

'I'll check my diary,' Honey had said. Pointless. There was nothing in it. No shindigs with fellow hoteliers, no invitations for drinks with Detective Inspector Steve Doherty. Where was he when she needed him?

'And it's my birthday.'

Mary Jane was kind. Mary Jane was a friend. She was also not on this planet. She believed in ghosts, spirits, poltergeists, table-tapping, guardian angels and fairies at the bottom of the garden.

'It's raining.'

'Ghosts don't mind a drop of rain.'

A drop? It was now raining cats and dogs, and Honey's trainers were sodden; a drop of water clung to the tip of her nose. She'd started sneezing — not one or two blasts with time in-between to dig deep for a packet of tissues, these were continuous, like a car engine trying to turn over again and again and again. This walk could be the death of her.

All around her, water gurgled down drainpipes, chuckled into drains, dripped from window ledges and cascaded in shimmering rods around amber-glowing street lights. It would have hammered off an umbrella if she'd brought one. She shoved the tissues back into her pocket. Water trickled in too. Dire! She reminded herself that it was Mary Jane's birthday. She had to stay bright. Now, how could she do that?

Rain, rain, rain. And umbrellas. She thought of Gene Kelly!

'*I'm singing in the rain . . .*'

Without the advantage of an umbrella or hitting the right key, she skipped into the road.

'Look out!' Mary Jane shouted, and tugged her back by the scruff of the neck.

A motorcycle had barely missed her.

'Maniac!' Honey shouted. As fast as he'd come, he disappeared into the darkness, leaving a plume of water in his wake.

'I didn't get his number. If I had done, he'd be toast,' said Mary Jane with a curse-ridden glower.

'Never mind. You got me. That's all that matters.'

Mary Jane was bright-eyed and bushy-tailed. She was a doctor of the paranormal who'd decamped from California to the Green River Hotel in Bath purely so she could be in closer touch with her relatives — dead relatives, that is. The old folk had passed over sometime in the eighteenth century. Mary Jane herself was on the plus side of three score years and ten and believed in forward planning.

'I'll be joining the spirit world before very long. It's dreadful being the newbie, don't you think? Always hated that at school and college and suchlike. Doesn't hurt to make contact with people before you actually join them.'

It was like listening to an aged aunt conveying her plans for visiting a long-lost relative in Australia.

Honey asked how long the walk would last. Mary Jane's response fell on her like a jumbo jet. She assured Honey it lasted two hours.

Honey's heart sank.

'Surely not tonight? Not in this weather?'

'It's bound to. Might even take longer. It's popular with seniors.'

This was bad news. Not all seniors were as fit as Mary Jane. Walking sticks and Zimmer frames sprung to mind. The world went hazy. Even the jolly lights of the Theatre Royal, next door to the Garrick's Head, seemed to dim as if the news was as spirit-sinking to them as it was to her.

A small group of people had gathered in the wide alley outside the main door of the pub. The guide, a slip of a woman with lank hair and a pale face, smiled nervously at her little group. She seemed in a worse state than any of them. The inclement weather gave the impression that the poor chick was slowly melting away. The rainwater drummed on her pink umbrella, ricocheting in a fine spray onto everyone else.

Honey shook a vision of her warm bed and a warm drink from her head and adopted what passed for an attentive expression. The guide was about to address them.

'My name is Pamela Windsor, and I'm very new at this so do bear with me. Unfortunately our more seasoned guides were unavailable this evening. I'm sure you'll understand.'

Droplets of water dripped from Honey's hood as she nodded. Of course she understood. She wished she'd been unavailable too.

'I have to take your names,' the unfortunate guide went on. 'And I'm giving you labels — just so I know who everyone is.' She laughed nervously. No one objected.

Pamela entered their details on a curling piece of paper attached to a clipboard. The heavy downpour was swiftly turning it to papier mâché and the ink was beginning to run, but full marks to Pamela for perseverance.

The group members, most of whom were wearing hoods or sporting umbrellas or both, gave their names.

While Mary Jane bubbled with enthusiasm, Honey studied the rest of the party, praying that anyone needing sticks or a walking frame had stayed at home.

There were four couples; two of them were American, one German and the other Swedish. There were also two middle-aged Australian women who appeared to be together. They were giggling like schoolgirls. They'd been the last to vacate the bar of the Garrick's Head, followed by the slight whiff of gin. There was also a young man wearing a green waterproof poncho and speaking with an accent Honey couldn't quite place.

No sign of anyone with a walking frame, but Honey's elation was short lived. A taxi pulled up. The front passenger door opened and an umbrella appeared, followed by a woman of advanced years wearing a bonnet and a shawl and using a walking stick.

The taxi drove off, the redness of its brake lights smudged by a mist of water. Its passenger pushed her way to the middle of the group.

'My name is *Lady* Templeton-Jones.'

She thrust her fist and the fee at the slender young woman.

'Hi. I'm Hamilton George,' said one of the American men, propelling his hand forward. 'Call me Hal. What do we call you?'

'Your Ladyship!'

Honey exchanged as much of a surprised look with Mary Jane as she could muster; it wasn't easy looking at or seeing anything from beneath her plastic hood.

'Was that a Midwest accent?' Honey muttered through the side of her mouth.

'Takes all sorts,' Mary Jane murmured back.

Of course it did. Bath was a Mecca for tourists from all over the world. Most came to suck up the atmosphere, do the Jane Austen stuff, wander around the Roman Baths and drool over the possibility that a centurion *à la* Russell Crowe had once bathed naked in its sulphuric waters.

Their guide issued them with name tags. 'So I can remember who everyone is,' she explained again.

Despite the lack of space on the labels, Her Ladyship insisted on using her full title. 'Lady Templeton-Jones is how I prefer to be addressed.'

'Lovely night for ducks,' chortled one of the Australian women as though it was the most original joke in the world.

'Jemima Puddle-Duck, you mean,' giggled her friend. For a brief moment the rain did nothing to obliterate the fug of Gordon's gin.

At least *they* were enjoying themselves.

'Right,' said their guide, tucking away her clipboard inside her roomy pink raincoat. 'We'll start here at the Garrick's Head. As most of you will know David Garrick was a great actor in his day, and many old pubs attached to theatres are named after him . . .'

She went on to recount the strange goings on in the Theatre Royal itself, referring to various performances in modern times and the amount of people who'd seen or heard ghostly apparitions.

'The Grey Lady actually appeared at a performance in front of eight hundred and fifty-seven people!'

The group was impressed. The number was so exact. Not eight hundred and fifty — eight hundred and fifty-*seven.* It had to be true.

'I never knew spirits were so brazen,' someone said.

Mary Jane was a bit sniffy. 'It's not a spirit. It's a ghost, the result of a traumatic happening. Spirits are different. They exist in a parallel plane and make contact when the mood takes them.' She said it with the air of someone quite used to getting a call from the other side.

Pamela Windsor nodded respectfully. 'Now, if anyone wants to use the restroom . . .' Half her group trooped back into the pub, including Lady Templeton-Jones. Once they returned she gave an in-depth history of both the pub and the theatre and the smell of jasmine that preceded the appearance of the Grey Lady.

'Next we're off to the Circus via Queen Square . . .'

Like a line of limp laundry, they followed.

The ghost of Queen Square came and went — or rather it didn't.

'No sighting.' Mary Jane sounded disappointed.

'Must be the weather,' said Honey under her breath.

As they made the gentle trek to their next stop, Mary Jane leaned close to Honey's ear. 'I don't think we're going to see anything interesting. I'm getting bad vibrations from this group. They're not spirit orientated.'

'Some are,' said Honey, eyeing the Australian women. They were playing hopscotch through the puddles. One of them had brought a hipflask. Whoever made the biggest splash had a sip.

'These people need spirit counselling,' Mary Jane muttered.

'I need a new pair of trainers.' Honey eyed the water squelching out through her lace holes. The laces kept coming undone, trailing behind her and getting soggier by the minute. Every few minutes she stopped to tie them up, and she began to get left behind.

Enthused with her favourite subject, Mary Jane kept pace with the guide.

Honey found herself trudging along next to Lady Templeton-Jones. She felt obliged to make conversation. 'So! You're titled. How come?'

'That's none of your business.'

'Sorry. No offence.'

They trudged on, along the raised gravel path where folk of substance used to strut their stuff. Black-leaved trees dripping with water rustled in the darkness.

Someone's comment on the sound drifted back to her. 'Like a stiff taffeta skirt.'

Honey promised herself hot chocolate and a hot-water bottle as soon as she got home.

She and Her Ladyship caught up with the rest of the group on the grass in the centre of the Circus.

Pamela's take on the Circus and its strange happenings flew over Honey's head. Her shoelaces were trailing again. She bent down.

'Ever onward! Next, the Assembly Rooms.'

Pamela stabbed at the air with her brolly.

The group trailed along behind her. Honey brought up the rear.

The tall buildings lining the road threw black shadows that even the street lights failed to cope with. They dropped back towards Gay Street, taking a right into an alley which took them down the back of the antique markets.

Thanks to her shoelaces she dropped back again, and it came to the point where she could neither see nor hear the group. Only Her Midwest Ladyship was close at hand. It seemed to Honey that the old dear was getting slower and slower. She stopped to let her catch up and chanced a smile when she did. 'You're not a psychic, I take it.'

'Certainly not!'

Honey tried again. 'And you're not afraid of ghosts?'

'It's the living you have to fear, not the dead.'

CHAPTER TWO

Was it her imagination, or was Her Ladyship trying to lose her? Honey was pretty certain that the old girl's stride lengthened every time she caught up with her.

She felt a great urge to explain that she wasn't as batty as the rest of them. 'I was at a loose end. My friend invited me along. She's into that kind of thing.'

Her Ladyship grunted.

'I'm not a psychic. I'm a hotelier,' she blurted. 'I run a hotel here in Bath.'

'You run a hotel?' Now she sounded interested.

'Worse than that; I own it, which in turn means that the bank owns me,' said Honey with a wry chuckle. It was a joke — and also a basic truth. But her companion wasn't laughing.

'Do you happen to have a spare room?'

She sounded deadly earnest.

'Yes, I do. When do you need it?'

'Tonight.'

That quick!

In her mind she was inspecting the mirror frame, fluffing up the pillows and running the credit card through the machine. 'Fine. OK. I presume you need to collect your stuff from where you're presently staying . . .'

'No! No need. I'll come with you after we've finished this absurdity.'

'Sure.'

This absurdity? The urge to ask questions tingled on her tongue.

Safe beneath the confines of her hood, she fixed her eyes on her feet splashing through the surface water at the point where the alley levelled out and cobbles became concrete. *Never look a gift horse in the mouth.* How very true. Take heart from the fact that another room was let out — without her potential guest asking the price. They'd come to that eventually, and titled people didn't usually quibble. Strapped for cash wasn't good for their image.

The downpour went into overdrive and she'd fallen behind. Well, if she lost the group, she lost them and that was all there was to it. She refused to poke her nose out from her hood to get a clearer picture. Happily, they were going downhill. The tour would soon be over.

The buildings behind the antique markets jostled for space alongside narrow alleys on varying levels. They were mostly small lock-up shops and single-storeys as old as the cobbled surface of the alley itself. In the past they might have been artisans' workshops or stables. It was darker here and even in daylight less frequented. An old copper gaslight hung from a wall bracket above one door. A candle flame flickering from a bow-fronted shop window caught her attention. It briefly occurred to her that a naked flame left like that could cause a fire. Hopefully it wouldn't. Whatever the outcome, she wasn't inclined to do anything about it. A warming drink and a rub-down with a rough towel beckoned.

The alley suddenly swept downhill, passing the second-floor windows of the buildings to her left. A narrow gully some twenty feet deep separated the walkway from the Regency facades.

Honey peered out from beneath her hood and tried to get her bearings. Cosy oblongs of light glowed from the upper windows onto the wet cobbles. They looked as though someone had brushed them with a coating of silicone.

Quaint they might be, but cobbles were slippery. She attempted a diagonal move to the left so she could hold onto the wall.

'Be careful,' she called to her companion.

She received no reply. Pompous cow! *Hope she slips and bruises her dignity.*

Honey kept her eyes fixed on the cobbles, her fingers gripping the harsh sandstone of the parapet.

She glanced away from the cobbles ahead of her. Not a soul in sight. How had the group got down this slope so quickly? The way ahead was shiny and wet — and empty. Very empty. Was it possible they'd passed the group without noticing?

She glanced over her shoulder. No one there either. Shadows, a flickering candle and driving rain — no stout woman with a pompous air and a walking stick in sight!

A sudden gust lifted rainwater from an overflowing gutter and the equivalent of a bucketful of water fell onto her head. Spluttering and blinking, she wiped her face with her sleeve. A contact lens popped out and fell earthwards, a tiny coracle for some drowning insect.

'Damn!'

Coming out from behind her hood, she found she was on level ground and on the right side of a large puddle.

She looked back up the slope. Rods of rain streaked across streetlamps. She thought she glimpsed the same motorbike she'd seen earlier. Apart from that, nobody and nothing, not even Her Midwest Ladyship. Presumably she'd rejoined the rest of the bunch. How, she couldn't quite figure out. On a night like this she didn't care.

'Please yourself,' she said with a sigh and bent down to retie her shoelace.

Losing a contact lens was almost as bad as losing a leg; everything was lopsided. Close up wasn't so bad. Distance was a nightmare.

A sudden movement attracted her attention further downhill. A group of people were jumping in and out of a puddle that had gathered between the alley and the main pavement. The Australian women, no doubt.

Just as she thought that, a pair of shiny shoes sauntered past. She glanced up and spied a broad-brimmed hat, pulled low over the face, and a cloak, flapping in the wind.

'Good evening,' she said.

Whoever it was didn't answer, which was something of a pity because she was dying to make a comment about his shiny patent shoes.

Shiny?

Patent?

In this weather?

How come they weren't wet — sodden, even? And how come she hadn't heard his footsteps? Not a ghost. No. Couldn't be. Could it? Her blood turned to ice — and the weather had nothing to do with it!

Taking off like Concorde from Heathrow, she raced and skidded her way over the cobbles crashing into the small group standing in the gap at the end.

'Hey!'

The blurred figures turned clear. Faces — young faces frowned at her. Nightclubbers.

'I'm sorry. Wrong group!'

CHAPTER THREE

Having eluded her companion, Lady Templeton-Jones headed quickly for the shop with the candle burning in its window.

Before trying the handle she looked over her shoulder. A lone figure was picking her way down over the cobbles towards the main road, concentrating on not slipping. Apart from her the alley was empty.

She pushed the door open and stepped into the darkness. The shop smelled dank and dusty. The candle in the window did little to aid her eyesight. Using her stick to feel ahead of her, she took a few steps forward, squinting into the darkness.

The sound of a creaking floorboard sounded overhead. She looked up. Anyone else might have been afraid. She was not. Her purpose for coming here far outweighed any fear she might have felt, and anyway, it was a matter of honour.

'I need to talk to you,' she called out. 'You might not like what I have to say.'

Her voice sounded thick in her throat but weakened as it bounced off the whitewashed walls.

Another floorboard creaked. The candle flickered behind her. The shop was empty and had been so for some time, hence no electricity, only a candle. Why hadn't she thought to bring a flashlight?

'Keep going,' she muttered to herself. She was determined to go through with this.

She fancied the outline of a door in the corner and made for it. Using her stick she poked at where the floor should be and found a ledge — no, a stair! The door opened onto a black-as-ink staircase winding upwards.

She paused with one foot on the bottom stair, hand clenching the handle of her walking stick — a weapon if need be.

'Hey! Are you up there?'

Perhaps there was another door. Perhaps it was difficult to hear her. After all, she'd only heard the creaking of floorboards. No voice. It was reasonable to assume that her voice might not be heard.

Placing one foot on the first stair, she leaned forward, twisting her head and shoulders so she could see the top of the stairs. A faint brightness appeared and was gone instantly. Perhaps the person she had come to see had opened a door and closed it again.

She was about to call out again when something brushed against her face. Cobwebs!

Since childhood she'd been terrified of spiders. Panic overcame her. The stick necessary for her to feel her way was now used to lash out. Thrown off balance, she tilted backwards, then forwards again. Momentum increased. She climbed the stairs more quickly. Her breath was coming in quick gasps. Her chest was wheezing.

Not far now! She had to be at or near the top of the stairs.

Something brushed gently across her chest. She climbed, stick held out in front of her.

This time she heard a door latch before the darkness lightened.

Convinced she'd reached her goal and everything would be worthwhile, she lunged for the top of the stairs. Whatever had lain on her chest tightened around her windpipe. She heard a springing sound, then the sound of her own breath as it was strangled from her throat.

CHAPTER FOUR

Fast as her soggy trainers would allow, Honey splish-splashed through the puddles. The best place to finish this walk was at the beginning. Her strategy proved correct. The ghost walkers were just sliding to a standstill outside the Theatre Royal.

'See anything?' someone asked her.

'No . . . Ha, ha, ha . . . Nothing at all.' Even to her ears her laughter sounded weak and wobbly.

The dripping-wet ghost walkers trooped into the Garrick's Head. The lounge bar took on the atmosphere of a launderette as their clothes began to steam.

The Australian women were first at the bar. Honey wasn't far behind. Mary Jane muscled in beside her.

'Didn't see or hear a thing,' she said miserably. 'I sure expected some kind of sign. Did you see anything?'

The shiny black patent shoes came to mind. Avoiding eye contact, Honey ordered another drink. 'No. Nothing.'

Mary Jane narrowed one eye and arched her eyebrow high above the other. How did she manage that?

'You look a little pale. You're swigging back the sauce like there's no tomorrow. I'm reading that you did. You saw something. Go on. Spill the beans — and take a handful of potato chips while you're at it.'

Honey ordered another drink but refrained from digging into the bowls of nuts and potato chips placed on the bar top. Mary Jane was sometimes intimidating. She was giving her that look, the one that said, *I'll turn you into a frog if you don't tell me the truth.*

'You ever lectured at Hogwarts?' Honey asked her.

Mary Jane raised both eyebrows. 'Of course not. That's only fiction.' Her smile widened suddenly. 'I'd make a good witch though, don't you think?'

Honey's reaction was to wrap both hands around her glass. 'Don't doctor my drink whatever you do. Ice and a slice are fine, but eye of newt gives me wind.'

Mary Jane made a grunting sound but bounced back for the kill. 'You saw but ain't telling.'

Honey shook her head. 'It was nothing.'

Mary Jane loomed over her. 'Tell!'

Another slurp of vodka. 'I saw a guy wearing a black cloak and black patent pumps. Fancy dress, I bet.'

'Oh, my giddy aunt! Oh, my word! You did see something! You did! You did!' The wrinkles of a lifetime rearranged themselves into an expression of awestruck envy. 'Well, that's not fair. How come you saw a ghost and I didn't?'

Everyone in the immediate vicinity fell to silence. All eyes were turned their way, waiting until Honey fired the shot that would get them going again.

'Nah! Just a toff in a tux. He'd probably been to an important dinner. I expect the woman from Ohio or wherever it was — Lady Whatshername — saw him too. I'll ask her.'

She presumed that Lady Templeton-Jones had scorched on ahead of her and quickly rejoined the group. Her eyes scooted from face to face. The dishevelled ghost walkers were now warming themselves up with bottled spirits. Lady Templeton-Jones was not among them.

'Oh. Looks as though she's already checked out.'

Of course she had. And she'd probably forgotten about checking into the Green River. People reserving rooms and not checking in were a nightmare.

Damn! I should have got her credit card number.

A sudden whack on the bar top sent the complimentary snacks skipping out of their dishes.

A big voice boomed out. 'Here's yer bag, Your Ladyship.'

Conversation paused. Uncomprehending faces turned in the direction of the voice.

'Oh. Where's your friend?' he added. 'She asked me to look after this for her. Couldn't say no to a lady.'

Adrian Harris was the pub landlord. He was tall, dark and bloated. His six-pack had become a beer barrel long ago. He also had the publican's sweaty pallor, indicative of people who came out at night and slept in the day. Think vampire but without the strong teeth and muscle tone.

'She's not here,' Honey explained. 'She's booking in with me, though. I presume she'll turn up at my place later.'

'It's all yours, then,' Adrian said abruptly. He slammed the bag down in front of Honey and turned away.

'But she might come back here for it.'

'She'll be out of luck. I'm closing at eleven on the dot.' Surly was Adrian's middle name. He didn't give a sod for anyone.

'I thought you usually stayed open later?'

'Sod that. I'm off to the Costa del Sol tomorrow, and I can't be having old bags left in my premises — of any sort.'

'Charmed, I'm sure,' Honey murmured, presuming that she was one of the old bags he referred to.

'Excuse me.'

She turned to see Pamela Windsor's pale face on a level with her own. Her eyes were brighter now, perhaps because of the impromptu steam bath.

'I'd better take it,' she said, reaching for the bag. 'I can leave a message at her hotel that I have it safely in my possession. I'm sure that would be all right.'

OK, it was a perfectly reasonable suggestion. So why was it that Honey suddenly found herself feeling protective about a brown leather bag? Was it because it resembled her favourite overlarge receptacle, though on a smaller scale? Or was it because their guide looked less wan, more animated than she'd been all evening?

'No need.' Honey hugged the bag to her as though it were a newborn babe due for a feed. 'Her Ladyship was checking into my hotel. She'll probably be there when I get back.'

There was no guarantee that Her Ladyship would appear at the Green River. Neither did she have any real reason to be suspicious of dear Pamela. The guide was well meaning, but Honey couldn't help but get the impression that something was wrong. The world and his wife passed through the doors of the Green River Hotel. You got to know how people behaved. No woman of a certain age would wander off home or wherever she was staying without a bag over her arm. Such a bag would contain everything she held dear and of value: a bunch of keys, her phone and money, perhaps a stub of lipstick and a powder compact, plus family photos.

She remarked on this.

Pamela glared. Strange, really, because she didn't look the sort who would glare. She was more the nervous fluttery-eyelash type, and sure enough, the latter kicked in. *Flutter, flutter.* At the same time her chin disappeared into the cowl of her bright red sweater. 'I didn't realise. But if you're quite sure . . . ?' Her voice was reed-thin and yet for a slip of a second Honey had detected strength, even a hint of the sultry.

Mary Jane suggested they call the police.

'We should wait,' Honey cautioned. 'It's not long enough to report her missing. She must have decided she needed her luggage after all but forgot about her bag.'

Pamela Windsor retreated further into her cowl, her eyes fixed on the bag. 'I fear she may presume I'm responsible for looking after her property.'

For a split second Honey considered handing the bag over. Mary Jane jumped in first. 'If the woman's moving into the Green River then Honey's the gal to take care of it. She has a huge green safe that she keeps in the office behind reception. It'll be fine in there until it's claimed.'

Honey touched Mary Jane's arm and in a low voice explained that it was never wise to discuss safes and valuables in the middle of a pub, no matter where it was.

'Makes sense, huh?'

Mary Jane jerked her chin. 'I see where you're coming from. You don't want to get done in.'

'Done over. Done in is getting killed, done over is getting burgled.'

'Right!'

Mary Jane was quickly picking up UK slang, most of it gained from soaps set in the north of England or the East End of London. She'd tried watching a Welsh soap, convinced she would pick up the language. She'd failed.

'OK. So Her Ladyship got topped.'

Honey didn't correct her. She might just be right.

* * *

When they arrived back at the Green River, Lindsey was sitting behind reception surfing the net. The desk was custom-built and had little alcoves hidden above it out of the guest's view but easily accessible to the receptionist. On seeing her mother, Lindsey brought out a half-bottle of Shiraz and an empty glass.

Honey felt a wave of relaxation fall over her. 'My daughter knows me well.'

'This first,' said Lindsey, handing her a towel.

'I saw nothing,' said a dismal Mary Jane as Honey dried her hair.

Towel draped over her head, Honey rolled a sip of wine around her mouth. 'I saw someone vanish.'

'You can't see someone vanish. If they've vanished you can't see them,' said Lindsey. Her daughter was good with words.

Mary Jane, on the other hand, was jaw-dropped and goggle-eyed.

Honey tapped the bag she'd been landed with. 'Apologies to the Queen for my poor use of her English. Let me explain.

A woman vanished on the ghost walk. This bag is all that's left of her.'

'Yes,' said Mary Jane, retrieving her jaw from her chest. 'Of course she didn't vanish. Not properly. She just got lost. But I didn't see anything,' she repeated, noticeably upset that she hadn't made contact with one single ghost, spirit, poltergeist or hobgoblin.

'Has Sir Cedric wished you a happy birthday yet?' Lindsey asked her.

Mary Jane's grin was like an eruption of wrinkles. 'I expect he'll sing it to me.'

'Happy birthday, Mary Jane. Sweet dreams,' said Lindsey.

'Happy birthday and thanks for a great night out,' said Honey.

'Great?' muttered Lindsey through a fixed smile.

'Wet,' Honey muttered back.

Lindsey was a younger version of her mother — except for her hair, which tended to change with the seasons. Lindsey had a more athletic look about her, mainly because she enjoyed a little exercise and Honey did not. A bit of salsa around the bedroom was OK for Honey. Lindsey preferred jogging and symphonies.

Mary Jane looked a bit like Adam West's Caped Crusader, though her tights were baggier around her bony knees and her cape of pink angora was devoid of bat insignia.

'So what's the story?' Lindsey asked once their one and only permanent guest had floated up the stairs.

Honey rested her arms on the desktop and her chin on her arm. She swirled the wine around the glass, watching it rise, ebb and subside. 'One minute the woman was walking with me, and then she wasn't.'

'Nice woman?'

'Overbearing. That reminds me, has your grandmother called?'

'Three times. She has a problem. Was whining that she might just as well have remained childless. She thought her daughter would look after her in her old age. Said she couldn't get you on your phone. I told her you were on a ghost walk and that mobile phones disturb the ectoplasm — or whatever.'

Honey did an eye-roll in one direction and repeated it in the other.

Lindsey grinned. Gloria Cross — Honey's mother, Lindsey's grandmother — was not your run-of-the-mill septuagenarian. Senior she might be, but senile she was not. She held strong opinions and a taste that only Donna Karan and Helena Rubinstein could cater for.

Honey checked her phone. Three calls, all from her mother. None from Steve Doherty. He's busy, she told herself. Cops usually are.

The bag was put in the safe, and the night porter checked in. Mother and daughter gave reception up to his care and headed for the coach house behind the hotel. The old place had been planned upside down in order to take advantage of the city view. The bedrooms were situated on the ground floor. The huge living room, kitchen and bathroom were above that and enjoyed views of mansard roofs and the green hills surrounding the city.

Kicking off soggy trainers and socks was followed by a warm shower. Like herself, the old house settled down for the night to the sound of water trickling down the roof and gushing throatily along its ancient gutters.

She closed her eyes and nestled into the pillow. This was *so* good. Comforting. Warm. And yet she could not, simply could *not*, drift into sleep.

Exasperated, she flung herself onto her back and stared up at the ceiling. What the hell was keeping her awake?

She sighed. It was like having a roundabout inside her head, the same observations and questions going around and around and around.

Why had the woman been so quick off the mark about moving into the Green River? Was the hotel she was staying at that bad? No point losing sleep over it. She'd probably turn up in the morning with a plausible excuse. No one could simply vanish.

CHAPTER FIVE

Sleep was elusive, even though the rain had stopped tap-dancing against the bedroom window. She checked the clock. One thirty. She tried closing her eyes. Her brain was doing a tap dance of its own.

How about the Zodiac Club? Steve might be sitting there on a bar stool expecting you to drop in. You could run this strange night past him.

Honey swung her legs out of bed and got dressed. Jeans, a sweater and loafers would do the job. The soggy shoes had found the bottom of the trash can and a fresh pair was dug out along with jeans and a red angora sweater. Her raincoat was still soaked. She left it draping over a radiator chancing that the rain would hold off.

The rain had gone off and the city had come alive. OK, it wasn't actually zinging along, but like nocturnal lemmings, the populace were poking twitching noses out into the night.

A big shiny motorcycle slowed and for a while seemed to keep pace with her. She looked round. Was the city being taken over by Kawasaki and Yamaha?

A police car surged into the space immediately behind the gleaming monster. A twist of the throttle, a throaty roar and it was gone.

The police car eased its pace, the officers inside scrutinising the shop fronts before moving off.

Honey watched it go, its brake lights glaring at the traffic lights before it disappeared. She found herself near Henrietta Park. Not liking the dark shadows thrown by the trees, she kept to the opposite side of the road. The air smelled of fresh foliage.

Two jogging figures came into focus on the other side of the road. Late-shifters, she thought. People who worked odd hours like she did, and found it difficult to fit in exercise.

Then she saw him. Doherty! Jogging? He'd never struck her as a fitness fanatic nor keen on sport.

Her attention jumped to his leggy companion. So that was his idea of sport! She was blonde, tall and athletically built. Her shoulders were square and her bosoms were firm, as though plaster of Paris had been applied to her and allowed to set. Either that or she was wearing a cast-iron brassiere.

Honey's heart did a quick cartwheel. She wasn't jealous, she told herself. Doherty was hardly Mr Wonderful. He wasn't even the best of coppers. But he'd held her hand since taking on her appointment as crime liaison officer on behalf of the Bath Hotels Association. She felt comfortable in his company — a bit like the old trainers that she'd thrown away.

Hovering like this, she was bound to be seen. He might think she'd been following him. She didn't want to appear needy or too keen. Heaven forbid!

There was nowhere to hide on her side of the street. Now what?

Just before she drew level with them, a black motorcycle slid into the kerb.

'Wanna lift?'

Never take a lift from a stranger. She gave him the once over: silver crash helmet, leather jacket, jeans and . . . wellington boots!

It was stupid. It was spur of the moment, but hey, nobody with dark deeds in mind wears wellies — do they?

Of course not!

She flung her leg over the pillion seat. Turning her face away from Doherty and his companion, she rested her cheek against the smooth leather of the biker's jacket.

The motorcyclist turned into the city centre and then headed for Lansdown Hill. Panic set in. 'Hey!' she shouted.

The Green River Hotel was in the opposite direction.

She tapped his back. 'Excuse me!'

Her voice was lost on the wind. They sped up Lansdown Hill, skirting parked cars and moving vehicles that dared to hog the middle of the road.

She daren't let go. The wind whistled through her hair. Elegant buildings gave way to squat cottages. They hurtled past the racecourse and the Blathwayt Arms. Where the hell was he taking her?

He followed the left-hand curve of the road. She recognised where she was. They were dropping down towards the village of Wick on the outskirts of Bristol. Perhaps he would pause there long enough for her to skip off.

Skip? She reminded herself of her age and the fact that her legs lacked the flexibility of a bouncy nine-year-old.

The bike barely paused at the bottom of the hill. A swift right and they were climbing again, this time up Tog Hill.

Honey recalled the views being stupendous at the top of this hill. Not that she'd have time to sit and stare, by the look of it.

The rider swooped around the island at the top and headed back down the A46 into Bath.

She tapped his back again. 'So, what's the point of the mystery tour?'

No response.

Hold on, girl, she told herself. This wasn't over yet. There had to be a point to him abducting her. Everything has a point, doesn't it?

She went over the options. Number one, he was trying to scare her. Why, she didn't know. OK, it wasn't everyday she went tearing around riding pillion on a motorbike. But was she really scared? No. No, she was not. All in all she was coping pretty well.

Number two, he'd truly been going to take her home but had lost his way. Rubbish!

Number three, he'd been going to stop in some dark place and ravish her but had realised she was old enough to be his mother and changed his mind.

This last option rankled, but was a relief.

Or maybe he was just biding his time . . .

Familiar streets and buildings were regained. With a squeal of brakes he came to a halt outside the Green River Hotel.

Home!

Ungainly but swiftly, she swung her leg. Both feet were once again on the ground.

Her hair was a mess, her face was cold, but she was in one piece. Now was he going to get a piece of her mind!

'Right,' she said, her best lecturing finger raised and at the ready.

He didn't give her chance. A flick of the wrist and he was off as fast as Superman.

She stood for a moment thinking that wellington boots were a bit innocuous, not standard uniform for a guy with a black-metal steed between his legs. Wellies were more suited to a four-legged steed, though mainly to the clearing up of the manure it left in its wake.

Never mind. She was tired now and would sleep. Her bed called. The biker had done some good. As for Doherty . . .

It had been an odd night.

'I'm ready for bed,' she said as she let herself back into the coach house. The interior was silvery still, moonlight pouring through the round window high up in the apex above the beams.

She shivered. She sneezed. Damn the rain. Damn getting a cold. The recipe required was well tried and tested. After fetching a Lemsip from the bathroom, she armed herself with the ingredients for a brandy balloon.

The brandy and coke tasted good and went down fast. She spied the unopened packet of powder through the empty glass. *Drat,* she thought, picking it up and tearing it open. I'll just have to drink another one.

Then something occurred to her that kept her up for a while — how did the guy on the motorcycle know where she lived?

CHAPTER SIX

Some minutes after Honey got home, a young man named Simon Taylor pulled up outside a Regency terrace in Green Park. The house had long ago been divided into flats — five floors, two flats on each. He parked his motorcycle in one of the allotted spaces next to a dark-red scooter. The light in the living-room window of the flat he shared with his mother was still on. He hoped she'd forgotten to turn it off and had gone to bed. Unlikely. His mother always waited up for him. She always had.

The doorway was wide and swollen in its frame, scuffing the black-and-white floor tiles of the threshold as he pushed it open. The hallway was far from welcoming. The walls and internal doors were faded burgundy by virtue of a job lot of paint the downstairs neighbour had acquired some years before. He'd attempted to brighten the décor by adding a series of pink and gold lines around the architrave of the door to his one-roomed apartment. It was hardly art and neither did it do anything to lift the atmosphere of neglect. Likewise, the plug-in air freshener was fighting a losing battle against the smell of damp caused by ferns growing from third-floor parapets and mould climbing up from the cellar.

Not wanting to answer any questions about why he was out so late, he shut the front door quietly behind him. The hallway on the ground floor was still and silent. Not a stick of furniture invaded its austere emptiness. The floor's cracked brown surface might shine if anyone ever got up the energy to attack it with a can of polish and a duster. No one ever had; a brief sweep and mop over was all it ever got. This was why he took his shoes off before going up the stairs to their flat. His soles would stick to the glutinous underside of the threadbare carpet covering the stairs and make a sucking sound. The woollen pile of his socks would snag and tear softly away.

By the time he got to the door of his apartment, he knew for sure she hadn't yet retired. The sound of car sirens on a late-night cop show told him she was still watching television. On gently turning the key and opening the front door, his suspicions were realised.

'That you, Simon?'

As if it was likely to be anyone else.

Her son of twenty-two years grimaced as he shook the rain from his coat. Why was she so deaf if anyone rang the doorbell but so alert when it was him coming in from a night out?

'Yes,' he replied in a cheery voice. His mother would hear it and think he was smiling.

He managed to bare his teeth in a fair imitation of one when he poked his head around the living-room door.

His mother was sitting in an armchair pulled to within four or five feet of the television screen. To either side of her were placed two small tables with piecrust tops and tripod legs. They were originally meant to take a gentleman's — or woman's — wine or spirit glass. In his mother's case, a box of Maltesers sat on one and a tumbler of Jameson sat on the other. Nutshells and sweet wrappers filled a porcelain dish. The dish was quite valuable, a pretty little Dresden thing. His mother wouldn't know that. Wouldn't know how much he'd bid for it on eBay.

He picked up the dish and took it into the kitchen to empty it. After swilling it beneath running water and wiping it carefully, he brought it back in.

'Did everything go according to plan?' she asked, without her eyes ever leaving the screen.

'Yes,' he answered. 'I'm going online now. See you in the morning. Goodnight, Mother.'

'Goodnight.'

He paused, mesmerised by the effect of the light shining on her face and through her thinning hair. He could distinguish the shape of her skull and the freckles on her scalp. Seemingly unaware she was doing it, she tapped her fingers compulsively on the chair arm. Her nerves were bad and getting worse. All those chocolates. All that booze. It was only to be expected.

He closed the door silently behind him and made his way up the stairs. His bedroom door locked against the world and his mother, Simon smiled at the screen saver as it soared from corner to corner. At present it was a Tudor Rose, an amalgamation of the white rose of York and the red rose of Lancaster, a great favourite of his.

He logged into his business site. This extra-curricular working life was a secret he kept from his mother. This was the work he enjoyed the most. It also made him quite a bit of money.

Rich shades of blue and burgundy flashed onto the screen — a coloured-in brass rubbing of a knight in full armour, a lady in flowing gown and pointed hat.

The Noble Present.
Purchase a noble title from the past as a present for your loved one — make her a lady, make yourself a lord.
Authentic antique titles for sale.

CHAPTER SEVEN

The phone rang early.

'Hannah. It's me. What are you doing?'

Only her mother ever called her Hannah. Honey closed her eyes and began counting to ten. She got to fifteen.

'I'm on my way to the kitchen.'

'Never mind that. I need to speak to you. It's important.'

Honey looked up at the ceiling. 'Mother, I've a hotel to run. The kitchen is the powerhouse of the Green River. There's work to be done.'

'You've got a chef!'

'It's his day off.'

This was a lie. Mark 'Smudger' Smith, head chef extraordinaire and one-time professional wrestler, had met some old friends the night before. Lindsey had rung from reception that morning to inform her mother that Smudger was sitting on the floor of the cold store with a bag of peas on his head and another on his groin. Honey had taken as read the reason for the peas being on his head. She made a mental note to check how much he'd drunk and what. Their stocks would be depleted. She decided not to ask about the other bag. Men did pretty strange things when they were drunk.

'Hannah, I'm very worried.'

Honey held her breath. Her mother was a born survivor. Anyone who'd had as many husbands as she had needed to be.

'Is it to do with a man?'

'Of course not. Why would I be worried about a man?'

'I thought you might . . . Never mind.' Her mother considered it her duty to find her daughter a new man. The trouble was that she had different tastes to her daughter. Besides, Honey felt she was mature enough to find her own. 'What's the problem?'

'It's about the shop. Secondhand Rose. We have a problem I need to run past you.'

Honey glanced at her watch. Juggling work and the little leisure she could manage was bad enough. Trying to fit in time for family was a bit of a squeeze.

'Mother, this is not a good time. The guests get ugly if they don't have their breakfast on time. Can we talk later?'

'Well, that's it! To think a daughter of mine prefers to take care of perfect strangers rather than help her poor old mother!'

Gloria Cross was far from being a frail old woman. In fact she was decidedly feisty, flirty and frightening to know. She was also selfish, irritating, domineering and downright testy when she wanted to be.

Honey used both hands to strangle the phone before gritting her teeth and diving back in.

'So, who's rattled your cage?'

Her mother's tone turned whiny. 'Well, that's pretty typical. You youngsters lead hectic lives and have no time for the problems of old folk, even your own mother! Never you mind about my problems. Your mother can look after herself despite being an old-age pensioner.'

This was serious! Never, *ever* had she heard her mother refer to herself as an OAP. Senior citizen, maybe. Mature lady, perhaps. Old-age pensioner conjured up a vision of a decrepit old woman in wrinkly stockings and squashed felt hat. Her mother was far from being that.

Honey immediately felt contrite.

'Mother, if there's a problem, tell me about it.'

'I wouldn't want to burden you.'

The voice on the other end of the phone took on a fragile tone.

As though she's drawing her last breath.

'Why don't you call in for coffee?'

'Fine! I'll ring reception and fix an appointment!'

Slam went the phone.

There always followed a sense of relief once her mother stopped talking. There was now, but there was also guilt. By the time Honey got to reception she was already unlocking her phone, ready to beg forgiveness. The line was engaged.

'Later,' she muttered to herself. 'I'll phone her later.'

Shirking responsibility meant hiding in the dry-goods store. There was something therapeutic about sorting out jars of rice, pasta, sugar and salt while she wiped the shelves. Borrowing Lindsey's iPod helped things go with a swing. She wiggled as she worked; she'd read it helped reduce the waistline. Kept her mind occupied too.

Honey scrubbed at a particularly vigorous stain. Keep focused. That was the secret. Everything was fine and would stay fine.

Then Murphy's Law kicked in. If something's likely to go wrong it will.

Lindsey poked her shoulder. Tina Turner and 'Simply the Best' were put on hold.

Lindsey's expression was bad news. 'There's water everywhere! It's pouring in.'

Recovered from his hangover, Smudger came running from the kitchen, his fair complexion pink with irritation and steam from the dishwasher.

'That bloody drain's blocked again.'

It was the third time that week. Honey began rolling up her sleeves. 'Here we go again. Fetch the wet and dry.'

While Lindsey went off to wrestle the vacuum from Dumpy Doris's meaty hands, Honey headed out to the yard at the back of the kitchen. Smudger followed her out.

The thought of donning rubber gloves, lifting a drain cover and hauling out all manner of gunge was not exactly appetising. Mentally, then verbally, she began to squirm. 'It's really a man's job . . . and by the way, that bag of peas . . .'

'I've got half a pound of cod roe to sauté.' Muttering something about 'severins', he began to beat a hasty retreat.

The kitchen door slammed shut. Smudger was gone. What were severins? Or had she misheard? Had he in fact said 'several things'? Whatever it was, it translated that she was on her lonesome.

The drain was situated in a narrow area bounded on three sides. The sides were formed by the hotel itself, a funny inlet set into the stone. The sun never reached here, so moss and ferns sprouted to their hearts content. It was a miniature ecosystem complete with a small lake when the drain blocked. A slope on the open end meant the water could not run away. The only way out was down the drain.

Honey gritted her teeth. 'The glamour of running a Bath hotel!'

The door opened again and Anna waddled out fumbling with a pair of wellies, a garden fork and a plunger. Anna used to run reception full-time, but was now six months pregnant and almost didn't fit behind the desk.

'Lindsey said you might need these.'

Setting aside her blue suede shoes with gold buttons on the side, Honey pulled on her green wellies. No gold buttons on these, just mud-encrusted toes.

'You can give them a quick brush over, if you like,' she said, handing the shoes to Anna, who frowned at them.

'I don't do cleaning shoes.'

'Just hold them for me.'

The drain in question took the output from the kitchen. Smudger had told everyone to lay off doing anything that needed water while she did her thing.

Taking the plunger and brandishing it aloft, she couldn't help identifying with the Statue of Liberty. 'Bring me your smelly drains.'

Looking confused, Anna passed her the garden fork and went back inside.

Wading through greasy water and floating carrot peel, she began prodding through with the fork. The prongs hit home, metal clanging against metal in the narrow space beneath the mucky grey stuff that passed as water. Just as she began to lift the drain cover, she became aware of a fine blue haze drifting around her head.

Fire!

She was just about to run back inside to grab a fire extinguisher when she glimpsed Mary Jane out of the corner of her eye.

'I've come to rid this house of evil spirits . . .' said Mary Jane in an eerie voice. Like a flute, it was haunting but slightly out of tune. She was waving her skinny arms above her head. A flurry of blue smoke whirled and writhed in the air.

'I've come to give you a hand sorting this out.'

Honey gave her the once over. 'I see no sign of a shovel or a drain-cleaning hose.'

'With this,' said Mary Jane.

Honey ducked as Mary Jane wafted a bunch of dried leaves towards her.

'Indian sage,' Mary Jane said, as if that said it all. 'Guaranteed to chase away evil spirits.'

'I'd prefer a plumber.'

'There's a poltergeist come to stay,' said Mary Jane. 'It was him who blocked your drain.'

'Didn't see him check in.'

Down-to-earth solutions didn't rate high on Mary Jane's agenda. At present she was out of this world, her head thrown back, her eyes closed. She was wearing an outsize pair of wellington boots, the heavy type with thick treads that workmen wear. Each leg looked like a small twig planted in an outsize pot. How she lifted her feet without stepping out of her boots, Honey couldn't fathom.

Honey stood with a silly smile on her face, watching as Mary Jane drifted back towards the kitchen door. She wondered if wafting Indian sage around could be construed as smoking in a public place. Visions of a two-thousand-pound fine now drifted before her eyes more clearly than the smoke.

'Mary Jane! Do you think you can do that elsewhere? In the garden, maybe? I do remember you saying that there was activity around where the rose garden used to be.'

Mary Jane stopped, pulled herself up to her full height and looked round. At first her face was implacable. Honey was about to apologise and say, 'Hey, what the hell? Who cares about a little fine and the customers coughing up their lungs? Carry on. Just watch the dried flower arrangements. They catch fire easily.'

Squeezing her eyes shut, Mary Jane took a deep, chest-heaving breath and made an *ommmmm* sound. If it went on long enough it set your teeth on edge.

'Right,' said Mary Jane once that was done. 'The nasty little sprite has gone back to sprite land.' She paused. 'I think you've got a point about the rose garden. I'll take a look at that PDQ. Shouldn't take too much sage burning to sort out.'

And the grass is damp so you can't set it on fire!

The sage had indeed had its uses, its smell having camouflaged the whiff of waste. Waste was like wine, thought Honey. The older it was, the more intense its bouquet.

Back inside, there was no one behind the reception desk when she got there. She frowned. It was Lindsey's shift. Where was she?

Then she saw her, hovering just outside main doors talking to someone she couldn't quite see.

Half turning, Lindsey spotted her. The other figure vanished. A smiling Lindsey swept back in.

Honey jerked her chin at the door. 'Anyone I know?'

'No,' returned Lindsey, suddenly turning into Mrs Busy. 'Just someone wanting directions.'

CHAPTER EIGHT

Reception smelled of beeswax and roses. The beeswax lent a golden glow to the rich mahogany of the reception desk. Cabbage roses in white and dusty pink were arranged with other flowers in a huge basin with ornate handles. The basin was of a deep Sèvres blue with gilded handles sticking out like elephant ears.

A Japanese family were checking in. The parents were sleek and slim, but the children chewed gum and, judging by the denim jeans straining over their pot bellies, were into fast food.

'Have a nice day,' said Lindsey once the formalities were complete. She turned to her mother. 'Worried?'

Honey was mindlessly fiddling with the pen for the register. 'She hasn't shown up.'

'Stop doing that. You'll make a mess.' Lindsey took charge of the register.

'Well, it makes a change. Usually it's the guest who gets to reception and reports lost baggage — not the other way round.'

Honey watched as her daughter typed the guests' names into the computer, but her mind was elsewhere. Should she open the bag? Her fingers were in danger of doing that awful nervous tapping thing. Best to get them occupied, she decided. The outer rose petals on the cabbage roses looked in need of attention.

'What are you doing?' asked Lindsey. She'd stopped typing and was throwing her that know-it-all look.

'Just dead-heading the roses.'

'Those are silk. Try the ones on the table.'

'Ah!'

The phone rang. Lindsey grabbed it more quickly than usual. 'Oh! Hi!'

Honey caught the tone of voice. Small words with a big message. Lindsey looked secretive, head bent over the phone, hair veiling her eyes. She told the caller she'd ring back.

Honey gave one of her knowing nods, the way only a mother with a daughter knows how.

'So who is he?'

Lindsey's movements were swift and mechanical, register to laundry list in six simple moves. She was humming, pretending she hadn't heard.

Honey tried again. 'You've got a boyfriend.'

'What makes you think that?'

Honey made a polishing movement along the countertop with her elbow. At the same time she rested her chin in her hand. 'You've got that moony look.'

Lindsey flicked at the sheets of paper comprising the laundry list. 'He's just a friend.'

'What else?'

'A musician — of sorts.'

This came as something of a relief. Knowing her daughter's interest in all things medieval, she stated the obvious. 'Tell me he plays the lute and wears tights. We could use him to entertain in the restaurant. Without the tights, of course.'

'He doesn't wear tights,' said Lindsey, studying the list of sheets, towels, pillowcases and tablecloths as though it formed the plot of a particularly thrilling novel. 'And he doesn't play the lute. He plays the bagpipes, actually.'

'And wears . . . ?'

'A kilt.'

The obvious question trembled on the tip of her tongue. Was it true what they said about Scotsmen?

She daren't! She daren't!

Her facial movements — chewing a smile, sucking in her cheeks — gave her away.

Lindsey glared.

'And before you say anything, I haven't asked.'

'Are you keen?'

Lindsey made a so-so shake of her head. 'He's cool. He's good company.'

Honey glanced at the old-school clock hanging on the wall immediately opposite the entrance. A sudden question occurred to her. 'Does he ride a motorbike?'

Lindsey stopped flicking the pages of the laundry list and frowned. 'What makes you say that?'

Not wishing to appear nosy, Honey shrugged. 'I need to get going.' But she'd love to know more. Mustn't pry, she thought. Lindsey was an adult.

'I'm off out. If Lady Whatsit-whatsit wants her bag she can go to Manvers Street Police Station. I'll take it now while I'm in the mood.'

'Give Steve my love,' said Lindsey.

'Not that kind of mood.'

'It's time you two stopped messing around.'

'I prefer being single — but don't tell your grandmother that.'

Lindsey's grin lit up her face. 'If you don't make it obvious that your trophy policeman is still on the scene, Grandma will find you a consolation prize.'

Honey made a choking sound. 'A booby prize more like!'

Honey's mother was one of the few people who insisted on calling her given name Hannah. Everyone else called her Honey, a nickname bestowed on her by her late father, who had died after absconding from his marriage with an exotic dancer less than half his age. Evidence of the fact that age and youth are not compatible, he'd snuffed it on his wedding night — much to his former wife's delight.

Like mother, like daughter, her own marriage hadn't made it long-term — or even halfway, come to that. A keen sailor, Carl had drowned in the middle of the Atlantic. Her mother had made it her mission to find a replacement. 'Someone ordinary but steady who doesn't go sailing off into the sunset with an all-female crew!'

Her mother's interpretation of ordinary meant an accountant or a dentist. Honey preferred DI Doherty. He was the bonus she acquired when landing the job of crime liaison officer. He was far from perfect, just like her.

CHAPTER NINE

Bath's elegant crescents and quaint alleys attracted tourists from all over the world. Tourists were welcome. Crime was not. The Hotels Association insisted on keeping a lid on it. That lid answered to the name of Honey Driver, crime liaison officer.

Detective Inspector Steve Doherty was divorced, jaded, stubble-chinned, blue-eyed, dark-haired and far from perfect. In short, he was the typically flawed man that every woman fell for despite her better instincts. He wasn't so much new man as caveman with clothes on. Most of the policewomen he worked with preferred him with his clothes off. Honey hadn't got to that point. It might happen. It might not. She wasn't going to push it.

Things had been threatening to bubble over ever since they'd met. Like making a soup, it was just a case of being fairly liberal when throwing the ingredients into the pot but being particular about the seasoning.

With Lady Templeton-Jones's bag slung over her left shoulder, her own slung over her right, she set off to Doherty's den — otherwise known as Manvers Street Police Station.

An overnight breeze had chased away the leaden sky of the night before. Spring flowers were budding from displays proliferating all over the city. The braver tourists and locals were carrying raincoats and windcheaters over their arms, believing the sun had come to stay. The pavements were glistening and a rainbow shone beyond Pulteney Bridge.

Honey meandered through the busy traffic of Manvers Street with a spring in her step. Losing those pounds had felt good. A taxi driver tooted his horn and winked at her as she traversed a zebra crossing. She pretended to be coy. How was that for a woman of forty-five? Her springy steps sprang higher as she gingerly avoided the wheel of a black motorcycle that had ventured too far onto the crossing. He revved his engine as though warning her to get out of his way. Honey gave him the finger.

The smell of flower-power air freshener wafted out through the door of the central police station. Before entering she checked the car park. There was no sign of Doherty's low-sprung sports car. Never mind, she told herself. Maybe he'd started jogging to the station on nice days. Her jaw stiffened. Perhaps the blonde Amazon jogged with him to work.

She smiled at the desk sergeant. He was male, thank goodness. Female desk sergeants had a 'competition for Doherty' radar that went doolally the moment they spotted her.

Older male police officers weren't so wary. Working behind the desk was the last post before hanging up their helmet and doing voluntary work for Help the Aged.

Close to retirement age, the desk sergeant had iron-grey hair and droopy eyes.

'Can I help you?'

'I've brought in this.' Honey brought the bag up onto the desk and started to explain.

He made a sucking sound. 'Ooow. It's not officially lost property, not if the owner indicated her intention that she was coming to stay at your hotel. In effect, she has tendered it to your safekeeping.'

Honey was only half listening, her neck swivelling round every time a door behind her opened and closed. It was never

Steve. She played for more time. 'But it'll have all her things in it. Perhaps even her hotel keys.'

He raised his iron-grey eyebrows. 'You haven't looked?' This sounded strange coming from a copper — surely it was illegal to open someone else's property and nose around?

'Certainly not!'

What was he thinking of? Not that she hadn't considered it, of course, but bringing it in as lost property had seemed the right thing to do. Now it didn't seem so clever.

'Look, dear,' he said in that condescending manner usually reserved for ladies of mature years. 'Give it a bit longer. She may have meant for you to take care of the bag until she got to you. Tell you what, you give me her name and I'll make a note of it. If she comes in asking for her property, then I'll point her in your direction. How does that suit?'

She eyed the bland smile, the pale, watery eyes. A queue was building up behind her. Her eyes travelled to the door leading to Steve's domain, wishing he would appear and offer her coffee.

'Is Steve Doherty in?'

'No. He's out on a case at present. Now, if you'll just give me that name . . .'

He indicated the queue with an impatient jerk of his chin.

'Lady Templeton-Jones.'

He wrote it down.

'And the last place you saw her?'

'Near the Assembly Rooms.'

He wrote that down too.

'Were you attending the Assembly Rooms for any particular reason?'

'Yes. It was part of a ghost walk. She was on the ghost walk too.'

'Oh! Right.' He sounded as though he didn't have much truck with ghost walkers, that they should be committed to an immediate custodial sentence along with shoplifters and willy-waggers. 'I'll let you know if she comes in asking about it.' He drew a line beneath what he'd written. 'Next?'

Dismissed and still carrying the brown leather handbag, she left the queue and the desk sergeant to their own devices.

Outside she paused and breathed a huge sigh of relief. The heat inside the police station was oppressive; no wonder they all worked in shirtsleeves.

The fresh air perked her up. A day to walk, she thought. Her feet reached the same conclusion and began to amble in the direction of Bath's premier auction house.

Collectables were her thing. Collectable underwear, stockings, garters, and sometimes gloves, shoes, reticules and parasols — the pretty, small and less noticeable particulars of historical wardrobes. Big frocks and hats fetched big prices. She left those to the big money.

CHAPTER TEN

Today's auction sale was not to her taste: General Household Effects.

She made a screwed-up face that betrayed her distaste. A host of second-hand furniture dealers would be sitting on chairs, waiting to bid on enough items to fill a pantechnicon for shipment to North America.

She wandered in for no other reason than to prove her point. And to say 'hello' to the auction clerk.

Red-bearded and big enough to fill a small living room himself, Alistair was in his usual spot behind the counter where bills were settled.

'Not your day, hen.' His voice was as big as his body, almost drowning out the auctioneer's methodical rant.

'No. When's the next collectables?'

His pursed lips slipped out from between the red hair that forested his chin and upper lip.

'There's one coming up, though not exactly in your sphere of interest. No naughty knickers or lace-trimmed garters. No buxom brassieres either.' He smirked, an obvious reference to a plus-size *büstenhalter* she'd bought some time back. 'Marine connotations,' he added with a smacking of lips and a faraway look in his eyes. 'Big-bucks stuff. Really big, from what I'm hearing.'

'Really?' Her eyebrows rose in puzzled interest. When Alistair spoke like that, it meant international.

'Some of it. There's some of that blue-and-white Chinese ware that went down on a Dutch ship sometime in the seventeenth century. That should make a packet. Then there's the really valuable stuff of world renown.'

'What sort of stuff?' she asked in a hushed voice, her eyes standing on stalks. Even if she herself wasn't interested in buying, her curiosity demanded satisfaction.

A slow smile made Alistair's beard appear to double in size as it spread across his face. He tapped the side of his nose. 'Nothing's confirmed yet. It's a secret, hen. For me to know and you to only guess at.'

'Spoilsport!'

She flounced off but lingered by the door.

'Are you sure . . . ?'

Alistair shook his head and made a sucking sound. 'Can't tell ye, hen. More than my job's worth. Anyway, you'll only get overexcited.'

'Shame,' she said. 'I could use some excitement in my life.'

* * *

The midday traffic was heavy. He nicked his toe beneath the clutch pedal and changed down. This was the third time he'd gone round Queen Square. He'd seen Mrs Honey Driver saunter into Spencers', the famous auction house in Queen Square Place. If he wasn't careful he'd miss her coming out. Anything on wheels had to come back out into Queen Square. Pedestrians had the option of cutting down into Quiet Street or even through Jolly's, the city's only department store.

Jaw clenched, he drove slowly towards the traffic lights fronting the Old King Street section of Queen Square. Once he was through those and there was no sign of his prey, he accelerated until he was facing King Street again. Four times he did this. Four times and there was no sign of her. On the fifth he saw her coming towards him. He held back, slowing the bike by dragging one foot behind him.

He couldn't tell if she saw him. He hoped not. He'd changed his mind about dealing with her right now. His stomach was in a knot at the thought of what he proposed to do — what he *must* do.

CHAPTER ELEVEN

Steve Doherty looked up at the skylight some twelve feet above his head in the narrow old stairwell. Something was blocking the light. A constable he'd sent up to investigate came back to say that the culprit was a piece of waterproof tarpaulin.

'Who found her?'

'I did.'

The small man with a wizened face and henna-dyed hair had stood silently and absolutely still up until now. His breath shook in time with his body.

'Mr Jim Porter. Builder and decorator,' explained Karen Sinclair. Karen was Doherty's new assistant who'd come up from uniform into the post of detective constable. She was young and keen, and he'd admired her before her promotion when she'd still been in uniform. Now she was plain clothes. Jeans and black sweater weren't exactly the stuff of fantasy, but he could still appreciate a fine-looking woman when he saw one.

'I only came to give an estimate for some work,' blurted out Jim Porter.

Doherty could see that poor old Jim's blood pressure was through the roof, the colour of his cheeks almost matching his hair. 'I didn't know her,' he added shakily, though no one had questioned whether he had.

'You had a key?' Doherty asked.

'Yeah. They told me to let meself in and take me time.'

'They?'

'The owners. Wallace and Gates.'

'You came through the front door?'

'Yes.'

'Was it locked?'

'Yes.'

'You're sure?'

'Yes.'

Jim Porter looked away as the body of the woman was laid carefully in a body bag.

'Didn't expect to see this,' he murmured. 'I was only 'ere to quote for a bit of glass in the back window and a lick of paint down in the shop.'

The sound of the zip being pulled made him jump.

'How about the skylight?' asked Doherty. 'Was it leaking?'

'No.'

'You had no reason to cover it with tarpaulin?'

'No, I didn't, and whoever did it done it only recent. It weren't there two days ago when I came to fix the sink.'

Steve Doherty jerked his chin in understanding. Already his mind was connecting the dots. Had the skylight been broken and covered purposely? The woman had to have been lured here with everything prepared in advance. But why?

Jim Porter asked if he could go.

'Leave your name and address. You're more than likely to be called as a witness.'

'Simple but clever,' said the medical examiner before closing his smart black bag. 'Strangled with a length of wire. She put her head in a noose as she walked up the stairs. Our boy pulled it tight from up there.' He pointed at a roof truss.

The medical examiner held up a bag containing the murder 'weapon' — what looked like a length of brown electrical cable.

Doherty inhaled and detected a pleasant hint of perfume. Karen was standing behind him.

'So, what do you think?'

'I think it's Conex.'

She looked at him blankly.

This was his chance to impress. 'Conex is used in computers, and more especially in television and satellite boxes. It's a communications cable rather than electrical.'

'My, you're so knowledgeable.'

She had a sugary tongue. He looked away. Hells bells, she was too young.

'Experience,' he replied tartly. 'No one saw or heard anything?'

Karen shook her head. 'No.' Her hair was blonde and fitted her head tightly like a rubber swimming cap. 'We've enquired of the residents in the building opposite. It's divided into student lets. Not all of them are back from the Easter break. We tried the shop next door, but there's no reply. It's a lock-up like this one with no living accommodation. They're mostly let to antique dealers and other arty-farty types.'

Doherty grunted and unzipped the body bag for one last look. Great effort was needed to keep his eyes fixed on the body. His nose was out of control, twitching in response to Karen's perfume.

'That perfume you're wearing . . .'

Karen's fresh-faced complexion blossomed into a deeper shade of pink. She was so polished, so self-assured. 'It's French.'

'Don't ever wear it again.'

'Oh . . .'

'Strong scents are likely to contaminate the crime scene.'

He sensed her mouth clamping shut and could imagine the disappointment in her eyes. Bending down he uncovered the dead woman a little more. He didn't know what he was looking for, only that he wished to be occupied so that Karen could not draw his attention.

'Sir, I can't come jogging this evening. I've got a date.'

'Fine. It wasn't working anyway.'

'It was for me.'

He glared at her. 'Try to remain professional, Karen.'

She looked crestfallen. 'Sorry, sir.'

The dead woman had dyed hair and a lined face. Sixty at least, he thought, possibly older. Her clothes were good. She was wearing a green cape and a high-necked sweater. There was something white stuck to the soft angora of the cape — a curled-up label. Someone had overlooked it.

'Gloves,' he ordered.

Karen provided them.

He set his jaw. This was serious stuff. Murder was as serious as it gets.

Carefully and without allowing the sticky backing to come away or adhere more strongly, he peered at the writing on the label.

'Ah! Looks as though we have a name.' Holding her lapel between finger and thumb, he turned his head sideways so he could see better. 'Lady Templeton-Jones. Well, that's something to circulate. Some old family must be missing her. It should be fairly easy to learn about her last movements.'

Basically, he was lying. In Steve Doherty's experience, nothing was ever easy in police work. He didn't expect it to be so now, but there are always exceptions to the rule.

He stared at the soft, round face, the hair, the clothes . . . especially the clothes. There was something about them that did not ring true.

'Karen. What's odd about these clothes?'

Karen's slim shadow fell over him. He could hear her breathing and felt her eyes boring into the back of his head before falling on the woman.

She shrugged. 'They're good-quality clothes, guv'nor.'

He grunted. 'I may be out of touch, but to my mind titled country ladies tend to wear tweeds and brogues.' He indicated the label, which had curled up again. 'I can't help thinking . . .' He didn't finish his sentence. 'Never mind. It's just my age. Call it the Jane Marple syndrome.'

Karen frowned. 'Who's she?'

He shook his head. 'You don't read books at bedtime?'

She smiled. 'No. I'm usually doing other things.'

CHAPTER TWELVE

The area outside the building had been cordoned off along with each end of the alley. Armies of interested tourists, shoppers and tradesmen pausing for a quiet smoke had gathered to gawp. An army of necks were craned in a crush at corners overlooking the site. They stared at Doherty as he came out and he stared right back before taking a left. The cobbles were uneven and still slippery after the rain. The moss growth surprised him, considering the number of footsteps that trod over it each day.

He walked slowly, his eyes flicking from side to side, though he didn't expect to see anything. Any items of interest had already been bagged and tagged. He made his way back up the slope.

On reaching the crowd of onlookers, he paused on the periphery, listening to their comments.

'Someone hung themselves.'

'I hear it was murder.'

'No. Not in God's little acre. Things like that don't 'appen 'ere.'

Doherty smiled to himself. Once a Bathonian, always a Bathonian, and no matter what part of the city you were from, there was no city like it in the whole world.

A slight movement made him look behind him. A man was coming out of the lock-up next door. The shop advertised old maritime memorabilia — a popular subsection of antique collection, though a curious one for a city twenty miles or more from the sea.

Still, he thought, Bristol wasn't that far away and hadn't the *Matthew* sailed from there just five years after Columbus got to the West Indies? At least the *Matthew* had reached mainland America — the cold bit. Nova Scotia.

On the spur of the moment he strolled over and looked in the old bow-fronted shop window. Three brass lanterns hung in the centre. He took it that the middle one carried a white masthead light. The ones on either side would carry the red of port and the green of starboard. On the right of the window a very intricate sextant perched half out of a mahogany box. The price tag said 'German, 1940, £675'.

Three plain-looking plates sat on a ledge on the left-hand side of the window. They were each priced at three hundred pounds. Doherty leaned closer and narrowed his eyes so that he could see better. Three thousand pounds seemed a lot for a very plain plate — until he saw the logo printed in the middle: RMS *Titanic*. A note underneath said, 'not verified'.

He blew a low whistle through his teeth.

A brass candleholder sat forward of the lanterns, similar to the one in the window of the empty shop. It had no price tag and didn't look as though it was worth much. Still, who knows? The most rubbishy-looking stuff went for a fortune to the right bidder — look at Honey Driver and her antique underwear.

Setting aside vivid daydreams, he stepped back and looked up at the blank windows above the shop. He tried the door. It was locked and a black-and-white 'closed' sign stared him in the face.

He looked around in an effort to see the man who had come out of the shop selling marine artefacts. He'd only caught a glimpse of his burgundy anorak and dark-coloured holdall. Probably long gone. To his surprise he found it was not so. The same anorak was standing on the edge of the onlookers peering at the crime scene from a distance.

'You,' he said, as he elbowed aside a senior citizen, who immediately elbowed him back.

'Back of the queue, sonny! I was here first.'

Doherty flashed his warrant card. 'I think I have priority, madam.'

She made a little sucking sound, surprise etched all over her powdered face. 'Well, of course, officer! Of course!'

Doherty flashed his card at the man in burgundy. 'Can I have a word?'

The colour drained from the man's face, or perhaps he was already pale. 'Why?'

'Just routine.'

The woman he'd elbowed nudged herself and a friend much closer. Their eyes were piggy in pink faces and their red lips were slightly parted. One woman nudged the other.

'He's asking this man questions.'

The man appeared more alarmed by the two women than he was by Doherty.

'A private word, I think,' said Doherty taking the man's elbow and moving away.

The two women looked peeved. The man looked relieved. He was tall, about mid-fifties and wearing spectacles. The lenses of the spectacles were as thick as bottle bottoms and made his eye colour indistinguishable. Poor soul, thought Doherty. He must have trouble seeing his own feet without them — or for that matter anything of interest in-between. His hair was hidden beneath a beanie the size of a tea cosy. A thick muffler was wound around his neck covering his chin and lower lip. 'I've got a chill,' he muttered. 'Best keep your distance if you don't want to catch it.'

The collar of his overcoat was turned up to further contain his germs and keep him warm. The cuffs were threadbare and bits of cotton hung from where buttons had once been. All in all he looked a bit downmarket as far as antiques went, though the prices in the shop were hardly bargain basement.

Saved from the curious onlookers, the man became impatient. 'Can we make it quick? I do have another job to go to.'

'The shop isn't yours?'

The man shook his head. 'No. I had to do a repair for the owner. The sink in the back was leaking.'

'Seems both these properties need work doing on them. Is the owner around?'

The man almost choked with derisive laughter. 'Good God, no. The owner rents the shop out. Nobody lives there and the bloke who rents it isn't there today. In fact I think he's out of the country on a buying trip.'

'Hmm. So no one would have been in there last night?'

'Shouldn't think so.'

'Shame. I was hoping someone might have seen something.'

''Fraid not.'

'And your name is . . . ?'

'Coulthard,' said the man. 'Reginald Coulthard.'

Doherty thanked him for his time, took one last glance at the crowd, then headed back to Manvers Street.

CHAPTER THIRTEEN

Steve Doherty was swinging through the corridor leading from the car park at the rear of the station. He got as far as the locker room, meaning to pick up an old pair of trainers he'd left there. He sniffed. His top lip curled upwards. Scruffy he could cope with. Smelly he could not.

'This better be worth it,' he said to himself.

Doherty went over it in his head again. Warren Price — a violent murderer serving a life sentence, and one of Doherty's first collars as a detective. Price had escaped and was thought to be somewhere in or around Bath. Clearly he felt he had a score to settle . . .

Three nights on the trot he'd been out jogging with Karen hoping to draw him out of cover, get him to make a move. No luck so far.

The locker room saw the most activity at shift-changing times. He'd timed himself to be exactly halfway between changeovers. Hopefully the locker room would be empty. No one would see him take the trainers from his locker and out to the boot of his car. All things being equal he would escape comments about 'middle-age spread' or 'pounding the beat with Kinky Karen', as the less-enlightened boys in blue called her.

One foot on a bench, the other on the ground, Sergeant Packer was the only one there. He was slipping on a pair of bicycle clips. What was left of his hair flopped grey and thin over his eyes. He looked up and grinned. 'Hello, hello, hello. If it isn't DI Doherty. What's this I 'ear about you taking up jogging?'

'Who told you that?'

'Guy Fawkes and Beau Bridges.'

The two men he referred to were actually called Guy Ford and Tony Bridges, but coppers can't resist an obvious nickname.

Steve opened his locker door and hid behind it. 'I need to get fit,' he said simply.

Sergeant Packer made no comment about exercise. Instead he said, 'Your girlfriend's been in.'

'Yeah, yeah,' said Steve, unwilling to go through another ribbing about getting free hotel rooms and someone to warm the other half of the bed.

'She brought in a bag that some woman left at the Garrick's. From what she said, it sounds like a batty old titled type going a bit absent-minded.'

Titled? He paused in the middle of lifting the trainers from the locker, mildly aware that they exuded a smell similar to a hunk of overripe Stilton. 'What time was that?'

'This morning,' said Packer, a lascivious grin splitting his shiny, spotty face. 'Now there's an excuse for you.' Packer winked.

The bloody sod was reading his mind.

Trainers tucked under his arm, he quickstepped past his own office and into the area behind the receiving sergeant's desk.

It was four thirty in the afternoon, and things hadn't yet heated up to fever pitch — a level of activity that usually only occurred between eleven and midnight.

Doherty said hello to the desk sergeant on duty and peered over her shoulder, his eyes quickly glancing at that morning's entries. His eyes scanned down the page and suddenly jolted to a halt. *Lady Templeton-Jones.* There she was.

The desk sergeant turned her head and eyed him with a withering stare. 'Are you looking down my top, DI Doherty?'

'No,' he said, taking his phone from his pocket, his eyes still fixed on the details entered in the log. 'Something much more interesting than that.'

CHAPTER FOURTEEN

The smell of freshly roasted coffee and freshly baked scones filled Honey's office. Doherty had finally phoned, and she was gleefully preparing for their early morning meeting.

On arrival Doherty seemed fairly relaxed. He told her about the murder. She told him about the bag plus the fact that she was probably the last person to see the deceased alive.

Silently and purposefully, he went into action. He settled himself on the edge of her desk and called into the station to relay the details as they appeared on the deceased's passport. 'She called herself Lady Templeton-Jones, but it seems her name was also Wanda Carpenter, age sixty-eight.' He nodded in response to whatever was being said on the other end of the phone.

'Absolutely. We'll leave them to take care of that.' He hung up. 'They'll contact the US police and inform the family. I've asked for some details to be sent to us.'

Doherty was wearing his serious expression. The deceased's brown leather bag was sitting centre stage on the desk — a bit like a coffin, though full of belongings rather than a body. It was down to Steve to itemise the contents for future reference just in case anything came to light that might have a bearing on the case.

Doherty began carrying out an inventory of the most important stuff — passport, money, crumpled receipts, leaflets of various attractions — the Jane Austen House, the Roman Baths and a concert at Bath Abbey. He dipped back into the bag for the final items, writing each down on his list.

'Hairbrush . . . lipstick . . . a box . . .' The box was about twelve by eight by two inches deep.

'Contact lenses,' said Honey, recognising the same green box she received every three months.

Doherty set it to one side. 'Powder compact . . . lipstick — two lipsticks? How many does a woman need?'

Honey put him straight. 'Depends on what she's wearing. My mother has a lipstick for every outfit.'

He pulled a face. 'I can believe that. I know your mother.'

'Two's fine,' said Honey with a casual shrug. Though the deceased hadn't struck her as a woman who did Helena Rubinstein — or even Tesco's own. She certainly couldn't recall her wearing make-up of any sort. The rain could have clouded her vision, of course. It had hardly been the night for keen observation.

He set the bag and his list to one side. 'I'll get back to this later.'

Honey caught him giving her a sidelong look.

'You OK?'

'I'm fine.'

It wasn't entirely true. She was rattled. Anyone could tell by the way she was fiddling with the rings on her fingers. She hadn't been this close to a victim of anything until taking on the job of Crime Liaison Officer for the Hotels Association. Up until that point her only brushes with violence of any kind had been a punch-up at a wedding the hotel had once hosted, when the bridegroom had called his newly acquired mother-in-law an interfering, ugly old bat. It hadn't boded well for the marriage, especially when said mother-in-law had retaliated with a swing of her handbag that had knocked him out cold. He couldn't possibly have known what kinds of heavyweight junk a woman carries in her handbag. But that was a domestic and had only resulted in concussion. This was murder.

As one of the last people to see Wanda Carpenter — Lady Templeton-Jones — alive, Mary Jane was called for. She arrived with a small Georgian writing slope tucked beneath her arm. Honey offered her a croissant.

She eyed the croissants dismissively. 'Can I have chocolate digestives?'

Lindsey was summoned to fetch some. She came back carrying a tray of biscuits and wearing a headset. Recently she'd begun making calls on the computer.

Steve lightened up. 'You look very hi-tech, Lindz. A bit Trekkie.'

Honey's daughter pulled a face. 'That's what Mum said. She said it was too Starship Enterprise — until I told her she's the only person in the known universe not making calls on Skype or Zoom.'

'So our lady wasn't a lady,' said Honey, wishing to change the subject. Technical matters left her cold — and that included computers, tablets, the timer on the microwave and even her ancient DVD player. Her phone was a necessary evil, though she only did calls and texts. The occasional photo, maybe. Anything else fried her brain.

'Ha!' said Mary Jane, loud enough to make Lindsey jump and the cups rattle. 'I just *knew* she wasn't a *real* lady. Real ladies have breeding. One look and you can tell whether they've got historic ancestry or not. Look at me, for instance.'

Everyone looked. No one said anything.

Mary Jane's ancestors must have been a little on the eccentric side, assuming dress sense and general behaviour were hereditary. Tall and thin with arms like broom handles, she was presently wearing a cerise pink trouser suit and lime-green Alice band. Her hair was tightly curled and dyed a fetching shade of cobalt blue. She clearly considered herself a lady. It was all to do with her ancestor, Sir Cedric, haunting the Green River Hotel, and, most specifically, the room Mary Jane presently occupied.

The silence was awkward.

Steve pricked it. 'If we stick to the point . . .'

Lindsey followed through. 'Mary Jane's probably right. Titles can be bought online for as little as three hundred dollars. The real ones are upwards of five thousand, some as much as thirty thousand pounds. Some even more.'

Mary Jane's jaw dropped. 'You don't say?'

Steve Doherty was all ears. 'So there's an official and an unofficial market?'

'Correct.'

'Tell me more.'

Lindsey, a fountain of historical knowledge, nodded into her microphone. 'There are a lot of old titles passed down in noble families, not used but still owned by them.'

'Did they earn these titles for services to the crown? To Henry the Eighth and people like that?' asked an enthralled Mary Jane.

Lindsey's smile was slow and slightly wicked. 'For services rendered. Some in battle. Some in bed.'

Steve closed in. 'Go on.'

Honey knew where he was coming from. Never mind the history, give us the lascivious details, please.

Lindsey, true to her soul, kept to the facts. 'It's no big deal for the old nobility to sell on defunct titles they no longer use. No property attached, of course, but they are listed by the Master of Arms — the keeper of titles in the heraldic process. But as with all things, especially online, there are sharks in the water. Hence the titles marked down for three hundred dollars — aimed at Americans, of course, though they're not the only partakers. Other colonials and even total foreigners buy defunct titles.'

Honey asked the obvious question. 'But why do people do it? What's the point of having a title you didn't inherit?'

Lindsey raised one eyebrow and eyed her mother with just a hint — a very small hint — of accusation. 'It impresses the flunkies.'

Honey felt her face getting warm. 'I'm never impressed by titles!'

Lindsey's eyebrow lifted a little higher. 'Maybe not, but you're canny around them, just in case they can do the business some good — recommendations to their friends or a mention in a glossy magazine.'

'That's different.'

Steve intervened. He addressed Lindsey. 'Are *you* impressed by titled people?'

Lindsey shook her head; this week her hair was a glossy beetroot colour, a single lick of blonde dissecting her fringe. 'No. I'm more interested in the nobility of the past, when they *made* history. Modern-day titles are no longer relevant. Nowadays I'm a republican.'

Mary Jane looked confused. Honey guessed that as an American national she was having trouble making her mind up as to where she stood. Should she declare for republicanism or defend her aristocratic heritage?

Lindsey made a comment about going off to beat the peasants in the kitchen.

Honey raised a disbelieving eyebrow at the thought of anyone attempting to beat Smudger the chef. Not healthy!

'Right,' said Doherty, turning to Mary Jane. 'I need you to make a statement.'

'The woman was a fraud!'

Doherty was a picture of forbearance. 'That isn't quite what I meant. I want you to think very carefully, Mary Jane. When did you see her last?'

Mary Jane screwed up her face, her pale eyebrows hovering around the bridge of her nose.

'Outside the Garrick's Head. That's when I last saw her clearly. I only kind of glimpsed her after that. Hell, it was as though God had turned on the faucet and was trying to wash us down the drain!'

'Right. "*I last saw the woman referred to as Lady Templeton-Jones, outside the Garrick's Head . . .*"'

Doherty was patient. He went on speaking each line out loud to Mary Jane, gaining her approval before writing it down. Eventually he had enough for her to sign.

Honey rolled her eyes as Mary Jane spread the letter on the writing slope, the whole thing perched on her knees.

Doherty looked on in amazement as she unfastened the brass clasps, then opened the lid of the inkwell. Last but not least out came the quill pen.

'The past is still alive with me,' she said. 'If I'm to write anything, I do it the way my ancestors did.'

She proceeded to sign the statement with a feathery flourish, writing her name with an ivory-handled blotter. Once that was done, she was told she was free to go.

Mary Jane half rose from her chair looking pretty thoughtful. She paused, her long legs bent like the stem of a desk lamp. 'I suppose I could try contacting her and ask her who did it.'

CHAPTER FIFTEEN

Once they were alone, Steve burst out laughing. 'A ghost walk! Are you kidding me?'

'Mary Jane's birthday. My treat.'

A lie, but necessary. She'd bought Mary Jane a pale-pink cameo broach for her birthday. The walk was part of her new lifestyle — walk whenever you can and the weight goes with it. Seemed a good mantra. It was working. Along with keeping away from rich, creamy sauces.

He continued to laugh.

'This isn't funny. Anyway, there could be life after death.'

'No one's ever come back to confirm it, have they?'

The laughter reduced to a gurgle deep in his throat.

Her phone rang. She checked the number. 'Casper.'

Steve met her eyes. The amusement died. 'You're unnerved.'

She nodded. 'Yes.'

'Is Casper on your back?'

She shook her head. 'No. Not yet. He must have only just found out. He'll want the details.'

Casper St John Gervais was chair of Bath Hotels Association, and it was Casper who'd appointed her as crime liaison officer for the association. The city of Bath depended on tourism for its living. The association had a vested interest in preventing crime from soiling its worldwide reputation.

'Don't phone him back. I'll call in and brief him on my way home. No problem.'

'Thanks.'

'You're very subdued.'

'I was the last person to see her. The last person . . .'

'I understand.' He cleared his throat, lowered his eyes. 'On another note, we've kind of cooled. Is that what you want?'

Seemingly of their own volition, her lips did a kind of hula dance as she considered an answer.

'You mean we only see each other over a dead body.'

Steve went back to listing and speaking each item.

'Set of keys . . . purse . . .' He opened the latter and began listing the contents. 'Fifty pounds in denominations of one twenty, two tens, two fives . . .' He began listing credit cards. 'And a key ring,' he said finally, tipping up the plastic tab so he could see the motif more clearly. 'RMS *Titanic*. Hmmm. Our victim had about as much luck as that did, sinking on her maiden voyage. A diary,' continued Doherty. He began leafing through. 'She's got the ghost walk pencilled in for the evening . . . followed by a squiggly doodle. During the day she went to . . .'

The fact that he paused attracted her attention. He was chewing his lip. She sat up and leaned forward, almost overbalancing the chair. 'Well, go on. What did she do during the day?'

She tried to read his expression, but he was keeping it deadpan. *Just to annoy me*, she thought.

'Steve! Are you going to tell me or what?'

He flipped her a sideways grin. 'You're curious?'

She growled, Rottweiler fashion.

Doherty took the hint. 'She had an appointment at some place with the initials ASS.'

'An unfortunate name.'

'I kid you not. There's a phone number.'

Honey met no resistance as she took the diary and scrutinised the details herself.

Doherty went on talking. 'You're looking good. Have you been going to the gym or just limiting the croissants?'

'Ditto. I mean . . . you look good too. Been jogging or something?'

He stumbled over his tongue.

'Shall I phone the number?'

He looked blank. 'What?'

'The telephone number.' She jerked her chin at the diary and reached for the desk phone. The tone trilled about five times before being answered.

'Assured Security Shredding. How may we help you?' The voice sounded young.

Honey thought on her feet. 'Hi. We have a delivery to make. Can you give me your full address, please?' She wrote the details down as she spoke.

Honey put down the phone. The address was recognisable as being on a trading estate between Bath and Trowbridge.

'Do you know it?' Honey asked as Doherty studied the details she'd written down.

'Assured Security Shredding. Can't say that I do.'

'ASS for short.'

He was frowning, and she could guess what he was thinking. What would an elderly American woman who'd bought an old English title want with a security shredding firm?

Doherty was good at his job and could withdraw into himself when he had a lot of thinking to do. He was doing that now; there was a closed look in his eyes as though he couldn't possibly let in any trivialities until he'd got rid of the serious stuff.

'I'll pay them a visit. Let's get the formalities out of the way first.' Pen in hand, he was ready for her to make her statement.

They went through the details: what time they'd left the hotel, what time they'd arrived outside the Garrick's Head.

'Are you sure of that? How did you get there?'

'I'm sure. We walked, obviously.'

He looked up. 'On a night like that? Why didn't you drive?'

'Hah!' She smiled, waving the idea aside. 'It was a short walk.'

He didn't pursue it. Just as well. The truth was delicate. When she'd relocated to England, Mary Jane had brought over her most cherished possession from the good old US of A: a pink, two-door Cadillac coupe convertible. One ride and Honey vowed never to go out in it again. She wasn't sure what she was more scared of — ghosts or Mary Jane's driving. But Mary Jane was a sensitive soul and Honey had no intention of spreading the word, intentionally or otherwise.

Instead she went on to explain that by the time they'd arrived the theatre crowd had already passed and were seated beneath the vaulted gilt ceilings of the Theatre Royal next door.

'So it was definitely around eight fifteen. There wasn't a single soul around — except us.'

'A bunch of nuts on a ghost walk. Right.' He wrote it down.

She gave him the evil eye. 'Two out of ten for your terminology. I resent you calling me a nut. It was a fun thing. Anyway, some people really do believe in all that stuff.'

He raised his eyes without raising his head, pen still gripped and ballpoint fixed to the notepad. 'Some kids still believe in Santa Claus.'

'So, are you calling me a nut or merely immature?'

'I didn't say that.'

'Anyway, I was there at Mary Jane's invitation, remember?'

'Now, she *is* a nut,' he said. He leaned closer. 'What I meant is that there you were, out in the pouring rain on my night off when you could have been tucked up somewhere warm.'

She leaned forward too, and they gazed into each other's eyes. 'You've left it long enough.'

He jerked his head away. 'You told me you'd been busy.'

'So did you. Anyway, I was getting myself into shape.'

'For what?' He spread his arms and shrugged his shoulders. 'For what?'

'No need to shout. I heard you the first time.' She sniffed and folded her arms. She could turn on Miss Huffy at the drop of a hat if she wanted. 'I wanted to achieve something.'

He grinned. 'So did I.'

'Have you ever thought about taking more exercise?'

'I'm fine as I am.'

She sensed a change of tone. He wouldn't be drawn towards making a confession about being out jogging. But she'd find out. In time she'd find out.

He turned serious. 'First things first.'

He took out his pen again and rested the paperwork on his knees, which meant drawing them both together like a maiden aunt.

'Right. So where were we?'

Step by step, sentence by sentence, she led him through the puddles and pavements of the ghost walk all the way to the alley sloping down past the antique shops onto George Street.

'I heard something. I looked over my shoulder.'

'Who was it?'

'I couldn't see anyone. But I think she — Lady Templeton-Jones — began to walk faster. Amazingly fast for a woman using a walking stick. Sometimes I think she was trying to leave me behind.'

'To lose you?'

She considered it. Yes, she thought. That was it. Her Ladyship had been trying to lose her. 'She obviously didn't care too much for my conversation. Too beneath her, do you think?'

'Cast your mind back. Was there anything else?'

Settling herself back in her chair, she closed her eyes. In her mind she could see the rumpled pavement slabs passing beneath her feet, the wetness lying like liquid sugar on the surface. She remembered the laces of her trainers coming undone and told him so.

'I stopped to tie them up, and when I next looked up, she was gone!'

He asked her the other question, the one she wasn't quite sure how to answer. What exactly had she seen? Rain. Darkness. Feet. Hat. She took so long considering it that he presumed she hadn't heard and repeated the question.

'Did you see anyone else?'

The answer was strangely elusive. Why did her lips flex and wobble like an elastic band when she found a question difficult to answer?

First things first. She took a deep breath. 'I saw people down at the end of the alley on George Street. Even though I'd dropped behind, I presumed the group had somehow managed to get ahead of me, though I couldn't understand how. I presumed she was with them, but then I reasoned she couldn't cover that much ground in a few seconds. It turned out not to be the group anyway.'

He dutifully jotted it down.

She entwined her hands around her knees, squeezing hard enough to make her bones crack. Perhaps he wouldn't ask the dreaded question, the one she wasn't sure how to answer.

He did.

'Did you see anyone else close by once you noticed she was gone?'

She nodded and put a brave face on it. 'Someone walked past. I didn't see his face. All I saw was a pair of black patent shoes, a cloak and a big hat.'

'Height? Weight? Anything?'

She shook her head. 'It was the classic dark and stormy night.'

Convinced she'd done her bit, she went back to entwining her hands around her knees. She also fixed her gaze on the toes of her brown suede shoes. It took a little time before she realised Doherty was giving her one of his intense, meaningful looks. Funny how he could do that and how she *knew* he was doing it, as though his eyes were on the end of fibre-optic cables and tickling the side of her head.

'Did you recognise him?'

'No.'

'There was something special about him. I can see it in your face. Go on. What was it?'

Now she squirmed. She had to completely envelope her knees with her arms to stop it. She took a deep breath. 'His shoes weren't wet. Not a spot of water on them.'

'OK. OK. He'd taken shelter from the storm. In a doorway. Beneath a parapet. There're tons of them along there.'

'I suppose so.'

'Was there anything else?'

She squirmed again beneath *that* look.

Tilting her head back, she looked up at the ceiling. Trailing her gaze along the ornate plasterwork she finally settled on bunches of grapes in the corners. If she'd been anything like a secretive person she would have kept her mouth shut. But she couldn't do that. She had to tell the truth.

'I'm not sure that he had a body.'

There was silence. And him looking askance. And her looking back up at the ceiling.

At last he said, 'OK. You saw a ghost.'

She heard the amusement.

'Did you go in the Garrick's Head beforehand?'

She stopped, seeing by his expression precisely where this was going. 'No I did not! He was wearing a black cloak — like an old-fashioned evening cloak. Maybe that's why I couldn't see his body.'

A smile drifted across his lips and into his eyes. He began shaking his head. 'You need a break. We both need a break.' The serious expression returned. He looked at her, glanced at the half-completed statement, and then back at her. 'We'll just say you thought you saw someone, but not enough to verify details. OK?'

'OK.' It was good enough for her. Superstition was based on suggestion. Deserted streets and dark nights only served to influence the imagination. Everything seemed so explicable in the cold light of day.

She took a deep breath. 'So what's next?'

'I'm planning to interview all those people who were last to see her alive. I'd like you to sit in, not just because of your position with the Hotels Association, but because you might be able to verify statements — remember where people were at the time she disappeared.'

'That reminds me, I need to let Casper know what's happening.'

* * *

A motley collection of clock chimes sounded as Casper answered the phone.

'What gives? What's the story? Have you made any progress yet?'

'Nothing concrete. I'm working closely with Detective Inspector Doherty.'

'Oh. Him. I have great faith in you, Honey. I'm sure you'll have this solved in no time. After all, you have first-hand knowledge of the woman. She must have said something useful.'

'Besides her name, the only other thing I know about Lady Templeton-Jones is that she wanted to check out of her hotel and into mine. I presume the one she was staying in wasn't up to scratch.'

The line seemed to freeze. Honey felt that she'd touched a raw nerve.

CHAPTER SIXTEEN

Casper St John Gervais turned pale as uncooked pastry. He put his hand over the receiver and held it slightly away from him as he locked eyes with Neville, his hotel manager.

'Neville. The empty room. Lady Templeton-Jones. Is that the name?' He spoke very slowly, very precisely, his tone rising with each word spoken as though stinging his throat.

Neville nodded. 'That's her. Her bed hasn't been slept in.'

Casper closed his eyes and took a deep breath. 'The woman decided to book into the Green River. How could she?'

Gathering himself together, he resumed speaking to Honey. 'I cannot believe that she was not satisfied with her hotel. Still. There is taste and there is taste-*less*.'

The penny dropped. By tone of voice alone, Casper had told her where the dead woman had been staying. La Reine Rouge!

Casper put the phone down before she could apologise.

* * *

Honey groaned and screwed up her face as she turned to Steve. 'Whoops!'

'What do you mean, whoops?'

'She was staying at Casper's place!'

'Whoops!'

Honey glared at him. 'It's not funny. Casper isn't good at taking criticism. I dread the next time I run into him. He'll be *so* sniffy.'

Steve grinned and shrugged. 'No change there, then.' His expression hardened as he called up a team and ordered them round to La Reine Rouge.

Honey's mind was skipping between clues to the murder and what Casper would say the next time she saw him.

Both thoughts were pretty heavy. All the good work of the last few months drowned in her preoccupied brain. Her fingers scurried over the last croissant.

Casper — or rather his hotel — was part of the murder, so worrying about him took precedence for the moment. 'I'll stay away from him for a few days . . .' She chewed. 'Give him chance to calm down . . .' More chewing. 'And then I'll explain . . . I expect it's as spick and span as ever by now. He'll—'

'Get him back!' Steve Doherty was on his feet.

Crumbs sprayed from her mouth as she gaped in horror. 'No! I couldn't!'

Steve dialled recall. Casper answered.

'Don't touch anything in that room. Don't let it and don't clean it. Not until we've looked at it,' Steve told Casper.

Honey brushed the crumbs from her bosom. 'We?'

'After we've done the interviews we'll take a look at the room. This woman had two separate identities. Maybe she also had two separate lives.'

CHAPTER SEVENTEEN

Hot water poured over Honey's closed eyes and naked body, helping her think, and there was a lot to think about since last night. She'd been the last person to see the victim alive — apart from the murderer. Lady Templeton-Jones had been there one minute and was gone the next. Quick as lightning. Steve Doherty had promised to keep her informed. The waiting was agonising.

Suddenly her mobile phone launched into the hallelujah chorus. Dripping wet, she sprang from the shower and grabbed it. Steam had made it slippery. Like a bar of soap it slid out of her hands and did an orbit of the toilet seat. She caught it just before it skittered off into the deep water of the toilet bowl. Casper was on the other end. Now she wished she'd let it drown.

'I don't like being involved in this,' he said coldly.

'Casper, I was in the shower . . .'

'The police are all over my premises.'

She knew this wasn't true. The police were at La Reine Rouge in the room lately occupied by Her Ladyship. It came as no surprise that Casper was being overdramatic. Crime happened to other people, in other hotels.

'They're only in one room, Casper, and shouldn't be there very long.'

'I hope not. The press are coming. I've insisted they give me a full-page spread.'

The line went dead. Despite everything, Casper was going to make the best of the deal. All publicity was good publicity.

Mildly satisfied that Casper wouldn't be boiling her in oil, she padded through into the living room wrapped in a towel. More thinking was needed. She went to the kitchen, poured a cup of black coffee and headed for the living room and her favourite 'thinking' chair.

A singular question kept running round in her head. Why had Her Ladyship decided to check out of Casper's hotel and into hers? OK, she was cheaper, but was that enough of a reason? And why make that decision so swiftly and so late in the day?

Honey breathed in the comparative calm of the old coach house she called home and shared with her daughter. This was her oasis away from it all. Her surroundings helped calm her nerves.

Whereas other people had watercolours hanging on their walls, Honey had antique underwear. Just like watercolours, her displays were safely behind glare-proof glass. The lace was fragile, the satin still shiny; sexy it was not. Vintage drawers were shaped like footballers' shorts — baggy and with plenty of room to manoeuvre.

The old station clock set halfway up the apex wall struck eight.

Honey finished drying herself, chose black trousers and a red sweater, tucked her hair up with a fixing comb and slid her feet into a pair of black ballet pumps decorated with gold bows. The dress code for today was quick and casual. No make-up. She'd been summoned to the Garrick's Head along with the rest of the ghost walkers; Doherty wanted to interview everybody back where everything had started.

'Get going, get going,' she muttered to herself. In her head she counted off the things she had to do before abandoning ship.

First she went to the kitchen and said hi to Smudger. She enquired if their stock of frozen veg was holding up. He blushed and mumbled something about having to order more peas.

Smudger's underlings scurried around, going about their business. The kitchen reverberated to the sound of clattering pans, hissing gas and the dull thud of a closing fridge door. The lack of conversation was nothing new. Smudger was not a morning person. The kitchen staff kept their heads down and got on with what they had to do. It beat getting your head snapped off.

The other sound Honey noticed was that of her stomach rumbling. Nerves, she decided. Damn the diet. It had to be dealt with.

There was toast in the dining room. She followed the smell, said good morning to the remaining guests and fixed herself a slice. Just a little butter . . .

Her stomach rumbled in protest. It wasn't wise to ignore it. Another, thicker application, then a smidgen of marmalade . . . then a more generous helping. Yummy!

She ate it on the hoof, the whole slice demolished by the time she reached reception. On her way she popped into the ladies' bathroom. A quick look in the mirror confirmed there were no crumbs around her mouth. No shiny smear of butter either.

Another quick glance. Did she look any fatter? It was difficult to tell. Yet. Time to give herself a good talking to.

'OK, so you've sinned. What the hell? A little of what you fancy does you good.' Her reflection looked guiltily back.

There was no getting away with the fact that sins tasted good. A salad for lunch should get her back on track. Same for supper. And no wine.

She headed for reception.

It was Lindsey's morning off and she was having a lie-in. Anna was on duty.

Honey checked the invoices made out for guests who were leaving that morning. Everything was in order.

'Everything is in order,' said Anna, echoing what she already knew.

Honey felt the receptionist's eyes scrutinising her.

'You know I always do this right, Mrs Driver.'

It was a questioning, almost hurt tone.

'Of course.'

Honey opened her leather-bound diary and entered her movements for that day and read them out to Anna as she wrote them down.

'First the Garrick's Head. Not sure how long I'll be,' she said.

'I almost forgot. Your mother called again,' Anna began. 'She said to make sure you're here. She's on her way.'

Honey was about to make a run for it when the double doors — warm mahogany with brass fingerplates and original handles — swung open.

'Hannah!'

Her mother's outfit contrasted vividly with the muted tones of a Regency-inspired interior. Purple-and-white Lacroix leggings with pistachio-green highlights teamed with a mauve blouson jacket. Her suede boots matched the jacket. So did her lipstick.

Anna blinked.

Honey slid on her sunglasses.

'Mother, I can't stop. I've got to go to the Garrick's Head.'

Taking a sharp intake of breath, her mother positively *glared* at her watch. 'This early in the morning?'

'I'm not drinking there. It's police business.'

There was a gap between her mother and the reception counter. She did a sliding movement, back flattened against the desk, in the direction of the doors. Not a very good avoidance tactic, though a quick sideways sashay should have been enough. Today Gloria Cross was on top form and could move alarmingly quick for a seventy-year-old. Vice-like fingers gripped Honey's wrist. Lacking her daughter's height, Gloria stood on tiptoe and sniffed.

'Are you sure about that? I wouldn't want you following in your father's footsteps. Other people have eggs for breakfast. He had Jack Daniel's with toast.'

'I've only had coffee and toast.' She failed to admit to the butter and marmalade. It didn't count as sinning if no one knew about it.

Her mother's fingers were long and tipped with red varnish. She had one hell of a grip, more peregrine falcon than pensioner.

'Mother, I have to go. This is a police investigation. I'm sitting in on interviewing the witnesses.'

Honey prised off each finger in turn, but they kept coming back.

Her mother went round-eyed in surprise and loosened her fingers. 'Is it a murder investigation?'

'Yes.'

'I hope it was a crime of passion. They're the best sort.'

Gloria Cross read a lot, but only romance; a flock of her sort could clear the library shelves of Mills and Boon in a matter of minutes.

'I don't know that it is,' Honey replied, though in all honesty she couldn't be sure. This case was a blank sheet. It could be some time before it was filled in.

'Will you get to ask some of the questions?' her mother asked.

'I don't know. I expect Doherty would prefer to ask the questions himself.'

'You could play good cop, bad cop,' said Gloria Cross with great enthusiasm. 'Best if you could be bad cop. Bad cop's the one who gets to do the physical stuff.'

'Physical stuff?'

'Torture. Nothing much. Just bending their fingers back or giving them a rabbit punch in the guts.'

Is that what they're putting in Mills and Boon these days?

'I have to go.'

Honey swung her bag over her shoulder, and swift as a Thomson's gazelle, though nowhere near as graceful, she sprang for the door.

'I've got a problem,' her mother called after her. 'I need your help.'

'Speak to Lindsey. I'll catch up later.'

She let the door slam shut behind her. Problems came to her mother in small packages listed under headings like house maintenance, noisy neighbours or choosing this year's cruise for the over-seventies club. Whatever it was could wait.

CHAPTER EIGHTEEN

Bath, a World Heritage Site, is noted for its elegance, culture and unrivalled history. That was how most people viewed it. But sometimes it turned weird.

Honey had never envisaged any of this murder stuff when she'd first entered the hotel industry. And now here she was sitting in on a murder inquiry.

The only problem was that this particular murder had come too close for comfort. Investigating a crime after the event was one thing. Being the last person to see the victim alive — possibly even seeing the murderer — was another.

Honey stopped outside the imposing facade of the Garrick's Head and took a deep breath. This part of Bath hadn't changed much since it was built back in the eighteenth century. She looked up at the gleaming windows. If it wasn't for the traffic she could easily imagine herself back then. As it was, she looked for signs of past residents. They said that the Grey Lady could sometimes be seen at an upstairs window or even peering over the parapet. At present the windows reflected nothing except sky and other buildings, the stuff she expected to see. She'd never spied anything else, much as she might want to — or not.

Mary Jane had once told her that ghosts and spirits are only seen when the mind least expects it. At present her mind was too full of other things.

'In there,' said a police constable, standing to one side of the steps leading in. The smell of something cooking smothered that of the traffic, dust and everything else. There were lots of restaurants around here, lots of kitchens in the basements of lofty houses.

Honey took a sniff. Her stomach rumbled. Shepherd's pie? Whatever it was, the smell was good.

The chest of the policeman expanded and contracted. It was accompanied by a hefty sigh. 'My favourite. Steak and kidney.'

Honey shook her head. 'No, shepherd's pie.'

He looked affronted. 'I know steak and kidney when I smell it. Bet you a fiver.'

'OK.'

He got out a fiver. Honey snatched it. 'Shepherd's pie,' she said, pointing to a chalkboard leaning against the wall in the vestibule behind him.

He muttered something inaudible.

Honey made her way into what had been termed the Green Room, where actors and the gay community had once gathered. Tables were neatly arranged and covered with tablecloths ready for lunch.

Two more constables stood just inside and parted to let her through.

Doherty was sitting at a table down at the far end of the room. The cloth had been removed, the cutlery replaced by notepads, witness statements and pens.

Doherty looked up when she entered. 'Good morning.' His eyes held hers for a moment. 'Take a seat. Would you like coffee?'

'No. I've had one.'

She sat down opposite him, surprised at her own nervousness.

Steve noticed her unease. 'Just here,' he said, patting the space beside him.

After moving around the table, she swung her bag from her shoulder and tucked it between her feet.

'Are you sure you wouldn't like a coffee? You can have a tot of something in it to steady your nerves.'

She shook her head. 'My mother would curse me. Can we begin? As long as you treat me gently. I'm feeling fragile.'

'That's a promise. Anything you want to ask me before we start?' He smiled. Fine lines radiated from the corners of his eyes.

'You look as though you got ready in a hurry. No make-up.'

He may not have meant it to, but it stung. She retaliated.

'I take it your razor's broken. You look like a tramp.'

He grinned, his fingertips making a rasping sound as they ran over his stubble.

'Designer stubble. It's hip in Hollywood. Touch it.' His chin jutted forward.

'No, thank you.'

They got down to business. She repeated the events once again, right up to the moment Wanda Carpenter had vanished.

'And you said you saw someone.'

She squirmed as she nodded. 'I was tying my lace when he passed by. He wasn't one of our group.'

'The one you thought might be a ghost.'

'I didn't say that.'

'OK. Could he have been part of the other group you bumped into at the end?'

She made a sharp guffaw. 'Are you kidding? They were more *Starlight Express* than *Phantom of the Opera*.'

'Phantom?'

'I've already told you. He wasn't a phantom.'

'Are you reassuring me or reassuring yourself?'

She went over the details in her mind. At some point she *had* regarded the dark stranger as some kind of phantom. He'd appeared from nowhere. Had vanished into nothing.

'Anything else you remember?'

She shook her head.

'Could he have been stalking her?'

Honey thought about it. She hadn't heard footsteps following them, but that didn't mean there were none. The sound of hammering rain and water gushing through pipes could have easily drowned out the sound of footsteps. She put this to him.

He agreed. 'If he was stalking her, he has to be our prime suspect. But who was he? Where did he come from?'

She nodded. 'Evening dress. It had to be evening dress.'

In the cold light of day logic replaced fantasy; dark clothes and patent shoes pointed to someone coming home from a dinner party, an official function or the theatre. Yes, that was it.

CHAPTER NINETEEN

Mr and Mrs Hamilton George the Fourth were first in. They were in late middle age, wore affable smiles and sported red tartan trousers and thick Aran sweaters. Their trainers were as big as buckets and they both carried backpacks that closely matched their trousers. Mr George also wore red earmuffs that were presently slipped just behind his ears. The wire from an iPod trailed over his broad chest. He was shorter than his wife though wide in the beam, and Honey tried hard not to stare at her impressive bosom.

On this occasion Steve had opted to interview each couple together. If their stories seemed suspect, he'd interview them separately down at the station.

The Georges hailed from San Diego, which explained why Mary Jane had floated off during the walk, catching up on news from home. Mary Jane came from La Jolla, just south of there.

After name and address came profession.

'Retired,' explained Mr George. 'I'm over here on vacation.'

'My husband used to be very big at IBM,' gushed his wife, who was pretty big herself — in body, that is. 'He held a very important position. He was well thought of.'

'And well paid,' her husband reminded her with a sideways smile.

Mrs George seemed barely to notice his intervention. 'But he keeps himself busy. And we travel. We've always wanted to travel. And now we do. We've been all over the world, haven't we, Hamilton?'

Her husband's mouth opened as though to answer, but he didn't get the chance. Mrs George was in full flow.

'We've been to Japan, Hawaii, China, France, Switzerland . . .' She went on counting out the countries they had visited on her fingers. It wasn't long before she ran out of fingers.

Out of sight of the devoted couple, Honey tapped her own finger against Steve's thigh. Steve reciprocated, acknowledging they were sharing the same thoughts. Mrs George was the sort of woman that, once she opened her mouth, couldn't close it.

'It's amazing what he can do with a computer. Why, I think he's probably one of the best people with a computer that's ever been. Not that I would know. I never worked in computers. I know how to turn it on and that's about all, but he's a real whiz, though of course I keep out of his domain because I might hit a button by mistake, and then all his work would be . . .'

Honey couldn't help staring, not really hearing what was being said. She was fascinated by Mrs George's mouth, the only part of her face that seemed to move. The woman had a severe case of verbal diarrhoea.

It was Steve who plunged in head first to plug the flow. 'So when did you last see Wanda Carpenter — the woman who introduced herself as Lady Templeton-Jones?'

Mr George was quick off the mark. 'I first noticed her when she was introduced by the guide. I was outside the pub with my wife.' He threw Mrs George a sideways look that was less than convivial. 'My wife doesn't drink . . .'

Mrs George interrupted. 'Only briefly and vaguely, Hamilton. We only saw her briefly and vaguely,' she said, slapping her thighs in unison. 'After that we were so swathed in raincoats, hoods and umbrellas that it was difficult to see anyone or anything. We kept close to our guide so we could hear what was being said, though we did peek at some interesting spots and feel cold air and all that, but Lady Templeton-Jones got left behind. She walked with a stick, you know, so it couldn't have been easy for her.'

Easy enough, thought Honey. The deceased could have held her own with a three-legged pony. Not a racehorse, but not a carthorse either.

'Did you see anyone else when you got to the Assembly Rooms?' Steve asked.

'Well, I certainly didn't,' said Mrs George, without time for a single thought to flash through her head. 'And I'm sure Hamilton didn't either, did you, Hamilton?'

Mr George had retreated into temporary silence, seemingly giving up trying to talk. Mrs George tugged at his leg and repeated the question.

'Did you see anyone when we got to the Assembly Rooms?'

'Someone in evening dress?' Honey added hopefully.

Mrs George repeated this to her husband. He shook his head. Mrs George shook hers.

Taking full advantage of the short burst of calm, Steve plunged in again. 'That's all, Mrs George, Mr George.'

Mrs George looked surprised at being shut up so abruptly, her mouth a red orifice among blank whiteness.

'So what do you think,' Steve asked Honey once they'd gone.

'I think Mr George suffers from a permanent headache.'

'That aside, can you remember where they were when our friend Lady Templeton-Jones disappeared?'

Narrowing her eyes, Honey tried desperately to resurrect the sight of that group glimpsed through the downpour. She shook her head. 'No. It was hard to see anything.'

'Could anyone have wandered off without the others noticing?'

'I did.'

* * *

Tami Burns and Dwight Denman were next to sit in the hot seat. They held hands, knees close together. They were younger than the other American couple, came from Washington and explained they were on a 'trial vacation'.

'We've both been married before — three times in fact — so this time we wanted to be sure, and vacations are when couples are thrown together and quarrel. We wanted to see if we could survive that . . .' They exchanged a sugary smile. 'And we have. It's been a whole week.'

Honey resisted the urge to poke her fingers down her throat and throw up.

Steve appeared unmoved and got straight to the point. 'Did you see anyone besides the ghost-walk group that night?'

Honey threw him a look. *Are you really that dumb?* The answer was obvious. Of course they hadn't seen anyone else. They only had eyes for each other.

The German couple — Herr Klaus and Frau Lotte Lowtz got straight to the point. 'We were soaked through but soldiered on. We saw nothing. Nothing at all.'

'Including ghosts?' asked Steve.

Frau Lowtz, who spoke with a deeper voice than her husband, fixed him with a toe-curling glare. 'Of course not! You will let us go now.'

Steve didn't argue. She was bigger than him. Her husband, Klaus, trundled off behind her.

'I wasn't entirely sure he agreed with her,' said Honey.

The last couple were the Karviks, who they discovered were from Norway, not Sweden. Arne differed from the stereotype by being dark-eyed and dark-haired. His wife had legs up to her shoulders and white-blonde hair that reached her waist. She fitted the Nordic image admirably.

'It was so atmospheric,' breathed his wife, an ample cleavage peeping above three pearl buttons. 'It made me tingle all over.' She accompanied her dulcet tone with a jiggling motion. Her boobs wobbled like jellies. The words 'my cup overfloweth' came to Honey's mind. In this case, two cups.

She butted in.

'Did you see anything — anyone at all?'

Mrs Karvik gave her husband's leg a quick squeeze. 'We lost ourselves in the atmosphere, did we not, Arne? We are so sensitive to atmosphere,' she said, facing forwards again, her words slow and throaty. 'We felt sure we were in the presence of spirits. It turned so cold at times that I tingled all over.'

Honey did not voice her opinion that this was probably down to the fact that the wind had been freezing cold and it had been peeing it down.

Once Steve had regained control of his jaw, he said they could go but must leave their address while here in the UK and that of their home in Norway.

'You let them off lightly,' said Honey.

Steve did a series of shifty movements and studied the doodles on his notepad as though they had hidden meaning. Most of them were balloons with large nipple-like dots in the middle.

Honey tutted. Steve took umbrage.

'I only said you could attend, not take over,' he warned while they awaited their next appointment. 'Anyway, your judgement was impaired as far as the Karviks were concerned. I could see it in your eyes.'

'I'm surprised you even noticed my eyes, given where you were looking. Chest height.'

'I was just being attentive.'

'Yeah, yeah, yeah. And she was just being friendly. If that cleavage had been any deeper you could have dived in, never to be seen again.'

'What a way to go!'

Jan Kowalski walked in minus his poncho. Green shirt, camouflage trousers and a black leather jacket. His hair was cut short.

He read his introduction from a sheet of paper folded into four. He held it at arm's length. 'I am from Gda□sk. I am a student of internet communications. I am looking for work.' He passed the piece of paper across to them. 'My details.'

It was on the tip of Honey's tongue to ask what sort of work he was expecting to get on a ghost walk. Was the spirit world hiring IT whizz-kids at the moment? She tried to think of some websites they might use. *Surfing for Spooks*? *Internet Intangibles*? *World Wide Weirdos*? Probably the latter was already taken, she decided. There were plenty of weirdos already out there.

Steve asked him how long he was staying in the country. Jan confirmed that if he didn't get work within the next two weeks, he would be returning home.

Honey asked him why he went on a ghost walk.

'Someone sent me a text message. Said they would meet me there and discuss work they could offer me.'

'And they didn't turn up?'

'No.'

He confirmed that he was looking for any kind of work. He seemed a likeable, presentable young man. Honey took his name and address. According to the sheet of paper he was staying at a youth hostel. Honey considered. At present she was fully staffed, but twenty-four hours was a long time in the catering industry.

'Keep in touch,' she said, handing him her card at the same time as explaining the situation.

His face lit up with pleasure as he took and pocketed her card.

'Thank you. Thank you very much.'

He prepared to leave.

'Just a moment,' said Steve. 'I need you to make a statement. No need for you to write it. I'll write it, read it out and you can sign it.'

For the briefest of moments, Honey perceived fear flash into the young man's dark-brown eyes. It was very quick, so fast that she wondered if it was her imagination. There again, sometimes immigrants were wary of officialdom. They were in a foreign land seeking work, and the local police made them nervous.

Steve Doherty gave no sign of having noticed.

Jan lowered himself back on to the chair.

Steve asked the same questions he'd asked of everyone else.

'Did you see anyone else besides those people on the walk?'

Jan Kowalski hesitated.

Steve had been looking down at the statement sheet in front of him. His eyes flicked upwards. 'You saw someone? A woman? A man?'

He nodded. 'A man. Yes, I saw a man.'

The tension was tangible. She sensed the stiffening of his body and saw his eyes narrowing.

'Can you describe him?'

Jan nodded. 'We had reached the top of an alley that took us back to the main road. He came out from a side street — a narrow side street. We were waiting at the top. Our guide had gone to pee.'

'An alley?'

Jan shrugged and gave a questioning flip of his hands. 'It was only a short moment.'

Steve asked him if he would recognise the man again. He was like a hungry animal following the scent, his body tense with anticipation.

'How was he dressed?'

'Black. In black. He wore a hat and a long coat.'

'Could it have been a cloak?'

Jan shrugged. 'It might have been.'

'Anything else you remember about him?'

'He had no smell.'

This was new. People normally reported what they saw with their eyes not what they sniffed with their nose.

'Not even of rain,' Jan went on. 'I could have been mistaken, but I do not think so. He came quite close. I have a sensitive nose. Those around me had smells. The women smelled mostly perfume and deodorant. The men of after-shave, brandy or a silent . . .' He looked up at the ceiling in search for the right word.

'I get the picture,' said Doherty.

'No one else saw him.'

Doherty met his eyes.

Honey stiffened.

'Nobody?' said Doherty.

'No. They did not seem to.'

'OK. Thank you. We'll be in touch.'

Jan seemed glad to leave.

'See! I told you I saw a guy in a dark suit, and this guy saw him too,' said Honey. She didn't remark on the fact that no one else had seen him. It was enough that she wasn't the only one.

'Great. Bloke in a dark suit. That narrows it down a bit.'

* * *

Pamela Windsor was the most cooperative and had written everything down, basically duplicating everything on her statement and a bit more besides. Surprised, Doherty thanked her and after perusing the details, could only thank her for her cooperation.

The last interview was with the two Australian women. They came in wreathed in smiles. Betty Smith and Sally Weston were middle-aged, single and out to enjoy themselves. They were overweight, dressed in tracksuits and trainers, and looked to be having a good time.

'Fire away,' said Betty, the chair legs creaking as they took her weight. Sally's chair did much the same. Not that she noticed. Her eyes were giving Steve a top to toe.

'You single?' she asked.

Steve sidestepped and cut to the chase. Had they seen anyone?

'Only ducks,' said Betty, and they both collapsed into tears of laughter.

Their laughter was infectious and brought smiles to both Honey and Steve. It fell to Steve to remind them that they were there for a very serious reason. A woman had been murdered.

They both coughed behind plump fists and apologised.

No. They hadn't seen anyone else, though in that weather it was impossible to be sure.

Steve didn't attempt to take up any more of their time.

'You can go, ladies, and enjoy your sightseeing.'

The plump faces resumed their former joviality, the pair of them giggling like a couple of schoolgirls. Betty winked. 'We don't just sightsee, Detective Inspector. You might say we like to try out local delicacies — if you know what I mean.'

Again a load of giggles.

Sally blew him a kiss on the way out and Betty shook her buttocks in an impromptu hula dance before the door was closed behind them.

Steve's expression was a mix of puzzlement and embarrassment.

The two uniformed police swaying on either side of the door fought to hide their smirks.

Steve looked to Honey. 'What?'

Honey did nothing to stop her grin from spreading. She poked a rose-tinted fingernail at his midriff. 'What are you? A local delicacy. That's what you are!'

CHAPTER TWENTY

Hamilton George took big strides to put space between himself and his wife. He'd pulled his earmuffs down over his ears and his woollen hat more tightly down on his head. His face was pickle red and his teeth ached because he was clenching his jaw so tightly.

He felt her hand grasping the sleeve of his jacket. Her short, fat legs were going nineteen to the dozen in her effort to keep up with him. He glanced at the piggy nose he'd thought so cute when she was young and slim. It was just as porcine as the rest of her now.

'What have I done wrong, Hamilton?'

He couldn't hear her too well, but then he didn't need to. He could see her mouth moving. He knew the words well, knew she was once again apologising for doing something wrong. Meredith was always doing things wrong. Wrong! Wrong! Wrong!

'You opened your big mouth!'

He shrugged her hand off and kept walking. She did her best to keep up with him, but he knew she was finding it difficult. By the time they got back to their hotel room she'd have her inhaler out and be fighting for breath, her breasts heaving up and down like sacks of oatmeal. Well, so be it! She deserved to suffer for what she'd done. And at least when she was fighting for breath she couldn't talk. That was Meredith's trouble. She talked too much. He hoped she was fighting for breath for a long while. At least then he'd have some peace.

The guy behind hotel reception handed him the room key just as Meredith came panting and puffing through the revolving door. Hamilton marched towards the lift, his wife padding along some distance behind him, her face bright red, her shoulders sloping forward as though she were in two minds whether to crawl.

The door closed before she got there. Her husband made no move to stop it. He went up. She waited at the bottom. At the exact same moment, a young man that the receptionist did not recognise bounded up the stairs to the right of the elevator shaft. The receptionist told the manager. The manager moved towards the stairs.

Meredith George chose that moment to collapse, landing belly up at the manager's feet.

'Get a doctor,' he shouted. 'Inform her husband. Room 471. Quickly!'

CHAPTER TWENTY-ONE

The bedroom recently occupied by Lady Templeton-Jones at La Reine Rouge was very French. The walls were covered in yellow-striped wallpaper. Noble silhouettes in gilt ovals were arranged in groups of four. Larger groupings, these too in oval frames, were gathered around a central portrait of a soft-bosomed lady in stiff lace. Judging by the pink cheeks and heart-shaped face, the portrait dated from the eighteenth or early nineteenth century. A light-oak French 'sleigh' bed of enormous proportion occupied the centre of the room.

As with every room at Casper St John Gervais's upmarket hotel, antique furniture of a certain age and the highest quality had been exquisitely arranged. Staging a room came naturally to Casper, and his work never failed to impress. As impressed as anyone, Honey stopped at the door and took off her shoes.

Steve didn't look as though he had any intention of following her example. 'It's not a mosque,' he snapped.

'Come on,' she urged, jerking her chin at the pale gold carpet. 'We can't clump street dirt over something that clean.'

'Your consideration is noted,' said a still-miffed Casper, who hadn't quite forgiven her for what he termed 'poaching'.

She'd insisted that she hadn't, that the suggestion had come from the lady herself, but he was still hurt.

A few more considerate comments and he'd be fine.

Doherty was a different matter. He wasn't exactly a rough diamond, but he didn't stand on ceremony for anybody or anything. Unimpressed by the luxurious surroundings, he kept his shoes on and waded straight in. 'So when did you last see the lady?'

Casper regarded Doherty's shoes with glaring distaste. He sniffed indignantly. 'Inspector! I do not keep tabs on my guests. I employ people to do that. You should ask Neville.'

Steve whirled round swiftly, taking Casper by surprise. 'I will. But for now I'm asking you!'

'*I don't know,*' Casper hissed with glassy-eyed distaste. 'I own the bloody place, I don't work in it!'

Casper using bad language? She'd never known it before. The chair of the Hotels Association was usually super cool, running rings around lesser mortals. The Noel Coward facade had been dropped entirely.

Doherty thrust his face within kissing distance to that of Casper. 'Think!'

The atmosphere was electric. Neither man would back down, yet someone had to.

Casper held himself stiff for what seemed like minutes. It didn't last. Doherty gained the upper hand.

'I only saw her once to speak to. We talked about the weather.'

Without a trace of triumph on his face, Steve wandered over to the window. He looked down on the street scene. 'How long had she been staying here?' His voice was low. Cool.

'Three days, so I understand.'

Steve frowned. 'Are you sure?'

'Positive.'

As Honey listened, her fingers sneaked across the dross sitting on the bedside cabinet. There was the usual rubbish that some people keep to remind them of their trip — bus, train and museum entrance tickets, money-off vouchers and leaflets for local attractions. There was also an auction catalogue for a sale two weeks hence. Being a girl addicted to things second-hand and valuable, she swooped on it.

Marine Collectables and Nostalgia. She leafed through it, recalling the items Alistair had mentioned; everything for sale at this particular auction had a marine connection. There were a number of listings for the blue-and-white china he'd mentioned. According to the blurb it had been carried by a Dutch ship that sunk following a storm. Apart from merchandise carried by ships, there were bits of ships — wooden tillers and wheels, their wood worn smooth by years of handling by rough-palmed men. There were listings for lanterns, clocks, navigation equipment and an inordinate number of telescopes. Some lot numbers were blank, with 'awaiting details' noted in the margin. Someone, most likely Wanda, had taken a pen and bracketed these unused page numbers together.

Alistair had hinted at expensive, world-famous items. She wondered what he'd meant.

'What's that?' asked Steve Doherty, interrupting his questioning to take a glance over Honey's shoulder.

'An auction catalogue.'

'Interesting?'

She made a *so-so* kind of face. 'I don't know. Why make a notation beside unlisted items?'

He looked perplexed, so she showed him the bracketing of four numbers. 'See? It's usual to make notes beside items that you're interested in. She's noted numbers with nothing listed beside them. Odd, huh?'

Their conversation caused a stirring in Casper's direction.

'Unless you're selling,' he said. 'Unused lot numbers are reserved just in case. Some people are not terribly organised.' Casper didn't fit into that category. Casper was *totally* organised, *totally* in control.

Honey, on the other hand, was *sometimes* organised. It wasn't that she was disorganised, it was just that when the pressure was on things could — and did — go awry. But on this occasion her thinking was clear. Alistair, the fountain of information at the auction house, would know if Lady

Templeton-Jones had been enquiring about putting items up for auction. If knowledge was power, the large, red-bearded Scotsman was very powerful.

Just then, someone knocked at the door. Neville, Casper's manager, stuck his head round the door. His voice was soft — and awestruck.

'Casper, Baron Ashwell Bridgewater's here.'

Casper grew straighter and taller like a palace guard who'd been told the Queen was imminent. 'Have you made him some lapsang souchong?'

'No!' Neville threw one of his forbearing looks, rolling his eyes until his gaze rested on Steve Doherty. 'He's come to collect his cousin's things — if you've finished, Mr Policeman.' Neville sounded contemptuous. Nothing new there. He always came over as hostile when Steve was around. Honey guessed it was due to some past brush with the law that he'd never quite got over, but like Steve she gave it no regard. The fact that Wanda had a cousin living in England came as something of a surprise.

Casper made to leave the room.

'Me first,' said Steve, pinning Casper to the wall with an outstretched arm. 'I'd like to speak to this cousin.'

Taking advantage of the moment, Honey slipped the auction catalogue behind her back and into her bag then followed Steve out. Like Batman and Robin, they swept along a landing bordered by chinoiserie cabinets. Persian carpets sucked at the soles of their shoes. From there they descended a staircase bounded by a deep-red mahogany banister.

Steve shook his head. 'What is it with these people? Why do they want to be called Lord this or Lady that?'

'Prestige,' said Honey. 'You can get a bigger overdraft at the bank.'

Steve nodded as though the idea appealed to him.

CHAPTER TWENTY-TWO

The middle-aged man waiting for them in reception was plump and pink-faced. Supposedly in an effort to look hip, he wore gold-rimmed dark glasses, a stud in one ear and a large floppy beret. The rest of his clothes were just as naff; Lord Cool Dude was trying to be something he was not.

His voice didn't fit his appearance.

'I came straight from work,' he said, displaying the sort of smile favoured by funeral directors. His voice was revoltingly smarmy, as sweet and thick as treacle poured straight from the tin.

Her Ladyship had hailed from Ohio, so Honey was surprised that her cousin lacked an American accent. It was plummy and smacked of elocution lessons. An add-on to go with the title? Extra charge, of course.

That by itself shouldn't have grieved her. But there was something about his tone that put her back up; it was conciliatory, almost condescending, and his smile was so fixed and so polished. She told herself that titles did that to people and wondered how much his had cost.

Doherty asked him for personal details.

'I live in Northend. You know it, Inspector?'

'Yes, I know it. I didn't know Her Ladyship had an English cousin.'

'We shared the same great-grandfather. He emigrated to America at the turn of the century. The last century that is. Nineteen hundred.' His smile never wavered despite his ambiguous response. 'Is it all right to take her things?' he asked, addressing Doherty directly.

Honey was again reminded of a funeral director — polite, oily and smiling, smiling, smiling all the time. She half expected him to secrete himself in the corner and start wringing his hands like Uriah Heep: '*I'm ever so 'umble.*' Not lordly at all.

'Not yet, and even then I'll need proof of identity,' said Steve.

'Here. I came prepared.' Lord Bridgewater dipped his hand into the inside pocket of his suit jacket and brought out his driving license. Steve scanned it fleetingly before handing it back. 'I also took the opportunity to contact her sister's son by email. I believe he's already been in touch with the local police department, who will also confirm my status.'

The voice pitch stayed the same. It was unnatural. No emotion. No overflowing tear ducts or the faintest tremble of his shiny, round chin. Honey decided she didn't like him.

Steve ran his eyes over the other paperwork Bridgewater had brought with him. Honey could tell by his expression that everything was in order.

'I can't release her things just yet, I'm afraid. Not until I've finished my investigation and am satisfied the items have no relevance to the case.'

'That's perfectly fine by me, Inspector. I know you're doing everything possible to apprehend Wanda's murderer. I'll keep in touch, if you don't mind.'

For no reason she could fathom — except perhaps that she didn't like his hat — Honey felt her toes curling up. The tone of voice was strangely familiar and irritated her. She forced herself to be positive and ask a question instead.

'Why was your cousin staying at a hotel in town? I thought long-lost cousins would stay together.'

His neck jerked and he was facing her. 'Are you with the police?' he asked. His smile was unwavering, but his eyes were wary.

'Well, actually . . .'

Steve saved her bacon. 'She's attached to my division.'

Casper had appeared now, trying to play everything down. 'Lord Bridgewater, I do apologise for this intrusion. But you understand how distressed we all are. I'm sure you're as keen as we are to apprehend whoever killed your cousin. And in Bath! Jane Austen's fair city!'

There was no perceptible variation in Bridgewater's smile, no hint of being even a little bit upset.

'I quite understand,' he said to Casper, then turned to Honey. 'In answer to your question, she did stay with me at first.'

'This is a fine hotel, Mr Bridgewater, but why did she move out on you and move here?'

'Distance and convenience. She'd been staying with me for a while, but she decided that Northend was too far out for sightseeing. She thought it made more sense to move into the city centre.'

Honey frowned.

Steve looked thoughtful. 'How can I contact you? I may want to speak to you further about this.'

Bridgewater's smile was undiminished, though his cheeks were deepening from pink to rose.

'Feel free, Inspector. You can get me at home. Here's my card. Or you can get me at work. We aim to please.'

The royal we?

Honey was having trouble dealing with Bridgewater. He made her squirm all over. She certainly wasn't impressed by his title. She'd proved Lindsey wrong about that. Another question blurted out.

'Where do you work, Mr Bridgewater?'

His mouth seemed to spasm in different directions at being addressed as 'Mister'. He managed to answer. 'APW Marketing. I lead a sales team in telephone marketing.'

Cold-calling! That was it! The tingling horror at the base of her spine! This man was responsible for the dozens of teeth-grinding telephone calls about goods and services she didn't need. And they all sounded the same, asking her to take part in surveys, to buy double glazing, kitchens and gadgets for clearing blocked drains. How many soaks in the bath had been interrupted by him and his team? Irritation bubbled up like magma.

Steve was not a mind-reader, but he must have known what she was thinking. She felt his warm palm resting on her arm. She got the message: *We can't hold his job against him.*

She couldn't resist one last question. 'Just one thing before you go, *Mr* Bridgewater. How did you and your cousin come to have titles?'

'She bought hers; I bought mine,' he said in that trained, even voice that annoyed a thousand or so households every day. 'I suggested it to her. It opens doors. It's amazing what a little name-dropping can do.'

She fancied that Steve hid a grin. Knowing he had fallen into a trap, Casper turned bright red.

'Why was she checking out?' she said once they were outside.

Steve shrugged. 'Price?'

'Possibly.' Honey pouted. La Reine Rouge was the most ostentatious hotel in town — a terry towelling bathrobe given away with every room. His and her basins in the bathrooms. A personal attendant allocated to every four rooms. How could anyone compete with that? But Steve was right. The price may well have been an issue.

CHAPTER TWENTY-THREE

The man who called himself Lord Ashwell Bridgewater marched smartly away from the centre of Bath, baggy corduroy trousers flapping around his legs. Everything would turn out fine as long as he kept his head. If his stupid cousin hadn't come along there wouldn't have been a problem. But only the gutless let problems stand in their way. His scowl turned to a smile. All's well that ends well. He'd had the guts to carry on and that was all that mattered.

Eventually he found himself walking along the towpath that would take him to Widcombe Basin. The day was fine, clouds scooting across the sky, a light breeze. Women with babies in strollers were sitting on benches or leaning over the railings throwing bread to the waterfowl.

In a clear space between family groups, he spotted a tall young man. The man's shoulders were hunched. He was leaning on the railings, staring at the water.

'Herr Klaus? Heinz?'

'Yes.'

The young man continued to stare at the water, his fly-away blond hair hiding the details of his face.

Unlike most people, Ashwell didn't mind not seeing the face of his contact. He was used to dealing with faceless people.

'So! Do you have it?'

'Not yet,' Ashwell replied with an air of confidence. 'But I will shortly. I'm the only relative to hand, so to speak.'

The young German nodded. 'That is good. You will give me what I want and I will pay you.'

Ashwell beamed. 'Half a million. Pounds, that is.'

'As agreed.' Heinz straightened. 'Phone me when you have it. You have my number.'

He walked off without a backward glance. Ashwell watched him go. He knew very well what he had to get to be paid his money.

He smiled to himself. Half a million pounds. He could have a jolly good time with such a grand sum of money. For now he would relish the thought of what was to come. He'd decide on the finer details once the money was his.

CHAPTER TWENTY-FOUR

Steve Doherty gave her a gentle pat on the shoulder blade. 'I can't believe you've let him get to you. Come on. Lighten up.'

'I can't help it. Did you notice how he smiled all the time? I mean *all* the time. His cousin's been murdered for Chrissake!'

'You need to relax. When the fog clears I'll whisk you away from all this. How does that sound?'

'I've been whisked away once already this week.'

'You have?'

She didn't really want to go into details about getting astride a complete stranger's motorcycle. With hindsight it was a totally stupid thing to do. Anything could have happened.

'Sort of.'

There was a disquieting intensity about the look he gave her. She couldn't help but spill the beans. Out it came.

'I saw you out jogging with the blonde with the biceps and didn't want you to see me. A spur of the moment thing, but that's why I did it.'

Steve stood in dead silence as she outlined the trip. A little more silence followed as he digested the details. His thoughtful frown made her think there was something else.

'She's a police officer. We were on duty.'

'I wasn't asking who she was.'

'You didn't need to. You're a woman. You're naturally competitive.'

She decided not to bite. Keep cool. Keep focused.

'Where's your car?'

Steve was about to respond, when a motorcycle swerved towards them then zoomed away in a cloud of blue smoke.

Honey recognised the black motorcycle.

'It's him!'

Doherty looked shocked. 'What?'

'Him. The guy who abducted me. He's always cruising around. Showing off like blokes on bikes do. It's a macho thing: *I've got a bigger one than you.* Bike I mean.'

Now his expression made her feel uncomfortable. What button had she pushed?

'Did you see his registration number?'

She shook her head.

'And you're sure he's the one who abducted you?'

'Absolutely sure.'

'Have you seen him anywhere else?'

She nodded. 'Yes. Here and there. Mostly when I'm about to step out into the road. Come to think of it, I've seen him hanging around the hotel.'

She frowned suddenly. Lindsey must have seen him too. Funny that she hadn't mentioned it.

Doherty closed his eyes and rubbed his forehead. 'Christ!'

When he reopened his eyes, he had that look, the one that looked everywhere except at her. 'I'm taking you home.'

'But I thought we were going for a meal, or a drink, or even . . .' She took a deep breath. 'Your place for supper?'

She attempted to put her arm through his. He pushed it away. At the same time he glanced nervously around him, his eyes seeking something . . . perhaps nothing.

'Don't let him see that we're close.' His eyes were still everywhere but on her.

'Well, if that's the way things are . . .'

'Don't be angry.'

His next words made her ears burn.

'I've got something to tell you, but it'll have to wait until we get into the car.'

* * *

Sitting together in the car after grabbing some takeaway coffee, Steve told her how it was.

'There's a guy I put away. His name's Warren Price and he wants revenge. He told a cellmate all about it. He lost his sweetheart while he was inside and blames me. So maybe to his mind it would only be fair for me to lose whoever's close to me. Don't ask me to explain his logic. Warren Price is not logical. But he is bloody dangerous.'

'Not exactly a barrel of laughs then!' Honey managed a nervous chuckle.

Steve's face remained grim. 'This isn't funny. If it was funny I wouldn't have opened up this distance between us.'

There was something else he wasn't telling her. She could see it in his eyes.

'Has something happened?'

He thought about it before nodding. 'That officer I was out jogging with is in hospital. He caught her out jogging by herself yesterday. Luckily he was interrupted. She'll live.'

'Oh my God, that's terrible,' cried Honey, then realisation dawned. 'He's stalking me? You think he may be the guy on the motorbike?'

He nodded. 'It's possible.'

He turned his attention to the traffic cruising around Queen Square. 'Did you see his face?'

She shook her head.

Steve blew on to the steaming coffee. 'Next time you see him, try and get the registration number — but carefully. If it is Warren Price, he's dangerous. Really dangerous.'

CHAPTER TWENTY-FIVE

Honey's jaw-clenching aversion to Ashwell Bridgewater simmered like stewed bones. Her teeth were still on edge by the time she got to the auction rooms. Alistair was just locking things up and was bending over one his many filing cabinets. He heard her come in and looked round.

'Hen! How can I assist you, lass?'

'Have you ever considered becoming a laird, Alistair?'

He stopped what he was doing and eyed her over his shoulder. 'You what?'

'You know, buying a title. You can do it online. You can be a baron, an earl or even a lord — laird, if you want to be.'

'Now what would I want with doing a thing like that, though it would have to be a laird for me.'

He rolled the 'r' in the Scottish version of lord.

She chuckled. Typical of Alistair. 'Some people quite like the idea. They reckon it gives them kudos.'

'All it would give me is a pain in the posterior and the undying disgust of my socialist relatives.'

Honey smiled and rebuked herself for bothering to ask. Alistair was totally devoid of airs and graces.

'I'm taking part in a murder inquiry,' she began.

After closing the filing cabinet, he turned and slammed his big hands down on the counter. It was a habit of his, and no matter how gently he seemed to perform the action, he always managed to make her jump.

'Aye, lass. The woman found in that lock-up. Terrible business.'

'Her name was Lady Templeton-Jones. I found this in her possession.' She brought out the auction catalogue and pointed to the bracketing. 'Could you check for her name on the sellers list for this auction — please?' she entreated, anxiously aware that the poor man was off home after a hard day flogging oak commodes and mahogany whatnots.

'Hmmmm . . . arghhhh.'

She recognised Alistair's grumbling sound. He always did this when he was trying to pretend he wasn't going to help her. But he would. Alistair was a big, red pussycat — most of the time.

'What was the name again?'

She gave him both — Lady Templeton-Jones and Wanda Carpenter. She wrote them down beneath the date of the auction.

Alistair was secretive about the red file he got out. Giving her a shifty glance, he ran his finger down the list it contained and finally made a sucking-in sound. He shook his head. 'No to each of the ladies.'

'They're . . . it's only one lady.'

'Right. No. No one of either name.'

Honey frowned. 'So why bracket those numbers?'

Alistair made a jerking motion with his head, nodding it from side to side as though he were deciding on the reason. 'Perhaps she intended bidding not buying. We sometimes list potential buyers, but rarely. People turn up or phone in. We list them that phone in or contact us on the internet.'

'Can you check?' she pleaded. 'It would be very helpful.'

It was the best explanation, and yet she wanted more. She asked herself *what* she wanted.

Treasure. Something of great value.

A brief glance at the catalogue and she knew she wasn't going to get it: marine items, instruments and so on. Now what would Her Ladyship want with marine items? There could be any number of reasons, though nothing immediately sprang to mind.

Sighing, she folded up the catalogue and put it in her pocket. Steve had suggested meeting later. 'Though not until about ten o'clock and I need to be home by twelve,' he'd told her.

'Or you turn into a pumpkin?'

He hadn't laughed. She guessed the ongoing case with Warren Price had something to do with it.

'OK. A salad at my place.'

He'd smiled. 'I don't mind a salad if you don't.'

'Tuna OK?'

He'd grimaced. 'I don't really like fish . . .'

'I'll find you something else.'

She considered offering herself as dessert, but Steve's thoughts seemed to be elsewhere. Another time, another place; their relationship was ongoing, but until he'd cracked this case he would remain distracted. She'd prefer him not to be. She wanted his undivided attention and didn't mind waiting.

CHAPTER TWENTY-SIX

The best laid plans and all that . . .

Honey had been looking forward to the evening. A little fun spliced into the humdrum life of a Bath hotelier. Then bedlam struck. First Steve phoned to say he'd been called back to the station. Then a guest at the Green River Hotel had pierced a shower tray with a stiletto heel.

'It must have been weak,' said the big South African girl. 'I shall be asking for compensation if you're not careful.'

Honey opened the shower door and looked inside. The stiletto shoe was still in situ.

The woman had followed her into the bathroom. Her husband, a scrawny guy with a concave chest and a forest of hair sticking out from his ears, stayed sitting on the bed. He looked downcast, his eyes fixed on the floor.

Honey addressed the woman. 'Mrs Van der Witt, why were you wearing stiletto heels in the shower?'

At this moment in time Mrs Van der Witt was wearing bright red Bermudas and matching sports shoes. Honey guessed she'd made a quick change.

'I was checking the heat of the water.'

'A hand is usually enough.'

'I couldn't reach that far. See?'

She bent over as she reached past Honey. Looking down on her broad backside was like viewing a particularly red sunset. Big and filling up one hell of a lot of sky.

Honey reached in, brought the shoe out and passed it to its owner. She held a rictus smile in place as she did it.

'I'm quite broad-minded, Mrs Van der Witt. I'll have someone come in to inspect the damage and put it on your bill. OK?'

Mrs Van der Witt's face went quite floppy. A look passed between husband and wife. Wife blushed. Husband went back to studying the floor. Neither said another word.

Honey went down to reception. Running a hotel meant that friends and relatives had be fitted into empty spaces. She had a question for her daughter. Her daughter got there first.

'Grandma said that she and Margaret and the others are talking things through and she'll be around when they've decided what to do.'

Honey eyed her daughter blankly. 'Have you any idea what she's talking about?'

Lindsey shook her head. 'None at all. But you know Grandma.'

She certainly did! But first things first.

'Lindsey, have you by any chance seen a motorcyclist hanging around the place?'

Lindsey was doing things on the computer. It looked complicated, though Honey couldn't really tell. Lindsey shrugged and looked quite diffident. 'I might have done.'

A wave of motherly protectiveness enveloped Honey's mind. 'Promise me you won't approach him. His name's Warren Price, he's an escaped prisoner and he's very, very dangerous.'

Laughter bubbled from Lindsey's throat.

'I don't believe it.'

'It's true,' said Honey, leaning close, her voice low and ominous. 'He's a murderer and it may be that he's stalking me. In fact, he carried me off only the other night. If I'd known before, I wouldn't have gone with him. Nothing happened, of course, and I'll never know why he dropped me off again unharmed. I think it could have been a warning.'

Lindsey carried on with what she was doing. One colourful web page after another. Honey saw what they were.

'Is that a dukedom I see before me?'

'Correct. There's a whole host of places where you can buy yourself a title,' said Lindsey, seemingly engrossed in the content. 'My, but these guys know how to make money.'

Honey frowned. 'I wonder whether our victim was fully satisfied with their service.'

'You're thinking she might have been about to spill the beans about a scam?'

'There are scams, I take it?'

'Of course there are. The web is a scammer's dream. But there are bona fide offers too.'

Honey rested her chin in her hands. Had Her Ladyship bought a bum title and, having found out, gone in search of the vendor? It was a strong possibility.

Honey raised her eyes to the ceiling and thought about it. 'People can get very obsessive about status. And there's the money, of course. How much do they go for?'

'Thirty thousand or more, from what I've seen. The real ones are the exception, not the norm. There's a surprising amount for sale at good money. Too many to be authentic.'

Honey sat down beside her daughter and fixed her gaze on the screen. Brass rubbings of medieval lords and ladies seemed to be the decoration of choice on these sites. The introductions were pretty similar too.

Be Lord and Lady of a small slice of England.

'This is for romantics not living in the real world.'

Lindsey shrugged.

Honey shook her head. 'I can't imagine spending *that* much.' She thought about it. 'So the victim found out that her title wasn't authentic and threatened to expose the site she bought it from. They had to silence her. How does that sound?'

'Feasible.' Lindsey's fingers scrolled and tapped. 'Some people get quite protective of their interests, even if it's just a dodgy online business.'

To Honey's mind it seemed like a waste of time. 'Doesn't seem like a very sensible way for someone to make money.'

Lindsey cocked an eyebrow. 'Not everyone is as *sensible* as you, Mum.'

Honey thoughtfully brushed a smudge from the toe of her fancy shoe. 'They've got to be obsessed. Perhaps it's not really about money, but the pleasure of doling out titles, in which case whoever it is may possibly be a bit touched. Or insane.'

CHAPTER TWENTY-SEVEN

Lindsey waited outside the door of the Catnip Club. She smiled on seeing the black motorcycle pull up and park. She saw him raise his visor before removing his helmet.

In days of old when knights were bold . . .

She smiled at her flight of fancy.

Just for once he'd left his leathers at home. He was wearing a beige jacket, dark trousers and a crisp white shirt. A small gold crucifix dangled at his throat.

He smiled when he saw her.

They kissed as she took his arm.

'Is your name really Warren Price?' she asked him.

He grinned. 'If you want me to be. Do you?'

'Not really. It's just that my mum's asking questions. Warren Price is a murderer. That wouldn't be you, would it?'

CHAPTER TWENTY-EIGHT

Breakfast had finished. The bills for guests departing that day were ready and waiting. Everything was rosy. And then Honey's mother arrived.

'Hannah! Me and the girls have racked our brains, but no deal. We've got a battle to fight and I need you to lend a hand. Come in here when you've finished. Is my granddaughter around? I might need her too.'

This was bad news. Honey had planned to check with Doherty whether there had been any progress on the case. No chance now.

Gloria Cross sounded like John Wayne getting ready for D-Day. She was striking the same poses too. Luckily she didn't look like him. Suntanned and incredibly vibrant for her age, she was wearing a pale-beige suede suit bordered with blue. Her hair was styled in short bouncy layers and dyed to match her suit. Pearl earrings the size of quails' eggs clung tenaciously to her ear lobes. A matching collar of pearls inset in gold — costume jewellery to die for — nestled around her neck. She was more vital than usual having just come back from a river cruise with the Senior Salsa Club.

'Just a minute, mother.' Honey was busy dealing with a ten-year-old Irish boy who had mislaid his skateboard. 'I'll get everyone looking for it, Kenny,' she promised the worried-looking lad. 'Come back after lunch. I bet it's turned up by then.'

She could tell by his expression that he believed her promise. Kenny was blond, blue-eyed and young enough to still have faith in grown-ups. Give it a year or two and he'd enter the grouchy in-between stage before finally, in five or six years' time, becoming a teenage stud.

One problem sorted — if only temporarily. One more to go.

French perfume wafted in Gloria's wake as they made their way into Honey's office.

'Close the door. This is private,' Gloria said.

Honey did as ordered. Once that was done, she slumped into a chair and kicked off her shoes. Hopefully her feet would not be swollen by the time she came to put them back on.

Her mother remained standing, floating even. Gloria Cross never slumped. Her pencil-thin eyebrows, courtesy of a top-class beauty parlour, frowned suddenly. 'Who's the guy in the wellington boots?'

'Was he riding a motorbike?'

'Lingering on it outside and peering in.' Her expression soured. 'Please don't tell me he's your latest beau. Please! Wellington boots?'

Honey was loath to admit anything. She wouldn't be doing the bike-ride thing again. Wouldn't admit to it either, and couldn't relate the details to her mother. Although he hadn't said so, she took it as read that what Steve had told her was privileged information.

'I don't know him. He's probably trying to get up the courage to come in and ask for a job. I thought you'd come to ask me about the murder inquiry.'

'Are you going to disappoint me and tell me you didn't beat any suspects?'

''Fraid so.'

'Then it's just as well I'm here about something else. Someone is out to destroy Secondhand Rose.'

Honey's eyebrows rose. 'What have you done?'

'Nothing. It's what they've done. It's underhand. It's criminal, but they needn't think they're going to get away with it. I've got the bit between my teeth on this one and I'm not letting go!'

Honey felt a sinking feeling as a worrying thought came to her. Her mother had a thing about fixing her up with unsuitable men — husband material of the worst kind. Honey fancied this might be one of those matchmaking moments. She fixed her mother with a wary look. 'Is this to do with a man, Mother?'

A deep frown wrinkled the smooth foundation of her mother's shiny brow. Her eyebrows made a pointy shape like a downturned arrow.

'Hannah! This is far more serious than men! This is about money!'

'Ah!'

Honey sat up straighter. Yes, her mother liked men and was convinced that she was the best person to find the right one for her daughter. Not that she was exactly off the market herself, though she merely dabbled now and again. No, money rated higher on her agenda. Money plus man equalled husband. What was that about a young man with a fortune being in need of a wife? Same thing. Jane Austen move over. Mother's coming through.

'OK. Take a deep breath and tell me all about it.'

Honey found herself taking a deep breath too.

Her mother's pink lips formed a waspish pout before she continued. 'As I've already mentioned, it's the shop.' She said it in a rush and got her handkerchief out, dabbing very carefully at her eyes so as not to smudge her mascara. 'We've received notice to vacate. Two weeks' notice! That's all we've got.'

'That's terrible,' said Honey, and meant it.

Secondhand Rose was a dress agency which was run as a kind of cooperative by her mother and half a dozen other well-heeled, socially motivated women. Clothes that had been outgrown or grown tired of were brought in for resale. Half of the proceeds went to the shop, the other half to charity. Her mother loved it, dealing as it did with top-quality merchandise. Never in her life had she served behind a shop counter; she'd always much preferred the other side, spending rather than selling. But this was different. Clothes and gossip came in and out of the shop with stunning rapidity. It was an enormous success — both as a business and a way of keeping her mother off Honey's back two days a week. Losing the shop would be bad news.

Honey felt a nervous tic flick like a neon light beneath her right eye. If she wasn't careful, her worse nightmare could come true. Her mother might want to help run the hotel. Nothing could be worse. Or so she thought.

Her mother sighed and tucked her handkerchief up her sleeve. 'I thought we could do our business here temporarily until we get a new shop and a new lease sorted out. Maurice Clout's old shop would serve us well after a bit of TLC.'

Honey turned cold. 'I had someone come in about it last week.'

A blatant lie. The old hairdressing salon was tacked onto the side of the hotel down a side street. Maurice Clout had run it for years until his arthritis — and the fact that he spent most business hours in the betting shop — had brought it to a grinding halt.

Honey's worst nightmare had come true, and yet it could still get worse! Honey was thinking ahead. What started out as temporary could easily turn permanent.

Gloria Cross narrowed her eyes into beady accusing slits. 'I may have to insist. You still owe me for that newfangled steam room you bought.'

The sauna. It had seemed a good idea at the time and the price was right. So was the salesman. Tall, blond-haired and Swedish with a lantern jaw and a tight butt.

Her mother's expression soured. 'You should never have bought that wooden steam kettle. Who the hell wants to be boiled pink like a hunk of pork?'

Honey rolled her eyes. She could have retorted that pink was Mary Jane's favourite colour, but there was some truth in her mother's argument. The sauna hadn't worked out to be as popular as she'd hoped and would come back to haunt her for all eternity — or for at least as long as her mother was alive and the bank still drawing on the direct debit.

'Let's not be hasty. This is all so sudden. Why don't we sit down? I'll pour coffee and you can tell me what happened.'

As Honey poured coffee, her mother began her tale.

'Wallace and Gates Holdings, who own the property, have been very good to us up until now. William Wallace is a real sweetie and would never have turned us out.' Suddenly she leaned forward, winked and patted Honey's knee. 'We're of an *age*, you know, and he was quite a stud before senility set in.'

'I get the picture. This means he's over seventy, unless he's the original William Wallace, in which case he's approaching about six or seven hundred, give a century or two.'

Her mother grimaced. 'Now you're being silly and we can do without that. You need to take this seriously.'

'Oh, yes, I am.' The implications of having her mother as a neighbour were enormous. Honey forced herself to think seriously. 'You've had that shop for five years. Why do they want you out now?'

More money, probably.

Her mother shrugged. 'I've no idea, but I'm going to find out. I'm off to beard the lion in his den, so to speak.'

Murder would have to wait. Honey sprang to her feet. 'I'm with you.'

She grabbed the car keys.

'Let's go!'

'I'm warning you; William Wallace can charm the pants off a girl.'

'Not this girl,' said Honey. 'Not unless he's Mel Gibson wearing a kilt,' she added, mostly to herself,

'This guy could.'

Honey looked at her mother. She had a dreamy look in her eyes. It could mean only one thing. She looked at her mother. 'You didn't!'

Her mother shrugged. 'I'm old enough to know my own mind.'

* * *

Steve Doherty rang just as Honey was fastening her seat belt.

'What news?'

'Not much. We're just waiting for word from the owners of the empty shop where the victim was found. The old place is earmarked for renovation. I've asked them to give me a list of contractors that might have visited there in the last few days. What are you up to?'

Honey explained about her mother's shop. 'We're off to speak to a Mr Wallace of Wallace and Gates, who own the shop my mother leases.'

'Now there's a coincidence. That's the same company who own our murder scene.'

CHAPTER TWENTY-NINE

The office of Wallace and Gates Holdings occupied the whole of a converted warehouse overlooking the river. What had once been grain silos jutting out over the water had been altered to form balconies of smoky glass and stainless steel. The space-like pod of a panoramic lift ran up the corner of the building nearest the river. Landscaping had replaced the rubbish and corrugated tin of the car park that used to be there.

Gloria Cross eyed the lift with childish glee. 'Can we go up in that?'

'We're not here for the ride, Mother.'

'Wouldn't have hurt.'

The peevish look descended. Honey didn't have time for this. She had a business to run, for God's sake. And a murderer to catch — in between dishing-up plats du jour and clearing the drains.

Honey guided her mother towards the plate-glass doors with copper trim that formed the main entrance. 'Let's hope Mr Wallace is willing to receive visitors.'

Stainless steel and sheet glass formed interior divisions against Victorian brick and cast-iron supports. Daylight falling through sheet glass walls gave a liquid look to the marble floor. Everything was shiny, designer. History clad in tinsel.

The receptionist was no exception. She was tanned and tall, her hair slicked back into a tight ponytail tamed to lie at the nape of her neck. She wore a charcoal-grey suit, a startlingly white blouse and a red enamel pin at her throat — WGH, the company logo.

Honey congratulated herself that she was wearing a fitted navy-blue dress with a gold chain hanging halfway between waist and bosom. The skirt was mid-calf and fitted. She always felt glamorous in this dress. Her waist looked smaller, her hips and bosom balanced. She was wearing navy-blue stockings to match her dress. The dress sleeves were long with tight cuffs.

Glowing with confidence, she explained why they'd come and who they wanted to see.

'I'm sorry,' said the receptionist with a flash of snow-white teeth. 'Mr Wallace Senior was taken ill some time ago. His son, Mr Cameron Wallace has taken over.'

Honey tried to tear her gaze away from the glare of her teeth, but it wasn't easy.

'Well, that could explain a lot. Could you tell him that Mrs Gloria Cross is here to discuss the lease of her shop, Secondhand Rose?'

The receptionist checked her computer screen. 'He is rather busy today . . .'

Gloria leaned across the grey expanse of the countertop. 'I'll let you into a secret. His father and I used to be an item. Tell him I've got a legal matter to settle.'

The receptionist's eyelashes, thickly caked with mascara, fluttered like bats wings. Rosy cheeks blushed through the Max Factor sheen. Seemingly unwilling to delve further into the love life of a septuagenarian couple, she turned her attention to Honey.

'And you are?'

'Her lawyer,' said Honey.

'My lawyer,' echoed her mother looking as though she were enjoying the subterfuge.

The protective facade crumbled. 'Do take a seat, ladies.' Her voice was as stiff as her smile.

Cool, thought Honey, half-inclined to shake the receptionist's hand. She surely deserved to be complimented on keeping a straight face. Behind the mask she had to be wondering what manner of dodos she had here.

There were sofas in reception — big, squashy, dark-brown ones arranged around a glass coffee table. *Vogue*, the *Financial Times* and *Commercial Property Monthly* were set out equidistant from each other on the polished glass top. Honey wondered if a ruler was used to make sure the distances were kept uniform. She'd heard they did that at royal banquets. The queen inspected afterwards — off with their heads if they didn't get it right.

'I think we impressed her,' Gloria whispered to her daughter.

Honey responded at the same level of whisper. 'Sure. She thinks we're nuts.'

Fifteen minutes later the phone rang and the receptionist looked pointedly in their direction. 'Mr Wallace will see you now.'

There was something about the way she said it — and her reaction to the phone call — that made Honey think the girl was in awe of her boss, either that or she fancied him. Good looking, perhaps?

Good guess.

Cameron Wallace rose to over six feet in an act of old-fashioned courtesy.

They shook hands and did the introductions.

'Please. Sit down,' he said.

His office was big enough to hold an orgy. Not that she considered him that type. Anyway, the décor wasn't orgy orientated. The floor was Italian marble. The desk was of chrome and crushed leather. If there were any filing cabinets they were well hidden. Probably the walls had panels that sprang open when pressed.

The black leather walls were relieved by a glass panel. Modernistic splashes of red, green and blue shimmered and changed depending on perspective.

He saw her give it the once over.

'Do you like it?'

She nodded. 'Yes.'

'What does it say to you?'

The answer came straight from the hip. 'Red sky, green land, blue sea.' She leaned closer, peering at the centre of the scene. 'And isn't that a boat, or a piece of boat?'

'The bow of a ship. It's sinking.'

'Oh.'

It seemed a sad subject, almost macabre. What did she know? She could barely draw a sausage dog with stick legs. Modern art wasn't her bag. She liked old things that had worn well — a bit like her.

As they settled into their chairs, Honey weighed Wallace up. He was wearing a white shirt, a dark-blue tie with a red rose motif and dark-blue trousers. His cufflinks looked like real gold in the shape of dice. They were studded with what could be — just could be — real diamonds.

He shrugged his shoulders in a stretching action. There was grace to his movement and a sparkle in his eyes.

To his credit he was courteous to both mother and daughter, perhaps more so to Honey, though it could be wishful thinking that he was paying her undue attention.

Her mother, having neither lust for nor loyalty to this guy, jumped in first. 'It's about our shop. The girls and I have been running it for some time. We're a respected item in the community, and just to get the gist of where I'm coming from, your father and I were also an item — and not that long ago. Now as I see it . . .' Cameron Wallace listened politely as Gloria Cross outlined the problem before blasting off at the bottom line. 'So now, explain yourself. What the hell do you think you're playing at?'

To his credit, Cameron didn't look surprised regarding the comment about Gloria Cross and his father.

For her part, Honey looked up at the ceiling. Her mother was quite the blunt object. If you did her wrong, then she wasted no time in asking for an explanation — and getting even. The latter swiftly followed the former.

Cameron Wallace divided his smile equally between them. 'I'm sorry this has happened, but the circumstances are beyond our control. I won't go into detail, but there have been problems within the company. Real estate that was thought to be securely under our control turned out not to be. My father was not as attentive as he should have been.'

Gloria was having none of it. 'I can't believe that. Your father was always on the ball. A powerhouse of a man. I can't believe he's gone downhill so fast. I only saw him a month or two ago.'

Honey was sure she detected a tightening of Cameron Wallace's jaw.

'I believe I know my father better than you. He's not well. He hasn't been for some time. I think only his family would know that.'

The last thing Honey wanted was for this to get ugly and have her mother storm out. The thought of a trio of seniors taking over the defunct hairdressers just around the corner loomed large in her mind. She waded in.

'Look, is there any other shop you happen to own on which a lease is available? Secondhand Rose raises money for charity, and my mother's been involved in the venture for a very long time. It gives her an interest and Secondhand Rose is very successful.'

His eyes pierced her. 'Your mother? I thought you were her lawyer.'

'Your receptionist was a little . . .'

'Stiff?'

'As a broom handle. My name's Hannah Driver. My friends call me Honey.'

He smiled. She decided that he was just a little too sure of himself.

'Honey or Hannah, they're nice names. I was about to suggest I find your mother another shop,' he said. 'Give me a few days and I'll see what I can come up with. Rest assured, ladies, we will have something — I guarantee it.'

'That's very kind of you.'

He moved towards her as he came out from behind his desk and was close — inches behind her back — all the way to the door. She could feel the heat of his body.

'I'm sorry about your shop,' he said to Honey.

'It's my mother's shop. I only came along for the ride.'

'Your mother's very lucky to have a daughter like you.'

'I agree.'

Once out on the landing, her mother glanced about her. 'Is there a powder room?'

'Just there.' He bobbed his head at the brushed steel effigy of a woman embedded in an American oak door.

'It's a hobby of hers,' said Honey, once the powder-room door was closed. 'Checking powder rooms, that is.'

An amused frown creased Cameron Wallace's noble brow. He stood with legs slightly parted, hands in pockets and head held to one side, eyeing her with interest.

'So! What *do* you do for a living?'

'I have a hotel. The Green River.'

She went on to say how important tourism was to Bath's economy, and that led to outlining her role as crime liaison officer the Bath Hotels Association.

'No hobbies?'

'Running a hotel doesn't leave much time for hobbies, but I guess you could call me an antique collector.'

'Your field?'

She felt her face growing hot. 'Lacy things. Victorian mostly. And foundation garments.'

'Women's underwear?'

Her blush deepened. 'Well . . . yes . . .'

He didn't seem to notice. It was as though her comment had unlocked a secret door.

He looked enthused — eyes shining, face aglow.

'I collect a little too. Auctions and collecting are like iron in the blood; one can so easily get carried away and bid far above the true value of an item.'

'One can indeed.'

The sound of water flushing preceded the reappearance of her mother. She beamed broadly at Cameron and thanked him again for his courtesy.

'Nice powder room,' she added. 'Though I'd have preferred pure white soap to turquoise. Turquoise soap is flashy. White is classy.'

'My receptionist chose it.'

'Figures,' Gloria muttered.

'Keep in touch,' he said, and shook their hands.

On the way down in the lift, her mother fixed Honey with a knowing eye. 'Clickety-click.'

'What's that supposed to mean?'

'Aw, come on. You're on the menu.'

'Can't be,' she said with a toss of her head. 'I didn't give him my phone number.' OK, she'd told him the name of her hotel, but that didn't count in the great scheme of things. It was information. Giving him her phone number would be invitation.

'I did,' said her mother with a furtive uplifting of eyebrows. 'I palmed it when I shook his hand.' She made a clicking sound. 'I always was a dab hand with a deck of cards.'

Honey was mortified. 'That is so embarrassing!'

'You're not forward enough.'

'Am too!'

The argument might have continued, but her phone interrupted. It was Steve. 'Hey. Where are you?'

'I've just been to see this very rich handsome guy called Cameron Wallace at Wallace and Gates.'

Steve paused before he spoke. 'The owner of the murder scene. Like I told you—'

'That's a macabre tone, Steve.'

'It's a macabre subject. How about we meet up at the Zodiac tonight? I'll be dropping in on Mr Wallace myself later. I'll tell you what transpires.'

'I wish I could.'

'You've got a date?'

'The Dentists' Association are having their annual award ceremony in the restaurant.'

He laughed. 'Does the winner get a little plaque?'

The joke flew over her mother's head. She was dead serious and ready with sound advice. 'Don't give them anything too chewy. It's a known fact that dentists don't look after their teeth — only other people's.'

Outside the building, Honey craned her neck back so she could see all the way to the penthouse.

'What price coincidence?' she murmured as she considered it once again.

Her mother heard. 'Some people think there's no such thing as coincidence.'

'They could be right,' said Honey, looking down again. 'They just could be right.'

CHAPTER THIRTY

Life amused Cameron Wallace. Some people are born into money, some are blessed with good looks and some are very clever. Cameron Wallace was one of the lucky sods who'd got the trinity. He'd always had money, always had the looks and always outsmarted the next guy — even his father.

He also had a secret. Some might call it a weakness, others an obsession.

He locked the door after his visitors, turned and smiled at the glass panel. Like a priest, he stood reverently before it. A light press of his finger and, hey presto, the glass panel opened. A series of downlighters targeted his favourite items. Some of them gleamed in the light. Others were not of the sort of material that gleamed. Some items were just too old, too stained and too scruffy. Yet they were all valuable. Some of the shabbier items were more valuable than others. This was his personal treasure trove and a very admirable one. And yet it was not entirely complete. There was one other item he coveted to make his collection absolute. One item he would kill for. If only that bloody American woman had stuck to her word. His jaw stiffened at the thought of her. Stupid bloody cow!

Every day he opened this panel, relishing the sight and smell, the look of his collection. The items contained were approaching or past a hundred years old. One look was enough. He closed the door. This part of the day was over.

He eyed the details on the card Mrs Cross had palmed him. Her daughter interested him. Hadn't she told him she was a collector? Underwear. Not quite his area, but interesting to some. His interest in Honey Driver faded once he was back behind his desk and more weighty matters pressed for his attention.

He tapped his password and security number into his computer. The company logo came up above a row of headings. He clicked into 'legal' and scrolled down. The freehold and leasehold details of a number of properties came up. The company legal department had been tardy in reassigning some of these. They were a month overdue, and in the meantime someone had stepped in and snatched the options to renew from under their noses. Someone with knowledge. Someone on the inside. He wasn't happy. He'd spent a few years building up a portfolio of property in the city. Wallace and Gates Holdings had grown considerably under his tenure and he was proud of his achievements.

Holding the card between finger and thumb he flicked it against his teeth. Honey Driver was a little older than he liked. Younger women were less complicated; they enjoyed the high life he could offer and were freer and easier than the older generation. All the same, he had his own reasons for wanting to see her again. He phoned her at six when the office was quiet and bereft of staff.

'Can I tempt you?' he asked her.

She sounded surprised, flattered even. Well, that was par for the course. He wasn't surprised. She made excuses about being busy, but he persuaded her. He was good at that.

'I'll pick you up at seven thirty. I'll drive.'

'I can't. Not tonight. I've got a big function on.'

Her hesitation was surprising, but hell, she was a businesswoman. She did have chores to perform. No guy though. He was pretty certain of that.

'What time do you finish?'

'Late.'

'Do you have a bar?'

'Yes.'

'I'll call in for a drink. Ten-ish?'

She didn't decline.

At five minutes past six, Debbie, the bronzed babe from reception, padded across the creamy-coloured carpet. She was carrying her shoes in her right hand. Her blouse was open to the waist and she was playing with her skirt so that it skidded up over her thighs, bunching there like a parcel waiting to be opened.

He smiled. 'You're coming undone.'

Smiling and smelling of high-street perfume, she wriggled between him and his desk. 'So are you,' she whispered huskily. Her fingers wandered down his trouser front.

Cameron clasped his hands behind his head, closed his eyes and leaned back. He let Debbie take over. Not that she was really taking over at all. She was doing exactly what he wanted her to do. He was good at that. Good at being in charge. An older woman like Honey Driver should be a pushover.

CHAPTER THIRTY-ONE

Somewhere around teatime Honey had fetched out the auction catalogue and phoned Alistair. Had he found out anything about the lot numbers? Any idea what the lots constituted?

'I did a quick search, hen. Let me get the details.'

She'd heard the turning of papers.

'Something photographic. Camera, photographic paraphernalia maybe. Perhaps even photographs or film of the old-fashioned variety.'

Did Cameron Wallace collect photographic equipment? He hadn't been specific.

Now the dentists' ceremony was in full swing, and it was all hands to the pumps in the restaurant, but the coffees had already been served, the speeches commenced and the staff could take a breather.

Honey was scraping dishes in the kitchen. Rodney Eastwood, known by all as Clint, their casual washer-upper, had got himself into a spot of bother. Word was that he'd gone for a 'wet lunch' at the Curfew, a pub just off the London Road, and was picked up a few hours later for urinating on a police car.

Hence Honey had landed the job of loading and unloading their very temperamental dishwasher. The thing liked to let off steam now and again. A lot of steam. Loading it was a nightmare. Who needed a sauna when you had this spitting monster?

'Mum. There's a man at the bar asking for you.'

Lindsey said this just as Honey was half buried in the hissing contraption in pursuit of a spoon that had fallen through the cutlery container. She backed out, face red, hair limp and plastered to her scalp. Panic set in.

'He's early!'

'It's nine thirty.'

'Already? I can't see him. Look at me.'

Lindsey looked. 'You look terrible.'

'I knew I could count on you to stroke my ego.'

'I'll tell him you're out on a date.'

'Yes!' Wait a minute. She remembered telling him about the gathering of dentists. 'No!' She entered panic mode and tried fluffing up her hair. It refused to be fluffed and remained determinedly flat.

'You've got a headache,' said Lindsey, who had watched her mother's efforts in silence.

'In other words you're saying he'll run a mile if he sees me like this.'

'You look a fright.'

'Do you want to be specific?'

Lindsey shook her head. 'I don't think you'd like it. In fact you might want to crawl into the dishwasher and not get out.'

'Damn it. Keep him occupied, will you, darling?'

Lindsey went off to make excuses. She came back looking slightly amused. Not that Honey could see her. Only her butt was visible to the outside world. The rest of her was stuffed in the machine.

Lindsey tapped her on her back. 'He says he's got a surprise for you. He's waiting outside.'

Honey backed out, banging her head on the way.

'Bloody Nora!'

She stood looking panic-stricken, spreading her hands helplessly.

'What do I do?'

Lindsey was Merlin the Magician among teenagers. Honey often blessed the day her one and only daughter had declined a university place.

Her daughter's advice was usually good. 'Your cheeks are *so* crimson!'

'We need camouflage.'

'White flour?'

Lindsey mugged Smudger Smith of the red kerchief he wore around his neck.

'Emergency,' she said in response to his surprised expression. 'You won't regret it.'

Smudger smiled. Lindsey never riled him. Affection hovered between them, though Honey had never dared suggest it.

'Here,' said Lindsey, shaking the white-spotted kerchief into its natural square. 'Wear it like this.'

She twisted the kerchief into a thin sausage shape, fatter in the middle, then wound it like an Alice band around her mother's head. She tied the ends into a bow.

'Voila! La crème de la custard!'

Honey eyed herself in the polished chrome of a refrigerator. The redness of the kerchief outdid that of her cheeks. 'Not bad.'

Cameron Wallace was waiting in the foyer between front of house and the 'engine room' — accepted phraseology for the kitchen. He was standing with his back to her, his hands in his pockets. His stance was self-assured — too self-assured for her taste. A sudden thought struck her.

'Tell him I won't be long,' she whispered to Lindsey, and dived into a closet.

The closet was opposite the kitchen. It contained disposables — paper napkins, toothpicks, tablets of soap and toilet paper.

She got out her phone and dialled Doherty's number. He answered fast. He always did.

'It's me,' she hissed.

'Are you in a cave? You sound kind of hollow.'

'No. I'm in a closet.'

'Did someone lock you in?'

'No. I just wanted to speak to you in private.'

'I see.'

It was obvious from the tone of his voice that he didn't see.

'Cameron Wallace is here and wants to speak to me. I wanted to speak to you first. I need to know how you got on when you went to see him.'

'Nothing much to report except that he owns all the shops in that rank. Four in total. Three are let out. One — the one in which the victim was found — is empty. He was going to sell it, but he changed his mind. Up until then there'd been a lot of surveyors and builders going in and out on behalf of interested purchasers.'

'OK. I'll bear that in mind.'

'How about making an ASS of yourself tomorrow?'

He emphasised the word ASS. Honey got the drift.

'I'll try. I'll ring you back.'

Cameron Wallace smiled when he saw her. White teeth flashed like a beacon on a dark night.

She reckoned she looked like a dog's dinner. He gave no sign that she did.

She smiled right back. 'Sorry, but the bar has a dress code. I don't think they'll let me in looking like this.' She indicated her chef's whites and striped butcher's apron.

'Another time, perhaps. Never mind. I've come to make you an offer.'

He passed her a folder. 'It's the lease of a shop I own, one suitable for Secondhand Rose. I trust your mother and her friends will approve.'

Somehow Honey had expected him to ask for a date, though she much preferred him offering her mother a shop.

'Ring me when you can.' He sauntered off.

Honey stood and stared. This was *good* news! She rang her mother first. Her response was much the same.

'Will you come with me to view it?'

'Yes!'

She rang Casper to give him an update on the murder case. She told him that Doherty had invited her to accompany him to Trowbridge to take a look at Associated Security Shredding.

'Excellent!' said an excited Casper.

She started to explain about her mother and the offer of the shop.

His tone turned cold. 'I've had an enquiry from a coach party for rooms next February. Are you able to take the booking?' A carrot to keep her on board this crime liaison thing. Trying to let rooms in February was like setting sail in a colander. To receive forward bookings this far ahead was nothing short of a miracle.

'I can catch up with my mother at teatime tomorrow.'

'Good girl.'

Things were good and getting better. Capturing Lady Templeton-Jones's murderer would be the icing on the cake. Solving this case above all others would be like laying a ghost to rest.

CHAPTER THIRTY-TWO

Doherty was in good form. As they motored along with the roof down, he filled her in on the details of the case. 'Her nephew informed the police in Ohio that she'd bought the title online. She reckoned it gave her kudos and had always fancied being a lady. At first she'd been happy about it. But the more she looked into it, the more she began to think she'd been duped.'

'So Her Ladyship was out to stick it to whoever might have sold her a duff budgie?'

'Possibly.'

'Do we know who she bought it from?'

'Not yet. We're getting it checked out.'

Trowbridge had a no-nonsense red-brick Victorian look. Railway, canal and weaving sheds had given work to the hard-pressed in years gone by. Now it was a dormitory town to Bath, an overspill for those who couldn't afford Georgian crescents, but could rise to a Victorian terrace.

A number of trading estates had been built around the town, catering for small industries that didn't require space for raw materials or production lines, ideal for the service sector.

A big sign at the entrance showed a long road leading through the estate to the very end, where Associated Security

Shredding was housed in a building slightly larger than the others. All the buildings were colour-coded on the plan. ASS was lilac.

'Wimpish kind of colour,' Honey remarked.

Steve grinned. 'It's the kind of colour your mother would choose.'

'Floaty and ultra-feminine.' She cast her gaze over the prefabricated building — huge compared to a garden shed, but just as mundane. 'Hardly the stuff dreams are made of. Not a turret in sight. What the hell was Her Ladyship doing here?'

'It's a start.' He switched the engine off on his low-slung MR2 and drummed his fingers on the steering wheel.

'Something up?' she queried.

'That guy Wallace, did he hit on you?'

'No.'

'Disappointed?'

'None of your business.'

'He's got false teeth.'

'Not so!'

'We caught him with his pants down.'

'No!'

'That receptionist of his was being *very* personal.'

Honey grinned. She had a sudden urge to make a return visit to Wallace and Gates Holdings, if only to smirk knowingly at the stuck-up bitch manning reception.

Doherty's grin rivalled that of Cameron Wallace — though the teeth were real, not porcelain enhanced. Wallace had perfect teeth, perfect tan, perfect features and the clothes and accoutrements to match. Doherty on the other hand was a little rough around the edges. They were like houses on *Location, Location, Location*. One was smooth and all together. The other had character and needed a bit of touching up here and there.

The guy manning reception at Assured Security Shredding was the total opposite of the young woman at Wallace and Gates. No smart suit and swept-back hairdo.

He had dreadlocks and wore a pinstriped T-shirt. A gold tooth flashed in the midst of his molars when he smiled. The tongue stud was stainless steel.

'Can I help you guys?'

One flash of Steve's warrant card and the gold tooth and the tongue stud vanished with the smile. Hostility replaced hospitality.

'I can't let you see nothing without Mr Bannister's permission, and I can't leave here to go and ask him.'

'Can you phone him?'

'No. He won't hear you.'

Steve frowned. 'You're being evasive.'

He rolled his eyes. 'Sheesh! You ain't never been in no shredding shed!'

'And where is this shredding shed?'

He pointed to a door on his right marked 'Authorised Personnel Only'.

Steve pushed through. Honey followed.

The shredding shed vibrated with sound. The noise was deafening. Up ahead of them were banks of shredding machines — big ones eating paper more quickly than McDonald's could produce burgers.

Men wearing rubber gloves were loading handfuls of A4 paper and computer printouts from plastic bags into the gaping mouth of giant shredders. Sometimes sheets of paper escaped and floated to the floor.

Another van load had just arrived at the loading bay. At present the big double doors were open and a draught was blowing in. Some of the paper had already escaped and was skidding around like big white leaves. Accountancy printouts were unravelling, flopping out like fish.

Steve did his thing with the warrant card. A kid in trainers sloped off to get Bannister.

A bald-headed man with a closed expression and a slack jaw looked up in response to someone pulling at his shoulder. He nodded to whatever was said and quickly left what he was doing.

He had a sloping forehead, pale eyes and shouted to make himself heard. 'Can I help you?'

Again Steve flashed his badge of office and shouted back. 'I'm here with regard to a murder inquiry.' He winced at the effort of shouting. 'Can we talk somewhere a bit quieter?'

Mr Bannister nodded and led them back through the door. Closing it behind them was like putting the lid on a bubbling stew. The noise subsided.

He peered at both of them with narrowed, questioning eyes. 'Did you say murder?'

Doherty nodded. 'A Lady Templeton-Jones was recently murdered in Bath.'

Bannister nodded back. 'I did hear about it.'

'We found your address and telephone number in her appointments' diary. Do you know why it might be there?'

Bannister thrust out his bottom lip when he shook his head. 'Name doesn't ring a bell.'

'Can you check your records?'

He shook his head. 'No need. We get very few private individuals using this facility. Our clients are big companies producing more paperwork than a normal office machine can cope with. We do a lot of government departments and big blue-chip companies and some smaller ones. And that's it.'

As Steve asked more questions, Honey watched Bannister's body language. Apart from dropping his top set of teeth now and again — here was a man in bad need of a fixative — he gave no sign of having something to hide.

Steve showed him a photo of the dead woman.

Bannister shook his head. 'Nope.'

'If I leave a photo with you, can you pass it around?' Doherty asked.

'No problem,' said Bannister.

* * *

Back in the car, Steve got out a packet of jelly babies from the glove compartment. He offered one to Honey. She eyed them warily.

'Devil dolls,' she said and shuddered.

Steve laughed. 'What?'

'Devil dolls. One rubbery little body between my teeth and I'm well over my calorie allowance for today.'

'It's only one jelly baby, for Christ's sake!'

She groaned and made a face. One! She couldn't resist a red one. And then there was a green one, an orange one, a white one . . .

'One little red one can lead to a whole rainbow of colour . . . Oh, go on then. Just one.' Red, green, orange, white and black swiftly followed.

Steve smiled. 'Did you skip breakfast this morning?'

The insinuation was obvious. She was being a pig. After rolling the bag up, she pushed it to the back of the glove compartment and snapped it shut.

'Get thee behind me, Satan.'

Still smiling and shaking his head, Steve restarted the engine.

A large van had parked alongside while they'd been inside. More cars had arrived in the car park. It was getting pretty full. Without them Doherty would have turned right to drive out. In order to avoid their back bumpers, he had to turn left.

Feeling guilty about guzzling the jelly babies, Honey gazed forlornly out of the window, mentally reciting that well-used mantra: *I must not yield to temptation. I must not yield to temptation.*

She stopped mid-mantra. Gold Tooth was sitting on the dock of the loading bay. There was another guy with him, slightly plump and wearing a dull green windcheater and polyester trousers. He appeared to be unloading the van — or was supposed to be. At this moment in time he was undoing one of the bags marked for shredding and going through the contents.

She pointed it out to Steve. 'What do you think they're up to?'

'Let's go and find out.'

The pair stiffened on seeing them approach. Doherty flashed his warrant card for the other guy's benefit. The guy became visibly nervous.

'And you are?'

'Simon Taylor.'

'You work here?'

'Yes.'

'Do you recognise this woman? Did she ever come here?' He showed the guy in the windcheater a copy of the photograph.

'No. Never seen her.'

'Are you sure?' urged Doherty.

The boy was adamant, and yet Honey had the impression he was holding something back.

CHAPTER THIRTY-THREE

Steve Doherty rang her in the middle of the happy hour, that dull time between six and seven when the workday dips and tips into night. The hotel bar was empty. Honey made herself comfortable.

'How about me whisking you away tonight?'

She agreed to be whisked away this time, but only as far as the Saracens Head. On her way out her eyes strayed to the traffic. A motorbike idled then skittered through the dawdling cars. She strained her neck to see if the man in wellies was the rider.

Steve had parked his car on double yellows.

'You'll get nicked.'

'No I won't. I'm on police business.'

'Is that what I am?'

It was a warm night as they strolled along Great Pulteney Street.

Honey had opted for smart casual — denim skirt, a white bouclé sweater and green earrings. Green — dark green, that is — made her skin glow and looked good against her dark hair. Light green made her look ill, or even ghostly. She'd opted for high heels. Not practical, but they did make her legs look longer.

'You look good,' he said and sniffed.

'Perfume or grease from the deep fat fryer?'

Obviously she hoped it was the former.

He leaned close and nuzzled behind her ear. 'Not fried fish. Definitely perfume.'

Steve went on to talk about Warren Price. 'I've had to pass him to a colleague. This murder takes priority now. Can't say I'm sorry. You can give jogging to the birds!'

It was eight o'clock and they were strolling past the Theatre Royal. Neither of them seemed particularly keen to get to the pub too quickly.

She sensed that Steve Doherty was doing his best to relax. A list of questions seemed to be ricocheting around his brain. Physically he was with her, but mentally he seemed to be still on duty.

Her guess was confirmed the moment he swept her past the welcoming entrance of the Theatre Royal. The play *Arcadia* by Tom Stoppard was playing. 'Let's take a rain check on the Saracens. I want another word with the landlord of the Garrick's Head.'

They turned right into the pedestrianised walkway outside the old pub. Actor David Garrick looked down at them from the creaking old inn sign.

Inside Adrian Harris loomed large behind the bar. As a keen angler, the word was that his prime objective in life was to land the biggest salmon for that year. Cultured he was not, odd for a man living next door to one of the finest theatres in England. He talked a lot about fishing and did a lot of drinking and socialising. He left serving the customers to his barmaid. Marion was grey-haired and kindly. Without her he would have gone broke years ago. Whether he appreciated it or not was another matter. And how she put up with him was something else again. Adrian was rude. How he managed to keep customers at all was a mystery.

Once they had drinks, ice and a slice, Steve asked to speak to Adrian.

Marion was true to form, overly defensive of the man who ruled her working day. 'He might not want to speak to you. He's busy. He's had a lot to do since coming back from Spain.'

Honey and Steve looked to where Adrian was indulging himself. Marion had made it sound as though he were in conference. Between swigs of whisky he was fiddling with a digital camera.

'This one was taken on the River Dee . . .'

Honey raised her eyebrows. 'No holiday snaps?'

'He likes fish,' said Steve.

'So do I,' said Honey. 'With chips.'

Steve was not to be brushed off. He laid his hand on Marion's wrist and leaned forward. 'I don't want to flash my warrant card, but I will if I have to.'

Marion got the message. A policeman in the midst of out-and-out theatrical types — especially in the Green Room — was not good for business. People got nervous when the fuzz was around.

Adrian's glass paused halfway to his mouth as Marion gave him the news, jerking her fluffed-up hairdo in their direction.

The landlord's expression of outright bonhomie faded. A wary look ensured. He downed his drink and stalked over.

'I don't know nothing. I told yer mate that.'

'You have not told me,' said Steve, his words evenly spaced and precisely delivered. There was no softness in his expression, no give in his jaw.

Adrian had attitude. The wrong attitude. The sort that made the mildest of manners want to put a dent in his jaw. To say he was surly was an understatement. Honey noted his lack of a tan. She guessed he'd trawled Spanish bars rather than Spanish beaches.

Steve asked his first question. 'Did she come in alone?'

Adrian nodded. 'Yes.'

'Why did she give you her handbag?'

'A lot of these walkers do it. Maybe in case they take a fright, wet themselves and do a runner.' He grinned. Honey was amazed to see he had small, pointed teeth — like a fish.

'Did you look inside it?'

'No.' The grin vanished. He looked defensive.

'What time did she come in?'

'Early. About six thirty.'

'So she had a long wait until the ghost walk started?'

'Yes.'

Adrian was being monosyllabic on purpose. The two men met and held each other's fierce glare. The two of them were like bulls snorting at each over a fence.

'So what did she do to while away the time?'

'Talked.'

'To you?'

'No. To her companion.'

Anyone who didn't know him wouldn't have seen the flicker of anger that crossed Steve's face.

'I thought you said she came in alone.' Doherty's tone was colder. His eyes stone-dead determined.

Adrian appeared unfazed. 'She did. He joined her a few minutes later.'

'Who was he?' said Steve.

Adrian shrugged. 'No one that I know.'

Honey tried to work out where this was going. It appeared that Lady Templeton-Jones had gone into the pub, left and come back again in a taxi in time for the ghost walk. Why was that?

If the landlord of the Garrick's Head thought he was going to be let off the hook, he was very much mistaken. Steve got a notebook and pencil from out of his pocket and pushed it across the brass drip tray on the countertop. 'I want a list of everyone who was here at that time. Anyone who might have seen her companion.'

Adrian's hands — great meaty hands with hairs growing out of the knuckles — still rested on the bar.

His hesitation was obvious to Honey. It was just as obvious to Steve. Being faced with a six-foot-four man was pretty forbidding, but Steve was in commando mode.

Leaning across the bar, he whispered in Adrian's ear. 'If I don't get it pronto I might spread a rumour to the drugs boys that you're selling more than Pimm's No. 1.'

The shielded look dropped from Adrian's face. 'We don't do that stuff in here!'

Steve shook his head disconsolately and pursed his lips in a low whistle. 'Doesn't matter. Those boys are always on the lookout for potential training exercises. They'd apologise afterwards, of course. They'd probably even apologise in writing. But that's not the point, is it? Bad publicity travels quickly. Not good for the supper crowd from the theatre.'

Adrian turned from one of Jonathan Swift's giants to one of Walt Disney's dwarfs. A meaty hand grudgingly snatched the notepad.

'Find your own pen,' said Steve, slipping a Parker into his breast pocket. 'I've lost too many that way.'

'I thought he was going to punch your lights out,' whispered Honey, between sips of vodka and tonic.

'Nah!' said Steve, grinning. 'I've got a reputation.'

'Oh, yeah,' she said with a mocking smile. 'What as?'

One more drink from the ever-faithful Marion, and Steve had his list.

Adrian was just as abrupt, just as gruff in speech though he did manage to string a whole sentence together. 'That's those who I can say for sure were 'ere, but only regulars. The rest that were in were just tourists.'

Just tourists, the city's lifeblood. He said it so flippantly.

Steve was running his eyes down the list. He paused about halfway before carrying on. He passed it to Honey. 'You'd better take a look.'

As they made for the door, she made the most of the light. The name popped out at her outside under a street light.

'Casper!'

'I'll interview the others. You interview Casper.'

The personal and professional had come crashing together. It had entered her head to make a night of it, but seeing Casper's name on the list intrigued her. She weighed up her options. It was no good. Responsibility came with having been the last person to see the victim alive — the last person beside the murderer, that is.

CHAPTER THIRTY-FOUR

The flagstones outside the Garrick's Head were roughly as old as the theatre and pub, and it showed. Knobbly bits, raised ridges and blobs of cement and mortar held them together and in place. Wads of green moss had taken over where no footsteps trod. All in all, they were lethal.

Honey was wearing her favourite shoes: plain black, higher heels than normal. Her heel caught in a groove; her foot moved onwards but her shoe didn't. With a girlish cry, she fell forwards, her skirt tearing and her nose making contact with the step.

Steve helped her to her feet. 'Upsy-daisy.'

She covered her nose with the flat of her hand. 'Och, my noche. My noche is broken.'

'Let me see,' Steve said. 'Get your hand away.'

She did so, holding her head back to help stem a slight blood flow.

Steve peered intently at her nose, turning her head this way and that, from the front and from each side. He kept smiling.

'You look good from all angles,' he said, looking at the exposed thigh where her skirt had torn.

She eyed him accusingly. 'You're not concentrating.'

His smile widened. 'Can I help it if my concentration wanders when you're around? At least you're not speaking a foreign language anymore.'

A few tourists from a 'See England in Two Hundred Hours' trip chose that moment to leave the pub. They all had a comment to make:

'My God. What happened? Has she been attacked?'

'She fell up the step.'

'My, my, honey pie, I would sue if I were you.'

'A broken nose can get you a whole lot of plastic surgery money. You could have your boobs done at the same time.'

'Take no notice,' said Steve, looking slightly perplexed by the last comment. 'They're fine as they are. As for your nose, well that's up to you.'

'Honey? I thought I heard your dulcet tones.'

She looked up to see Casper St John Gervais on his way into the pub. 'Casper. I was just on my way to see you.'

'Too hurriedly,' he quipped. 'No need to bow and scrape, dear thing.' He was in company and the company was vaguely familiar. Wasn't he the Hollywood actor who'd got famous in some medical drama but didn't admit to being gay? Was it for his benefit that Casper was putting on his Noel Coward performance? Casper was what he termed *casually dressed*. Midnight-blue velvet jacket, cherry-red neckerchief, black T-shirt and trousers.

His attitude was as aloof as ever. 'Dust yourself off,' he said as he stepped around her. His handsome companion threw her a winning smile — and did the same.

Feeing livid, Honey watched Casper casually stroll off. *Damn that man!*

Steve helped her to her feet. 'Old Casper's certainly got a way about him.'

Honey erupted. 'That man is the most selfish, rude, arrogant . . . Interview be damned. Interrogation! That's what this will be. Hold it right there, Casper! I want a word with you.'

Turning round he raised his elegant eyebrows. 'Such an aggressive tone!'

She heard the warning in his voice. *Whoops! Steady on, girl. Remember how much you like jam on your bread and butter.*

Room reservations were put her way in return for being crime liaison officer on behalf of the Hotels Association. Reminding herself of this curbed her temper. Her tone turned as sweet as brown demerara.

'This is a police investigation. It's generating a lot of media interest and you might have some useful information. Who knows, you could make the front page. Hang on and I'll take a photograph.' Honey's trusty bag came off her shoulder and she delved for her mobile.

At mention of taking a photograph and making the front page, the handsome actor became nervous. 'Ahem,' he said, stepping back with all the elegance of a ballroom dancer. 'Another time, Casper. There's an old girlfriend I promised to see . . .' He gave a swift wave before the slow waltz became a backward quickstep.

Casper looked as though he'd been hit in the face with a smoked kipper. The smug smile and flared nostrils were suddenly flat-packed. But Casper was not a man to be down for long. A group of women recognised the handsome actor. A murmur of excitement ran from one to the other. Casper saw them.

'Ladies! He fancies me a lot more than he fancies you!'

There was momentary confusion among the group of women, probably out for a hen night judging by their raucous laughter and smutty comments. Then they were off.

'Oi! Come back here!'

'Tell us it's not true!'

'*Show* us it's not true!'

A stampede of clattering heels and hoots of laughter accompanied their running.

Casper sighed. 'I could do with a drink.'

Now the tourists had gone, the bar took on a more sedate atmosphere. They headed for the corner nearest the window.

Over a large sherry, Casper told them what he'd seen — such as it was. 'She was in the lounge bar, and so was I. That's all there is to it.'

Still slightly angry with Casper, Honey buried her mouth in a large vodka and tonic. Her hand shook. Casper presumed it was due to the fall.

'Steady on there,' said Casper covering her hand with his. 'Take deep breaths. Count to ten.'

'My, Casper, you sound so fatherly.'

He pulled a face. 'Heaven forbid!'

She tried to pull herself and her torn skirt together.

Casper glanced and raised his eyebrows. 'A black lining to a beige skirt?' He looked affronted at the prospect.

She put him wise. 'No. That's my underwear.'

'Thank heavens.' He went on to describe the young man he'd seen in the company of Lady Templeton-Jones.

'He was a lumpy youth whose only redeeming feature was the fact that he could blend into a crowd very easily. *Nondescript* is the right word. Clothes were memorable only for their superior blandness. Green anorak. Dark *polyester* trousers.'

Casper said the word polyester as though he was spitting out something that stung.

'I know where we can find him!' Honey exclaimed, falling back in her chair. 'He works at ASS.'

Casper eyed her disdainfully. 'What was that you said?'

'Associated Security Shredding. It's a company.'

'An unfortunate name.'

'My sentiments exactly.'

Steve had a thoughtful expression. His eyes were trained on Honey's. 'So she did visit that place. But not to use their services. She went there to see Simon Taylor. But why?'

* * *

Doherty was parked in Queen Square and insisted on taking her home.

'I can walk.'

'Your knees look sore. So does your nose.'

She gently touched her nose. 'It's still sore.'

The lights of Queen Square passed over their shoulders as they swung into George Street. They took a left, swinging up towards the Circus. The Green River Hotel was in the other direction.

'Why are we taking the scenic route?' Honey asked.

'We're being followed.'

'Oh.' She suppressed a shiver. She tried to casually look out of the window. Was it the guy on the motorcycle?

'Is it Warren Price?'

'I shouldn't worry too much about him.'

'But you said . . .'

He made a snorting sound. 'Trust me. Everything will be fine.'

'Relax,' she said mostly to herself. 'Admire the view.'

That's exactly what she did. No big deal. The old Georgian buildings looked just as good at night as they did in the day — only different. Less traffic gave vent to more imagination.

Unblinking, she studied shadows she would never have noticed before. Could she see a figure hiding there? It was possible. A few late-night gropers might be around, grunting and humping in the gloom.

The curiosity reached up from where it was hidden and took hold of her. 'So this murderer, this Warren Price, who is he?'

'You don't want to know.'

'I wouldn't ask you if I didn't want to know.'

She couldn't quite get this evasiveness. Since they'd started working together he'd always been pretty open with her.

'Are you trying to frighten me?'

'Hey!' he exclaimed, and laughed nervously. He took his eyes off the road to look at her. 'Would I do a thing like that?'

There was something about the way he said it that just wasn't right. His laugh didn't ring true.

Something was going on with Steve Doherty. Something he didn't want to let go. It made her wonder about the motorcyclist.

She couldn't let things lie.

'Go on. Tell me more.'

'OK.' He said it slowly as though giving himself time to think. 'Now let me see . . . right . . . Warren Price . . . I got him locked up. I hadn't been a detective for very long. Then, he was nearing the end of his sentence and got moved to a low-security prison for good behaviour. Before legging it, he swore he'd make me suffer. Not a forgiving type.'

'Who did he murder?'

'Girlfriend. Slit her throat in a fit of temper.'

Honey took a moment to mull. Steve drove around the Circus and took the exit onto the long hill sloping from Lansdown.

'And he wants to slit your throat too?'

'Not quite. That's why he attacked Karen. He wanted to hurt me by disposing of someone close to me. That's why I was out jogging with Karen late at night, trying to draw him out. Looks like our course of action paid off — all too well. He thought she was my girlfriend. That's the premise we're working on anyway. Can't get at me, hurt her. It was a warning.'

Honey's ugly green monster shrunk to the size of a grape. Then another niggling worry followed the first one.

'Am I in danger?'

He made a non-committal kind of sound. 'I don't think so.'

'But you don't know for sure.'

'It's me he wants to get at . . .'

She knew the rest, remembering when Steve had told her not to put her arm through his. In case they were being watched. In case Warren Price would reach an obvious conclusion. 'Which is why you haven't come calling too much of late.'

He made a grunting noise. 'That's about it. It's been hard, babe, but I didn't want to put you at risk. Karen drew him out quicker than we'd thought.'

The big green monster sprouted arms and legs again. 'So, were you having a thing with her?'

She saw a grin crease his cheek. 'A training thing. I didn't mind the jogging that much. Besides, I saw you'd lost weight, and you were looking good on it. I figured I needed to get into shape. Karen's a qualified personal trainer.' He glanced at her sideways. 'But not that personal.'

She hit his arm. 'Steve Doherty, is this really what this is all about? I saw you out jogging and you're embarrassed about it. This Warren Price thing is a load of rubbish!'

She saw him wince as they dropped down onto the main road. They continued past the Star Inn and the park. At the lights he took a right on to the Warminster Road.

'About that jogging . . .'

'Forget it, Steve.' She said it with force and feeling. 'Anyway, if what you say about Warren Price is true, I can throw in a googly.'

He pulled in outside the hotel and looked at her. 'What do you mean by that?'

'Cameron Wallace has asked me out.'

He looked surprised. 'You'd go out with him? After what I told you about him and his receptionist?'

'All in the line of duty. I'm working on him to get my mother another shop. There's no way I can cope with her camped around the corner. I'd go mad.'

'I can see where you're coming from. Just decline his offer to go up and view his etchings.'

'Funny you should say that. He's a collector. Like me.'

'Underwear? The man collects underwear?'

She shrugged. 'I don't know what he collects. Only *that* he collects.'

'Oh, well. No doubt you'll hold him off.'

'I may not want to. Had you considered that?'

'Don't need to. I've met the guy. Smooth, yes, but hey, you can't say he's better looking and more charming than me.'

'You've a high opinion of yourself, Steve Doherty.'

He winked again. 'I've had good feedback.'

'Not from me.'

'Yet.'

'I won't kiss you goodnight just in case we're being watched.'

'We are,' said Honey. She pointed to where a head bobbed at one of the windows of the Green River Hotel. 'My mother's staying over.'

'One little piece of information,' said Steve, his right hand diving into his inside pocket. 'We've had a breakthrough with the website where Wanda Carpenter bought the Lady Templeton-Jones title. I had our computer bods look into it. It's called Noble Present, and it's a worldwide thing. Whoever runs it from here is only a franchisee. The real brains is this guy. Be surprised.'

She took the piece of paper he passed her.

Her gaze swept over the name. 'Hamilton George!' She couldn't help sounding surprised. Hamilton George had been on the ghost walk.

Steve raised his eyebrows questioningly. 'Something of a coincidence?'

She nodded. 'You bet it was! Didn't his wife say that he was a whizz on computers?'

'I don't know whether his business and Wanda's murder are linked, but I don't believe in coincidences.'

He told her Hamilton George had been traced to a cottage in Bradford on Avon. 'That's according to the hotel they checked out of.'

Honey refolded the piece of paper and tucked it into her bra.

Steve noticed. 'Hey. I may need that.' He grinned. 'Never mind. Keep it there. I promise to warm my hands before I retrieve it.'

They fell silent. It was great to maintain their usual camaraderie, but underlying it all was a murder. All they could do was work through it. All the same it was hard not to feel nervous.

'This Warren Price. Does he wear wellies when he's riding a motorbike?'

Doherty frowned. 'I don't know.'

'The guy that keeps dogging me definitely wears rubber wellington boots.'

'Has he approached you?'

'He abducted me for Christ's sake! Isn't that enough?'

'Hmm. But he let you go. Out of character for Warren. I'd be digging you up by now.'

'Perhaps he was having one of his off days.'

'Perhaps he just wasn't Warren Price. Or perhaps he was, but he's changed tactics.'

CHAPTER THIRTY-FIVE

The lights of the city spangled the tall buildings and sweeping crescents. Lindsey strolled along Alfred Street. The street ran from the Assembly Rooms to Lansdown Hill. What traffic there was passed at knee level due to the fact that the pavement was four-feet higher than the road and was interspersed with worn stone steps at regular intervals. Ironwork that had once held braziers to light the way for footfall and carriage arched over each set of steps. Nowadays they were empty, their job taken over by the overhead street lights.

Lindsey was on her way home from a recital given by the Medieval Minstrels. She had been hoping for company, but her date hadn't turned up. She was feeling glum about it. She liked him a lot, but absence didn't necessarily make the heart fonder.

She consoled herself that his profession caused him to keep odd hours. *He told you that*, she reminded herself. Normally such a relationship would have floundered, but he was hard-working. And different. Certainly different.

She forced herself to think pleasant thoughts. Naturally the concert she'd attended sprang to mind. Her mind filled with music. She hummed as she walked.

The sound of a motorcycle coming up behind her interrupted the flow.

She stopped and turned round.

He pulled up by the steps and pushed up his visor. 'Sorry I couldn't make it. I had a delivery. Came straight from work.'

She glanced down at his boots. 'So I see.'

'Hop on.'

She smiled. The evening had turned out even better. 'Don't mind if I do.'

CHAPTER THIRTY-SIX

It was late and past the witching hour.

The courtyard between the back of the hotel and the coach house was totally enclosed by high walls on each side and the buildings on the others. The sound of Honey's footsteps ricocheted from all four corners.

Something slightly out of sight, slightly out of hearing, made her pause at the halfway point. She glanced at the gate dividing her private domain from the lawns and patio reserved for guests.

The plants climbing up the wall looked the same. So did the tubs of parsley, rosemary, sage and lavender. That was the great thing about a courtyard garden. No weeding. No lawn mowing. Just pluck the weeds and trim the plants. Simple.

A climbing rose ran riot in one shadowy corner. It shivered in the night breeze. She peered at it. Had it shivered of its own volition or did the shadow move?

Calm down. Think logically. A bird could have caused it to shiver. Were there many birds out and about at this time of night?

A more worrying prospect wouldn't go away. Was that a pair of wellington boots sticking out at its base?

In daylight she wouldn't have given a fig for it. At night it was a different matter.

Steps quickening, she headed for her front door whistling 'Who's Afraid of the Big Bad Wolf?'

The door thudded shut behind her. That was the great thing about old doors; they had substance, they had character. Best of all was the thickness of the wood. A whole oak or elm had been cut down to make this door. She lay back against it, her heart thudding. The door felt good. Strong.

Home! There was nothing like it.

A cup of fresh coffee crossed her mind but she kept on going. A sip of water would be enough. Her bed was calling her. Freshly laundered bedlinen was heaven on earth. Shoes were kicked off, clothes were discarded. Sleep came but was beset with nightmares about shadows coming to life. A man in a woolly hat jumped out. He was wearing earmuffs and his wife was shrieking in the background.

CHAPTER THIRTY-SEVEN

The morning broke bright and clear but with its usual run of problems. Chef had run out of eggs and needed them for breakfast. Honey trotted along the road to the deli and bought three dozen farm-fresh organic ones. Of all the people sharing her life, Smudger Smith was the man she went most out of her way to look after. Family members weren't exactly replaceable, but they were forgiving. Chefs were neither. Like a good car they had to be run in. You had to get used to their foibles and irritating little habits. Good chefs were hard to come by.

Once the eggs were delivered and grunted and grumbled over, she roused Lindsey from her bed.

'Want to go snooping with me?'

'Is it dangerous?'

Honey shrugged. 'Could be.'

She'd checked with Steve Doherty. Hamilton George and partner had decamped to a rented cottage at Winsley, a village on the outskirts of Bradford on Avon.

Lindsey yawned as she swung her legs out of bed. 'Sounds like fun. Where are we going?'

'Winsley. I need to speak to a Mr Hamilton George about his online business dealings. I warn you, his wife talks a lot. That's why I'm taking you. I'll keep her occupied while you do the computer stuff.'

Lindsey nodded and yawned again. 'Ah-huh.'

Honey paused. Lindsey didn't usually fit into the lack-lustre teenager bracket. Even in the morning she had more bounce than a beach ball. 'You look tired. Had a good night with your kilted beau?'

Lindsey nodded, smiled and changed the subject. 'So, what are we dealing with?'

Honey took the hint. Lindsey didn't want to talk about the boyfriend. Fine. She filled her in on the Noble Present website. 'It's some kind of franchise operation. There's a guy named Simon Taylor involved, but I'm unsure how deeply. That's all I know.'

Lindsey told her she'd handle with it.

Honey found herself wondering about her daughter. Lindsey knew all about great men from history. But like her mother, she wasn't so clever with men from the here and now. It had been a surprise when she'd heard of her involvement with Oliver Stafford, a married, and later murdered, chef. But there, the girl couldn't be good at everything.

'Do you want breakfast?'

'I'll grab a coffee then see you outside.'

'We'll go in your car. Is that OK?'

'The Green Goblin is at your disposal, Mother.' Lindsey's green Citroen was a constant standby, small but reliable.

Reception was unusually quiet. Anna had sorted out most of the bills for leaving guests. But it wasn't just that. Mary Jane was nowhere in sight. Unusual for Mary Jane. It had to be said that she had presence. Both physically and mentally, she was pretty unusual. Perhaps, just for once, she was having a lie-in, thought Honey.

She addressed Anna, who was swiftly outgrowing reception thanks to her six-month lump. 'No Mary Jane?'

'No. She went out with Lindsey. She was chatting a lot.'

A cold chill rippled down Honey's spine. She was kind of so-so about premonitions and suchlike, but was sure she was having one now. Something awful was about to happen and she could make a good guess what it was.

Outside on the pavement, her eyes scoured the traffic for Lindsey's green VW. No sign of lime green. Instead she saw pink. She muttered, 'Oh, no,' under her breath.

Mary Jane's pink Cadillac, affectionately termed the Chick-mobile, glided against the kerb. She'd shipped it over with a few other precious things. The rest of her stuff that she hadn't wanted to dispose of she'd put in storage. The uninformed visualise all Cadillacs as long, low things with dagger-like wings sticking up at the back. But this was a coupe, a neat alternative to the Elvis-mobile.

Mary Jane had owned it since her high-school days and insisted it could tell a few 'hot' stories. No doubt it could, but a lot of years had gone by. The car had aged and so had Mary Jane. All the same, both still turned heads; admiration for the car, amazement for Mary Jane.

Over the years the city of Bath had seen a lot of transport come and go. Sturdy ponies and sledges in Celtic times, litters for the Romans, sedan chairs in the eighteenth century, and self-steering invalid carriages in the nineteenth. Cadillacs were a rarity. So were the likes of Mary Jane and her driving.

She'd never quite got used to the rule about keeping to the left side of the road. To travel with her was something of an adventure — comparable to bungee jumping on the end of an elastic band that had lost its bounce.

People stopped and stared. A group of tourists took a photograph, and a man, possibly a Russian, waved a fistful of money.

Lindsey was sitting in the passenger seat and had wound down the window.

Standing like a lump of limp dough at the kerb, Honey made a face. *What's she doing here?*

Lindsey mouthed a reply.

She insisted.

Mary Jane was not so much an insistent person but oblivious that others might not care to partake in what she wanted to do.

Knowing resistance was futile, Honey slid over the cracked white leather of the car's rear seat. She was loath to appear scared. But she needed to say something, if only to keep from admitting how she was really feeling.

'So,' Honey asked, 'how did your table-tapping go?'

She shouldn't have said it. She realised this the moment that Mary Jane broke into fast-forward animation at the same time as pulling out into the traffic.

'Badly,' she said with a scowl. Her scrawny neck turned like an owl's, so she was close to facing backwards. 'Badly. And when I say badly, I mean b-a-d-l-y! The yeses got mixed up with the noes until I didn't know who I was talking to. Sheesh!' She shook her head forlornly. 'I've never got this muddled before. The table did a damned jig when I asked my spirit guide if he knew anything about this Wanda Carpenter, otherwise known as Lady Templeton-Jones. I'm sure she was doing her damnedest to override him. Did she strike you as an impatient woman?'

'I never really got to know her that well,' said Honey, her eyes squeezed tightly shut. Not seeing what was happening was preferable to witnessing Mary Jane's dodgem-style car driving.

Mary Jane slowly shook her head. 'Well, it sure could have been her. Pushy type at that. Forcing her way to the front of the queue. Sir Cedric didn't like it one little bit! Manners matter regardless of the circumstances of a person's demise.'

Feeling more worried about her own demise, Honey opened one eye: 'Watch that zebra crossing! Brake, Mary Jane, brake!'

'Sorry!' Mary Jane shouted to a group of Japanese tourists, who parted as she ploughed on through.

Honey closed her eyes again. Her whole body had gone into rigor mortis. Mary Jane, on the other hand, was still waving her arms emphatically. And how could she turn her head like that? A certain eighties horror film came to mind.

Taxis were blowing their horns, brakes were squealing like pigs with slit throats, and white-van men were giving two-fingered salutes.

Lindsey grabbed the steering wheel, swinging it away from a sandwich board that was sent rocking in its frame.

Honey felt guilty about leaving her daughter in the front seat. It might be a fleeting fancy, but she'd quite like her genes to go on for a few more generations at least. And Lindsey was the only contribution to the gene pool she was likely to leave behind.

Strange how much eternity and the afterlife came up when Mary Jane was around. The lanky, lean Californian saw and heard nothing. Her mouth was in overdrive.

'Mark my words, that Midwestern woman was not on that walk to look at ghosts. She didn't have the right aura. Do you remember I told you that at the time?'

Honey had to agree. 'I remember.'

None of those interviewed had mentioned ghosts as a subject close to their hearts. They'd all been there for the fun of it. Lady Templeton-Jones had seemed the most unlikely of all.

G-force kicked in as Mary Jane jabbed her foot on the gas. The car shot forward, sending a trio of cyclists shooting up a disabled ramp.

Lindsey shouted, 'Whoa!'

Mary Jane carried on regardless. 'Something definitely stinks!'

More by luck than judgement, Mary Jane managed to manoeuvre out onto the main road, though by a very roundabout method. Rather than chance cutting through the city, she opted to head towards Bristol, then turn up past Green Park. They bowled out onto Queen Square causing the driver of a rubbish truck to stand on his brakes.

'Nasty temper,' Mary Jane said with an air of disbelief.

Lindsey put her straight — or so she thought. 'You didn't look before emerging.'

'Oh, yes, I did,' Mary Jane replied, sounding offended. 'Didn't I do just that, Honey? You saw me do it, didn't you? It's you Brits! You drive on the wrong side!'

Lindsey sighed and resumed giving her directions. 'Head out along Lambridge. I'll direct you from there.'

'Right!'

Things calmed a little. They were heading east in the general direction of Bradford on Avon. The village of Winsley was on the outskirts. By hook or by crook, they would get to where they were going. Luckily they were heading in a straight line until they got to the roundabout where the Bradford on Avon turning went off to the right. Mary Jane drove straight on.

Honey's nerves were too shredded to point this out. Lindsey was more diplomatic.

'I think we should have gone right back there, Mary Jane. It said right to Bradford on Avon. It might be best if you turned round.'

'Darn!' Mary Jane exclaimed. 'I don't like turning round. I like to keep going. I used to be good at turning round and going backwards, but I only like going forwards nowadays. Betcha we can bear off up here a way,' she said brightly.

Honey noticed her daughter's shoulders stiffen into a perfect square. Likewise, every muscle in her own body was rock hard. Every sense was on high alert.

Honey had a brainwave. She leaned forward so her head was between Mary Jane's and her daughters. Lindsey's face was white, worrying on a girl who tanned easily.

'I'd like a word with Ashwell Bridgewater. He's the dead woman's cousin and he lives in Northend. Do you mind making a diversion, Mary Jane?'

'Nope! Where's the turning?'

'Next on the left, but—'

Too late. No signal, a swift turn of the wheel and they'd shot up a cul-de-sac, leaving behind protesting car horns and skidpan manoeuvres. Mary Jane slammed on the brakes. 'This it?'

'Sure is.' Remarkably, they arrived in the right place in one piece. All's well that ends well. Ashwell Bridgewater lived in one of a terraced row of cottages at the Batch, Northend. Honey got out of the car. 'Stay here. I won't be long.'

Lindsey also got out. 'I'm coming with you.'

Mary Jane looked alarmed. 'Have I got to stay out here all by myself?'

Honey thought quickly. 'Of course you do. I need you to block his escape. If he comes running out, nail him.'

Mary Jane's eyes positively glittered at the prospect of nailing a real live criminal. She bent forward rummaging beneath her seat and brought out a tyre wrench. 'I'll nail him with this.'

'She insisted,' said Lindsey as she followed her mother through the gate. 'I couldn't stop her. I did try . . . Hey, what are we doing here? Do you have more questions for him?'

'No,' said Honey. 'I just hate people who get me out of the bath. His sort have hassled me, now I'm hassling him.'

CHAPTER THIRTY-EIGHT

The terraced houses lining the Batch dated from the late seventeenth century. They were tall and thin, three storeys high with stone mullion windows and slate mansard roofs. Number 17 had a well-kept garden with chocolate-box roses growing over a frame around the front door. Hollyhocks snuggled against the boundary walls. Purple, pink and white border plants jostled for space either side of the path. It was pretty in a Hansel and Gretel kind of way.

Lindsey asked, 'Is this guy dangerous?'

'Only on the other end of the telephone.' Honey gritted her teeth. She told herself not to let those interrupted baths get to her. Bridgewater might not be personally responsible for them.

There was no doorbell, just a cast-iron knocker — a naked naiad bent like a horseshoe, her feet touching the back of her head.

Mother and daughter eyed it speculatively.

'Tawdry,' said Lindsey.

'Physically impossible.'

Honey gave it a stout rap, stood back and looked up at the first-floor windows. A pasty face appeared and disappeared. People who spent a lot of time on the telephone and in front of a computer were always pasty. Except Lindsey, of course. Lindsey was exceptional. *But I'm biased*, thought Honey.

Feet descending on stairs sounded from the other side of the door. Honey took a deep breath and mentally listed the questions she needed to ask. She pushed her opinion about telephone harassment to the back of her mind.

The door was stiff in its frame and juddered as it was tugged open. Ashwell Bridgewater was dressed in dark chinos, a pale shirt and even a tie. He recognised her immediately. His smile was instant, like flicking on a light switch.

'Hello. My, you're lucky to find me here. Did the office tell you I was working from home today?'

Despite the molasses smile, Honey couldn't help the feeling that he wasn't pleased about her visit.

'I took a chance,' she said, matching his smile with one of her own.

She guessed he didn't believe her. Woe betide any poor soul he suspected of telling her he was home. They'd be for the high jump — probably off the edge of a cliff.

'Can we come in?'

For a moment his smile faltered. His eyes flickered as they darted between mother and daughter.

Suddenly he seemed desperate to please.

'Of course you can.' Oozing enthusiasm, he stood back against the wall, waving them in. 'Do come in. Would you like tea? Or coffee? The coffee's filtered. The tea's Darjeeling.'

Mindful that Mary Jane's driving could quite easily lead to a wet seat from the strongest bladder, Honey declined. Being a chip off the old block, Lindsey did the same.

The front door led directly into a single reception room. A wrought-iron staircase wound upwards in the right-hand corner.

'It's small but exquisitely built,' said Bridgewater as though he'd just read her thoughts. 'It still has character. I think character is so very important in a house. That's why I like old houses.'

'It was left to you by your grandfather?'

'Yes, it was.'

He invited them to sit down. As she did so, Honey got out her notebook and tried not to covet the delightful old furniture, the paintings and the porcelain. Shabby chic sprung to mind. All this stuff had been handed down. Overall it needed sorting out, refurbishing, reupholstering, refinishing. And there was too much of it, giving the cottage an overstuffed feel.

She noticed a few cardboard boxes on the floor to either side of a small, oak table. Old cameras spilled over the top of one box. Old film reels filled the other. Another small pile of reels sat on the table, barely discernible through bubble wrap.

His steely gaze followed hers.

'My grandfather collected old cameras and projectors. I'm sorting them out. He left the house to me, but it was full of bric-a-brac. He particularly liked old cameras and suchlike — anything to do with early movies, as opposed to photographs.'

'But you're not so inclined?'

His low laugh was something between a chuckle and a grimace. 'Not at all. Besides, I need more room. I only have two bedrooms, one on each floor above here.' He casually pointed at the ceiling. 'And a bathroom, of course. Think chocolate-box prettiness. No one could fail to fall in love with it.'

He spoke with an easy amiability, typical of those involved in telephone marketing companies. A salesman through and through.

'It's a very pretty cottage,' said Lindsey. 'How come you're selling it?'

Bridgewater's implacable expression changed to alarm. Pink spots flashed onto his cheeks and leaked colour. 'How did you know that?'

Lindsey pointed at the window. 'There's a man putting a 'For Sale' sign up in your garden.'

Honey fanned a hand over her mouth to hide a smile. Full marks, Lindsey. If the man putting up the sign had seen

Bridgewater's expression, he'd have legged it. But why react like that? Why not sell if he wanted to?

She dived in with her own question. 'Did your cousin travel a lot?'

He shrugged. 'I don't really know. She only stayed with me a short while, so I couldn't really say whether she's adventurous in that way, though it runs in the family somewhat.'

But not in you, she decided. Ashwell Bridgewater had nothing adventurous about him. Honey wondered at the propensity of genes to scatter indiscriminately. Someone in his family *had* been adventurous.

'So how come you've got an American cousin?' asked Lindsey.

'As I explained to your mother before, my great-grandfather went over at the beginning of the last century. One son stayed there, the other came back. The other was my grandfather, the man who owned this house.'

'And collected old movies and suchlike,' Honey added.

He nodded. 'That's right.'

The sound of the 'For Sale' sign being beaten into the ground punctuated proceedings.

'Why didn't she stay with you longer?'

He sighed and gritted his teeth. 'I've already told you. She wanted to be in the city centre so she could see all the sights.'

'Did you like her?'

'I didn't know her well enough.'

He didn't blink when he said it.

She didn't ask him when he'd last seen his cousin.

Their interview at an end, there was nothing to do but leave. Their appearance at the cottage had seemingly touched a raw nerve.

Steeling herself to stay that bit longer, she asked if he was taking the old cameras and film reels to auction.

'Yes. They're not worth much, but I need to de-clutter.' He said it with a smug smile.

Honey remembered the auction catalogue. Were these the items that hadn't made it? Or were there similar but more valuable items?

'Tell me,' she said, adopting as much of a smile as he deserved, 'did your cousin place anything for auction?'

He shook his head. 'Not that I know of.'

'Were you joint heirs?'

'Yes, and before you ask, her demise means that I do indeed inherit everything.'

'Thank you for that, though I wasn't going to ask.'

Because I didn't really need to, she thought. *I'd already guessed.*

* * *

The door knocker rattled as he shut the door behind them.

Honey shuddered. 'That man gives me the creeps.'

'It's a nice cottage though,' said Lindsey, looking back over her shoulder. She frowned suddenly.

Lindsey's expression jerked Honey out of her brooding. 'What is it?'

'I can see him through the window.'

'Is he watching us? I bet he is. The pervert.'

Lindsey glanced back again. 'He's not looking at us. He's got something in his hands. He looks as though he loves it.'

'There! I told you. A pervert!'

CHAPTER THIRTY-NINE

Hugging the film cans to his chest, Ashwell Bridgewater congratulated himself on handling things so well. Now the women were gone he adopted his true smile. The other smile he'd given them was the plastered-on false kind, the one that matched the smarmy voice he used at the call centre. This smile, his real one, was lopsided and twisted. Only one side of his mouth stretched into it properly. The other half jerked against a paralysed muscle. No one looking at him would be aware of his facial deformity simply because he took care they never did.

Stupid women! There it was lying there in front of their eyes, loosely covered with a scrap of bubble wrap. He'd seen her glance fall on it. She'd paid it no more attention than the other stuff — the rubbish. The rubbish was worth just a few hundred. But these! He patted them, feeling the cold hard tin beneath his fingers.

CHAPTER FORTY

Mary Jane was away from there and burning rubber before they had chance to fasten their seat belts. Honey checked the Georges' address.

'Winsley,' she ordered. 'It's down a lane behind the Seven Stars.'

Unlike the cottage in Northend, this was of a later vintage and had only two storeys. Instead of stone-edged mullions it had a large bay window. A purple-blossoming wisteria clambered up around the door and across the roof of the bay. A yellow climbing rose formed a barrier between the parking place and the rear garden. There was a small drive in-between the cottage and its ramshackle garage. The garage was constructed of corrugated tin with a concrete apron in front of it. The cottage was still recognisable as such. So far no development fanatic had ripped out its old windows or sold the lead from its slate roof.

The small garden was chock-a-block with old-fashioned flowers — pimpernel, foxgloves, cabbage roses and lavender. What looked like a rental car was parked outside. Mary Jane parked close enough to be out of the lane and only inches away from the rental.

Honey slid across the back seat and got out of the offside door. Lindsey slid out of the right-hand passenger seat. Not keen on being left behind this time, Mary Jane clambered across the propshaft housing to get out the same side.

A face appeared at the cottage window and then disappeared.

Honey told daughter and chauffeur to wait while she headed for the door. They did so reluctantly.

'I could be your sidekick,' said Lindsey, one eyebrow raised quizzically. 'You never know when you might need somebody to kick down a door or wrestle somebody to the ground.'

'I couldn't do that,' said Mary Jane, shaking her head. 'I haven't been physical for years.'

Honey and Lindsey looked at her for further explanation. None was forthcoming.

'So?' said Lindsey.

'So nothing,' said Honey. 'I reason that three's a crowd, two is unnecessary, and as I've already met Mr George, I do not foresee any trouble, so one is enough.'

As at Northend, she left Mary Jane with explicit instructions not to let anyone get away if they came running out.

As a result of recent updates, this cottage had a doorbell — not as provocative as the naked nymph in Northend, perhaps, but more efficient. As the face she'd seen at the window hadn't come to answer the door, she pressed the bell.

The top half of the door was formed by leaded light panels in a leafy design. The pattern altered in response to the shadow falling across it from the hallway.

Honey felt a fluttering in her stomach. As shadows went, it seemed a bit slim for Mrs George, who she remembered as being beefy.

She plastered on a friendly smile. The door opened. The smile froze on her face. This was not part of the script. There before her stood a woman dressed in something slinky and silky — silvery grey and figure defining. Her eyes matched the dress and her brandy-brown hair fell straight and sleek around a face she vaguely recognised.

Honey frowned and pretended to be puzzled. 'Do I know you?'

A faint haze of colour leaked over her pale white cheeks. She smelled of flowery perfume. What was more, she could tell by the woman's blushing cheeks that she too had been recognised. What the hell was going on here?

It might have been the perfume. It might have been the pollen floating in from the garden, but suddenly Miss Slinky sneezed. It was the opening Honey needed.

'I remember! You were the guide on the ghost walk. Pamela Windsor,' Honey added with a click and a pointed finger.

Hamilton George ambled up to fill the gap between her and the door surround.

'My wife's dead,' said Mr George, before she had a chance to accuse. 'She had breathing difficulties. She suffered from asthma.' He glanced at Pamela. 'Pammy helped me make all the arrangements.'

'Pammy' now, is it?

These two had more than ghosts in common, and they couldn't be that newly acquainted.

CHAPTER FORTY-ONE

At sight of Hamilton George, Mary Jane who had remained with the car outside the garden gate with Lindsey, leaped to her feet. 'Hey,' she shouted, waving the tyre iron above her head. 'Remember me?'

Hamilton George did not wave back.

Mary Jane's bottom lip quivered in a disappointed pout. 'He didn't wave back.'

Gently but firmly, Lindsey stopped her from going to the house.

'The tyre iron might have had something to do with that.'

Mary Jane hardly seemed to hear her. 'That's not his wife, you know. She's a trollop — an out-and-out trollop. How could he treat her so bad? And he never bothered to wave back. Don't you think that's just too rude?'

'Some people are like that.'

Mary Jane's face went blank, her eyes like slits in silk. 'I recognise that woman. That's the tour guide.'

'I think my mother knows that,' Lindsey replied.

Even from this distance Lindsey could see her mother's expression. Dracula's victims take on the same one when they see the count's pointy teeth.

Mary Jane shrugged suddenly. 'I may be prejudging here. It might not be physical attraction. Wonder where his wife is, though?'

A murder, an absent wife and a mistress. Telling Mary Jane to stay put, Lindsey was off up the garden path. She couldn't be sure that Mr George and this new woman in his life had murder in mind, but she wasn't willing to take the chance. She only had one mother and didn't intend losing her. OK, she was far from perfect. Like Grandma Cross, she was never going to grow old gracefully, never going to be a size twelve, let alone the dimensions of a stick insect. A series of old flagstones, like stepping stones set in loose gravel formed the path to the door.

Honey heard her coming and looked over her shoulder. Her expression was one of relief.

'My daughter,' she said. She went on to introduce Hamilton George and Pamela Windsor.

Lindsey gave a brief nod of acknowledgement to each and managed a smile.

'Mr George has just lost his wife,' Honey explained. Mr George hadn't gone into detail as to how he'd found Pamela so she couldn't pass this on.

Lindsey expressed sympathy. At the same time she took in her mother's expression. Shocked. Also a little disappointed. She made a brief stab at what the problem might be. Sleuthing was a nosey business. Her mother needed to get in the house. No one had invited her in. The old standby was called for.

'I need to use the bathroom. Do you mind?'

Lindsey could charm the birds off the trees. She'd never done drugs, never got drunk and was not promiscuous. Sometimes she was just too good to be true; lots of women would want their babies to grow up like her.

Pamela Windsor was no different from anyone else. She pointed vaguely upwards. 'Upstairs. First on the left.'

Lindsey looked for the stairs but couldn't see them. Old cottages were quirky like that. Nooks and crannies and things on the periphery in a new house could be anywhere in a cottage.

Lindsey adopted her Sunday-best smile. 'Do you . . . have any stairs?'

Pamela huffed and puffed her exasperation but did the polite thing. She led her to a simple plank door that was almost invisible, set as it was in wainscot panelling. A steep staircase spiralled upwards. Lindsey thanked her.

She was only on the third stair when the door slammed behind her. At first she thought it was Pamela conveying her temper. Then she saw the strong spring. In the past someone had got fed up of asking people to shut the door and had fitted this. Regardless, the shock had put her on edge.

The stairs creaked underfoot and turned back on themselves. By the time she got to the top she was facing the opposite way. The landing was dark and narrow. Pamela had told her the second door on the right, but today she would take a leaf out of her grandmother's book. Today would be her 'forgetful' day. All the doors were identical to the one at the bottom of the stairs. She wondered if they had the same strong spring. Now, which door should she try? Earlier Mary Jane had been gabbling on about reading signs before you do anything in life. She said this just as they'd run a red. She'd also run over a hedgehog.

'Look for the signs. You'll know them when you see them.'

She took a deep breath, pitying the poor hedgehog.

Right! Look for the signs.

Old paintings lined the walls and filled gaps where nothing else would fit. For the most part they were late-Victorian landscapes, bought fairly cheaply at auction. There was only one portrait, larger than the others. The subject had bushy whiskers and staring eyes; he wouldn't be troubling a catwalk any time soon, but it filled the space.

He was placed to one side of a door like a pictorial 'No Entry' sign. His eyes said it all, but stop looking at them and they'll stop looking at you. What better room to go fishing in than the one with a warning notice outside?

The bedroom had a low ceiling sloping down almost to floor level. A small, square window with a deep ledge let in some light. The walls were pale pink and the curtains were scattered with tiny rosebuds. At one end was a bed with frilly covers. At the other was a computer sitting on an old pine dressing table. The red standby light blinked enticingly perhaps proclaiming recent use

Lindsey flexed her fingers then gave them a little 'piano playing' kind of exercise.

She moved the mouse. The screen lit up. *The Noble Present. You too can be lord of the manor, lady in title and in deed . . .*

Lindsey pulled a face. 'Hmmm!'

She was not impressed by old titles. That's exactly what they were. Old. Worn out. Done and dusted. A thing of the past.

'A rather very lucrative way of making a living,' she muttered. She closed in on the screen, her face becoming bathed in its blue light. She scrolled down. Looked at page one. Dipped into page two.

Favourable Prices! From only $3,000.

Favourable? These prices were only favourable to the vendor, by the looks of it. Why work for a living when there were deals like this to be done simply by playing with a keyboard?

A third page was reserved for testimonials from satisfied clients, merry middle-aged faces smiling out from passport-sized photographs. She recognised the name — Lady Templeton-Jones. Her smile was as wide as anyone's, but there was one big difference. The captions beneath the other photographs mentioned initials only, not full names. In Wanda's case, it gave her full name and where she came from. The title had been bought from this site, though not from Hamilton George. Lindsey recognised one name that her mother had mentioned, Simon Taylor had provided a testimonial. On cross-referencing with Companies House, she found he was also listed as a franchisee based in Bath. She punched the air and mouthed a silent 'Yes!'

In a last effort to glean as much information as she could, she rummaged through the pieces of paper on the desk. Most of it was online receipts printed off for services rendered. As she flipped them down onto the desk, a catalogue for Spencers' Auction Rooms caught her eye. *Marine Collectables and Nostalgia.*

She thumbed through. There was nothing there that caught her eye — nothing medieval, that is. The Middle Ages were of particular interest to her and lately she'd got very interested in the Tudor period. But the items in the catalogue were all nineteenth and early twentieth century. Neither was her sphere of interest, i.e., there was nothing here brought up from the *Mary Rose*, a ship named after Henry VIII's sister.

After a quick flip through, she began retracing her steps, turning the pages, but more slowly, taking her time. Again, nothing interested her at first, until she read the heading '*Titanic* Memorabilia'.

She thought she heard a sound, perhaps someone coming up the stairs. She put the catalogue back where she'd found it. She needed to get back downstairs, but not before pulling the flush in the bathroom. The sound would be heard downstairs. Her cover would hold.

Like the bedroom, the ceiling in the bathroom sloped like a ski jump. The loo was at the lowest point. Put in by a woman as a final act of revenge on a man who constantly left the lid up?

Downstairs, Honey asked to go over the details again. She asked her questions in a carrying voice after accepting the cup of tea that was offered and a slightly soggy chocolate-coated biscuit. Anything to give Lindsey a little more time. There wasn't time to find out much, only enough to confirm what they did know or what could be gleaned from any website. There was no guarantee her daughter would find anything. If only there was more time.

'So,' she began, 'how long have you two known each other?'

'I was a friend of Fran, Hamilton's wife.'

She saw them exchange what was a frankly affectionate look and guessed they'd been close even before his wife had passed on. Not your job to criticise, she said to herself, and went on to ask about the ghost walk, wracking her brains for other questions that might lead them to slip up and give her and Doherty an opening to further explore.

'You know, I never knew you could buy titles before this case came about.' She addressed Hamilton George directly. 'Have you ever considered buying one for yourself?'

'I think I have enough of a superior name without adding to it. That's how it started by the way. People assuming I was titled.' He smirked. 'Hamilton is quite an aristocratic name and George, well, there have been four kings named George haven't there. So people tended to assume.'

All heads turned her way as she came back downstairs. Her mother's eyes fixed on her for a half beat longer than was necessary. Lindsey couldn't help looking smug. Her mother would see that. Her mother would know.

'I'm sorry about your wife,' Honey called over her shoulder as she and Lindsey alighted on the moss-covered stone path.

'Thanks a bundle,' said Hamilton.

'So kind,' said the one-time ghost-walk guide. Too sugary a smile. Too self-satisfied.

CHAPTER FORTY-TWO

'Simon Taylor!' Lindsey hissed as she followed her mother down the path. 'Noble Presence — or Noble Present or whatever it's called. I checked with Companies House while I was up there. It's run by Hamilton George, and Simon Taylor, that guy you questioned in Trowbridge, is one of his operatives. They work on a franchise. See? Simon Taylor bought into the franchise. It was him that sold that woman the title. And another thing: reference to a listing for *Marine Collectables and Nostalgia*.'

'Marine!' Honey did a quick about-turn. 'Her Ladyship — Wanda — whatever, circled the heading of marine collectables in the catalogue.'

Lindsey kept pace.

'So that was her interest?'

'It would appear so. I'm glad you think so.'

'You're quite sneaky and that makes me proud of you. It's a definite asset to my — our — investigation.' And wait till I tell him.

'I am when I want to be. Right,' she said, rubbing her hands together, 'what next?'

'More questions for those two lovebirds in there.'

'I'm right with you.'

'No you're not. Leave this to me, Lindsey.'

'I'm coming with you.'

'It's not your job.'

'You can't outpace me.'

It was true. Lindsey was fit.

Honey tried lengthening her stride into a loping jog. Not a good idea. Lindsey was wearing trainers and a very fetching pink and grey jogging suit. Honey had opted for skirt, sheer tights and high heels. None of it was made for jogging. Especially the shoes. One of her heels connected with gravel instead of stone and snapped off.

'Damn!'

She threw said heel a 'you're dead' look before bending down to pick it up.

'I loved these shoes,' she whined, then noticed the blister on her right foot had popped. 'But they don't love me!'

She took both shoes off. A gentle throw, and — hey presto — they landed in the goldfish pond, where they promptly sank to the bottom.

Lindsey nodded encouragingly. 'The fish will appreciate them.'

Honey decided she was probably right. Fish must get fed up with looking at the same rocks and weeds all day long.

She saw a head bob at the window. One of the pair had spotted her coming back up the garden path. From a distance it looked like Hamilton George.

The door was wide open by the time she got there. Pamela was no longer the innocent little waif who had sneezed her way around the ghost walk. Slender arms were folded across her chest and her eyes flashed intensely.

No more innocent excuses. What was the link between the Noble Present and the murder of the woman who had started life as Wanda Carpenter? And how could a plain Jane like Pamela change into a swan overnight? She'd come over as a bit of a drab on the ghost walk, though the weather hadn't helped. No one looked good in the rain. Well, that was her excuse and she was sticking to it.

Now Pamela Windsor was a picture of pissed-off self-righteousness. 'What now?'

'Did you know where Wanda Carpenter — Lady Templeton-Jones — bought her title?'

Pamela's jaw snapped shut. She shrugged over her folded arms. 'How the bloody hell should I know?'

So much for the dormouse demeanour.

Honey brought her notepad out from the sack she called a handbag and tried to look officious. 'We've made inquiries. We know you have dealings with a site selling earldoms, dukedoms and suchlike. Can you confirm?'

'No, I cannot.'

'Never heard of it?'

'Never heard of it.'

'The police have experts. They keep tabs on interesting and perhaps illegal websites.'

Honey saw the hint of a flinch.

'It's not illegal!'

Honey resisted the urge to grin. 'So you do know of it?'

Pamela squirmed then called for re-enforcements. 'Hamilton!'

He must have been listening behind the door. He slid out, half his bulk hiding behind his svelte lover. He rested his hand on her waist, his palm flat on her hip, fingers spread. He was mountain man to her woodland sprite, broad and beefy to her lean and lithesome.

'It's my website,' he said. His look was even, his eyes not shifting from her face. 'It's all legit.'

Honey recalled his deceased wife saying how clever he was with computers and that he'd retired from IBM.

'So you sold Wanda Carpenter the title of Lady Templeton-Jones.'

'Not personally.'

Honey was about to say, OK, but the company belonged to him and that amounted to the same thing. Lindsey butted in.

'You run a worldwide team. They use your website on a franchise basis, operate the enquiries, collate a database and get a percentage of the take. Correct?'

Hamilton George looked amazed. He nodded.

Honey threw her daughter a sideways mutter. 'Smart-arse!'

Lindsey looked pleased with herself. 'May I continue?'

Honey nodded. 'Go for it.'

Lindsey turned back to Hamilton George. 'So which of your team did the honours?'

Chewing worriedly at his lips, he seemed in dire danger of eating his moustache. Suddenly he seemed to wake up. 'Hey, I don't need to tell you anything. You're not the police.'

Honey scribbled a quick doodle in her notebook. 'I'm working with the police. I've made a note of your refusal to cooperate.'

On the page, a bug-eyed Mr Magoo-type character squinted back at her.

'Did you know Lady Templeton-Jones's cousin, Ashwell Bridgewater?'

'No,' said Hamilton.

'Now!' said Honey with an air of finality for this was the crunch question. 'I understand you have an interest in marine memorabilia. I also know that a copy of an auction catalogue in Her Ladyship's possession had such items circled. Did you ever meet? Was there some reason for friction between you? Perhaps you fleeced her for the title or the two of you were in competition for something at auction? If so, what?'

'Oh, for goodness' sake! Let's get this over with.' Pamela Windsor pushed him aside. 'His name's Simon Taylor, he lives with his mother at number seventeen, Fair Alice Avenue, and he works at Assured Security Shredding. He's a creep. You're welcome to him.'

The door slammed before Honey had chance to ask her what manner of creep he was.

'Creeps seem to be on the increase nowadays,' she said to Lindsey as they wandered back to the car, thinking of Warren Price.

Lindsey fell to silence and seemed to turn into herself.

Honey resisted the urge to ask what was wrong. She guessed it was something to do with this elusive boyfriend. She looked away, determined not to pry. Lindsey would talk when she wanted to. Until then, Honey trusted her to be sensible.

CHAPTER FORTY-THREE

Steve Doherty was standing in front of the reception desk at the Green River Hotel. His hands were hidden in the deep pockets of his black leather jacket.

The Green River wasn't top of the tree as regards hotels, but it certainly made him feel shabby. The faded jeans had a lot to do with it. So did the scuffed leather jacket. But he couldn't allow himself to be intimidated. This was business. Police business.

He was standing with his legs slightly apart. It was a defiant stance, a defensive demeanour. Did no good, though.

Unimpressed, Honey's mother was peering over the top of her gold-rimmed glasses. As usual she was beautifully groomed. Today she was sporting a lime-green dress with a low-slung waistline and a navy trim. He'd supposed that she would give him short shrift. He wasn't wrong.

'She's not hiding under this desk, just in case you think I'm lying.'

Steve's face broke into a self-conscious smile. Only Gloria Cross could do that to him. 'That's OK.'

He backed off. Once he was back out in Great Pulteney Street, he wondered what Gloria was doing there anyway. Didn't she have some shop to tend to on Wednesdays?

Sod it, he wasn't about to ask. He knew a brick wall when he saw one.

Outside in the city, the traffic was building up, tailing back from the island at the end of the road. A white box van was attempting to turn into the narrow road at the side of the hotel. Harking back to the days of traffic duty, he stepped out into the road and put up his hand. The traffic stopped. The van manoeuvred, giving him a thank you blast on the horn as it turned into the side road. It stopped outside a shopfront. He craned his neck to see better. As far as he remembered there was nothing for sale in that shop; it was empty. Must be a new tenant, he thought to himself. Well, it just went to show how out of touch he was.

Steve took a deep breath and sauntered back onto the pavement. He looked at his watch, then looked over his shoulder. No one was following him, but then he hadn't expected there to be. Strange the depths a man will go to in order to hide the truth. Terrible to be a liar. He'd come along fired up with the urge to make things right with Honey. Now that she'd guessed the full truth . . . Shame, in a way, because he wasn't sure when he'd have that courage again.

Will she understand? he asked himself.

He ran the conversation in his head.

'What a wonderful coincidence,' she'd say. 'We both decided to shape up at the same time.'

He'd nod and say, 'Sure, Honey. You with your diet and me with my jogging. Everyone should have a personal trainer. Karen was brilliant at it.'

The bit about Karen was the stumbling block. The lie about Warren Price had rolled off his tongue so easily. Wasn't it grim that women automatically suspected extra-curricular activities when a blonde was involved?

Nah! Honey will understand. She'll be fine. She'll kick the whole thing into touch — either that or kick me!

CHAPTER FORTY-FOUR

Gloria Cross had given up wearing four-inch stilettos sometime after her sixtieth birthday. Tripping over loose paving slabs did nothing for the dignity or bones of an ageing woman. As a compromise she'd gone quite overboard on kitten-heeled shoes in all the colours of the rainbow. Black, brown, beige, red, navy blue, purple and pale mauve. If she didn't have an outfit to wear them with, then she'd go out and buy one.

'Gotta go now,' she snapped to Anna, who had only just got back from a comfort break.

Like a keen-nosed gun dog, she was off across reception. The main doors swung and slammed as she burst outwards. She skitted off round the corner into the side street, stopped dead and swelled with satisfaction. The van was here and she had the keys in her pocket. Honey would be fine about it. She'd assured Anna she would be.

Just as she made the corner, two of the women who helped run Secondhand Rose waved to her and broke into a run.

'I've got the keys!' she called. She waved the trio of keys above her head.

Excited, the three of them clustered around the lock. Gloria turned the key. The door opened. A smell of mildew and old paint met them.

Margaret, who was a touch older than Gloria, wrinkled her nose. 'Pongs a bit.'

'Is Joe OK to do this?' asked Gloria, addressing Linda, who was married to a very successful builder.

'Easy-peasy,' said Linda, whose sunbed skin tone almost matched her dress. A dull orange was the best way to describe it. 'I've brought a mop and bucket. Can we borrow the hotel's vacuum cleaner?'

'I don't see why not . . .'

'What's going on here?'

Gloria's exuberance melted away.

Honey was standing the doorway. 'What's going on?'

'We need somewhere to put our stock. Gloria said we could put it here until we relocate.'

Honey raised a questioning eyebrow in her mother's direction. When it came to taking things for granted, Gloria Cross was second to none.

'I don't recall saying that.'

'You intimated!' Gloria was getting huffy.

'I said no such thing.'

'You'd turn us out on the street?'

Honey threw back her head and rolled her eyes. The delivery men were lifting the shutter on the box van. Her mother took advantage, breezed in, took over.

'Guys, you are the kindest men on earth. Now, would you like to roll the first trolley out . . . ?'

Honey knew a wheedling voice when she heard one. She also knew there was something of a challenge hidden behind that tone — help me or hinder me. And think of your image.

Difficult times. Honey ground her teeth. Too much of that and she'd be making an emergency appointment with a dentist. This was a two-pronged problem; on the one hand she didn't want to appear mean, and on the other she had a business to consider. Bills to pay. A bank manager to placate.

There was a third problem that she didn't really wish to admit to. Her mother's close proximity would drive her nuts.

Upset mother or go nuts. There was no contest. Her mind was made up. 'Hold it right there.'

The high buildings on either side of a narrow street acted like a megaphone.

The two men froze.

She should have known what would happen next. Her mother went into defence mode. A lacy handkerchief was tugged from a hidden pocket. She pursed her lips and her chin trembled.

'Do you see how my daughter treats me? And just when I need her. Isn't that typical? Children are just *so* ungrateful!'

Her mother's two friends made sympathetic sounds. Honey felt like puking. How could they fall for this? Her mother was a born actress and puppeteer. She certainly knew how to pull the strings!

'Mother!'

'A daughter should help her mother.'

It went on and on, whingeing and whining, a wringing of the handkerchief and a dabbing of the eyes. Her compatriots from Secondhand Rose made sympathetic sounds.

'Stop it!' said Honey, putting up her hand. 'Just stop it, OK? You can store that stuff here, but only for . . .'

'Great!'

They didn't give her time to finish. The back of the truck was opened, the platform lowered and rails and rails and rails of second-hand designer wear was trundled in through the open door.

Struggling to find words, Honey watched round-eyed. Her mother and pals were all talking at once. The poor guys on the delivery run were being ordered around like puppies on a leash.

'Not here, there . . .'

'Go easy with that.'

'No. I said parallel with the window. Parallel! Like this.'

A military operation it was not, but it wasn't far off. Honey darted in and out of all of them, trying not to be helpful but accidentally being roped in.

Mature these girls might be, but they knew what they wanted and went all out to get it. After a while she was sure she could hear them clucking like broody old hens.

For a while Honey had lost control, but she couldn't allow that to go on for too long. She had to pull rank here.

'Only until you find a new place. Is that clear?'

If they heard, they didn't acknowledge her. They were too engrossed in their world, cooing over shantung, drooling over French lace.

She smiled, hoping that she'd be as focused on something as they were once she got to their age.

But they can't stay, she reminded herself. And if they're not willing to find a new place for themselves, then you have to do it. And hadn't she made overtures already?

'Hold it. Hold it right there.'

The three elderly women regarded her, two of them blinking from behind prescription spectacles.

She took a deep breath. Drastic events called for drastic measures. Cameron Wallace had promised an alternative. She'd avoided phoning him. Cameron was a champagne and truffles man — not really her type. His offer of another shop had come combined with a dinner invitation, but now was the time to bite the bullet.

He answered after one ring.

'Hi. How are you?'

The sound of his voice caught her off balance. Cameron Wallace had given her a direct number. She'd been psyching herself up to deal with his receptionist.

'About that shop you promised my mother, how quickly can you arrange it?'

She imagined him smiling triumphantly. She knew what was coming.

'Are you free tonight?'

It had to be a yes.

'Yes. I can arrange that.'

'When can your mother and her friends take over the lease?'

'Is that the same thing as when can they move in?'

'If you wish.'

'How about today?'

He laughed. It was full and throaty — like a character named Blade in one of her mother's Mills and Boon historical romances.

'I'll get the keys sent round right away. Can your mother be there within the hour?'

'You bet she can.'

He ran off the address. Number six, Beau Nash Passage. Something about it jarred in Honey's mind, but just now she was too wound up to give it much mind.

She repeated what he'd said to the three women hovering around the driver and his truck.

'Oooow! That's a good location,' said Linda. 'Plenty of passing trade by day *and* it has ambience!'

Ambience seemed the right word to throw at her mother.

'Out with the gear! Get it reloaded — *pronto*!'

The women worked as quickly getting the stuff back out again as they had getting it in.

Her mother was in charge. 'Right. Let's get the hell over there! Driver! Get back in. We'll direct you.'

The driver didn't look too pleased at this suggestion. He also looked too scared to protest or tell them it was illegal to carry more than one passenger. With his unwilling help the three women clambered in, one of them sitting on his partner's lap.

Honey exhaled the biggest, most grateful sigh in the whole wide world.

'Thanks,' she murmured.

Cameron heard her. 'Now, about this dinner . . .'

She had no choice but to agree to meet the guy she'd mentally christened Mr Smoothie. Fast worker too, if his fixing her mother and friends up with a new shop was anything to go by.

'OK. I give in.'

'Do you always give in so easily?'

‘That depends. In this case I’m really grateful for helping me out. My mother’s a doll, but only at a distance. I grew up with her and now I’ve grown out of her. We’d clash big time if she was camping on the doorstep.’

That’s when it came to her. The shop on Beau Nash Passage — that was where Lady Templeton-Jones had met her end.

‘Is it empty? Have the police given the all-clear?’ she asked.

‘Yes, of course. Look, let’s talk about it tonight. Over dinner.’

CHAPTER FORTY-FIVE

Emergency over, she trotted back round to the hotel in a pair of shoes that weren't her favourite but matched the grey suit she was wearing. They were grey edged with white around the instep. The suit echoed the effect: white piping around the neck and running down the sleeves. Shame about the ones she'd ditched in the pond. But there were plenty more shoes in the sea.

Doherty was waiting for her.

'Are you free?'

She folded her arms. 'Am I free for what?'

He grinned. 'A bit of investigative work first. Then we'll see where things go.'

She guessed he'd ask her to meet him tonight. Should she tell him about Cameron Wallace or take a rain check? *Cross that bridge when you come to it*, she told herself.

Clint, their casual dishwasher, strolled through reception on his way to the evening shift. He wiggled his fingers in a silent 'Hi' when he saw her. He gave the finger to Doherty.

'Behave yourself next time.'

It was normal for kitchen staff to use the rear entrance. Honey asked him why he was using reception.

'Smudger's got the back door locked. Drain's blocked.'

Honey groaned.

Clint offered to sort it out for her.

'Of course, I'll have to charge you extra. It's above and beyond me normal duties.'

Honey leaped on him, grabbed his jaw and kissed him on both cheeks. 'Done!' Clint moved away. 'And you have been,' she muttered.

'Grim job, huh?' said Doherty.

'Gross!'

Outside she stopped and phoned her mother.

'Are you in?'

'All signed, sealed and delivered.'

'You've signed the lease?'

'I just told you that.'

'Great.'

Next she phoned Cameron Wallace and told him the bad news. 'I'm sorry. An emergency has arisen here at the hotel. Can we take a rain check?'

'I trust your mother is settled?'

She felt herself blushing. OK, it was a little underhand, but hell, he had terminated the lease on Second-hand Rose in the first place.

'We can do it again. How's that with you?'

He made her agree to another date.

'Had to,' she said to Doherty, who'd heard every word.

'Your mother could have kept the date.'

'You're being fractious. Why is that?'

He twisted his mouth this way and that.

She peered up into his face. 'Got something to say?'

'I got myself a personal trainer. She's very good.'

She purposely skewered him with her eyes. 'A *blonde* personal trainer?'

He shrugged. 'She was available.'

'I bet she was!'

CHAPTER FORTY-SIX

Together, Honey and Steve headed for Simon Taylor's place.

A busker and a living statue argued over a pitch at the top of pedestrianised Union Street. A pavement artist calmly took advantage of the situation, pictures of coloured chalk spreading swiftly around them.

A daytime tour was trooping through Queen Square. The traffic was fairly light. Rush hour would see a dramatic increase, with everyone trying to get round the square and head for home. Once it was over something of the old city magic returned. In some places you could imagine what it had once been like. Some said a ghostly Roman legion still marched at midnight.

They sped up on Snow Hill behind the high-rise council flats. Dating from the 1930s, the Taylor house had curved bay windows, dark-green paint and net curtains. Net curtains do little for most houses. For this place they shouted, '*I don't give a stuff about fashion. I don't even care if the windows fall out!*'

One look at Mrs Taylor confirmed that both she and her house were made for each other. Like the house, she was the Woman that Time Forgot, the product of a decade she had chosen never to move out of. She wore a beige cardigan, brown slippers that totally covered her feet and a plaid skirt with wide box pleats. A headscarf patterned with riding whips and jumping horses snuggled cravat fashion around her neck. Loose skin quivered like a turkey's gizzard around her slack jaw. The scarf helped keep the saggy skin in check.

Swiftly following the introductions, Steve asked to speak to her son.

Her eyebrows were no more than two plucked lines traced over with pencil. They formed a perfect V when she frowned.

'What d'ya wan 'im fur?'

'Just routine inquiries,' said Doherty.

'Well, 'e ain't 'ere.'

'So where is he?'

'At work, of course.'

At last. It sounded like English.

'At Assured Security Shredding. Is that right?'

'S'right'

* * *

On the way to ASS, Honey mulled over some niggling doubts. OK, maybe the title may have been a dud. But was that reason enough for Simon to kill Wanda Carpenter? And why was Wanda on the ghost walk?

She voiced the question.

Steve took his eyes off the road and glanced at her. 'Seeking cheap thrills like the rest of you?'

Honey threw him a look of condemnation. 'I wasn't seeking cheap thrills. I can get those in a sports car. Your foot's pretty heavy on the pedal you know.'

'Cheeky cow.'

Doherty loved his car. More than that, he loved driving it with the top down, the wind whipping his hair around his face.

Honey wrapped her arms around herself. There was fresh air and there was cold air. Today the latter was making her nose go numb.

Thinking about murder helped keep the cold at bay. 'There's definitely something we're missing here. Why go tramping about in the rain for no reason?'

'To meet someone on the ghost walk?'

'Could be.'

She'd told Doherty about Hamilton and Pamela and the website. He'd checked out the details. Mrs George had died of a heart attack brought on by asthma.

'She's being shipped back to the States.'

'Poor woman. And her husband already dallying with someone new.'

'Had been for a while, according to him. Virtual dating.'

Honey shook her head disconsolately. 'Virtual means not real. It's *virtually* the same, but not really.'

'Like virtual sex.' Steve grinned. 'I prefer the real thing myself.'

'Virtual is less tiring.'

Steve looked surprised. 'You've tried it? What's it like?'

'A bit like dreaming. You wake up when you get to the best bit.'

They eventually slid to a halt in the ASS car park beside a gleaming Aston Martin. Steve's eyes positively caressed the bodywork — purple with chrome hubcaps and wire wheels. Vintage. DBS. A grown man's wet dream!

'Nice car.'

Honey was trying to remember where she'd seen it before.

'Wallace and Gates! It belongs to Cameron Wallace.'

Doherty looked from the car to the office. 'What the hell is he doing here?'

CHAPTER FORTY-SEVEN

Cameron Wallace regarded himself as a man of style and culture. He rated fashion too. Not tacky high-street stuff, but the good shirts, suits and shoes that only London's West End, Paris, New York or Rome could offer. Out of the four, Rome was his favourite. The old saying was spot on: always buy Italian.

He was thinking this as he straightened his eighteen-carat cufflinks — tiny anchors, each tipped with a tiny ruby.

As he patted his tie flat, he looked out of the office window onto the car park. One of the lads employed by Associated Security Shredding had been washing his car and cleaning the interior with a portable vacuum cleaner. The lad had done a good job, probably because he'd known the boss would be watching. He'd smiled at that. His smile vanished on seeing Honey Driver getting out of a low-slung sports car.

His eyes narrowed. 'What the devil's she doing here?'

Bannister heard his remark and came to the window.

'That's the bird that was asking questions about the Templeton-Jones woman. She was with that bloke before. He's a copper.'

Cameron nodded, his lips tight against his teeth. There was no reason for undue concern. She was way off course, as far as he was concerned.

Wallace and Gates's golden boy spun round. His expression darkened. 'I don't want to see them. I'll let myself out the back way.'

CHAPTER FORTY-EIGHT

Out front, Gold Tooth was behind the counter as before. He saw Honey and Steve, did a quick take and remembered.

'Mr Bannister's in conference.'

Steve flashed his warrant card. 'What about Simon Taylor? Is he in conference too?'

The ropes of hair stayed still. The look was wary. 'What d'ya want 'im for?'

'Where is he?'

'Home, I s'pose. He called in sick.'

Doherty raised an eyebrow. 'Funny. We didn't see him when we called there just now.'

Someone chose that moment to come crashing in from the shredding shop, holding a bunch of crumpled paper in one hand.

'You'll never believe . . .' Seeing strangers, he stopped mid-sentence. 'Sorry. Didn't know we had visitors.'

The scrawny adolescent looked scared as a rabbit.

'Can I see those?' said Honey, snatching the pieces of paper. She frowned as she began to read. 'Private and Confidential.' She looked at the two youths, then at Steve.

Steve took a couple of sheets and had a quick glance. 'Good game while it lasted? Private and confidential information can fetch a packet if you know where to sell it. Instead of shredding sensitive information you've been selling it.'

The two behind the counter exchanged looks.

'It wasn't us,' blurted the first. 'Bannister said that it was the boss's orders.'

'The boss?'

'Is there a problem?'

Bannister appeared. He looked shifty, though that wasn't hard in his case.

'Aren't you supposed to shred this stuff?' Steve held aloft the crumpled sheets of paper. Honey copied holding up the ones she still had.

Bannister shifted from one foot to the other and attempted to look innocent. It didn't work.

Doherty outlined the problem. 'Sifting through stuff scheduled for shredding. Selling on the information to interested parties. Isn't that what you've been doing?'

Bannister's jaw dropped. 'You're both sacked,' he said suddenly.

'Stuff yer job!' said the first, starting to head out the back.

'Stuff it,' said the second and followed his friend.

'Hold it!' Steve's voice hit the walls and ceiling. 'Come on, Bannister. You're not kidding anybody. These two numpties would be hard pushed to sell ice creams to ten-year-olds. This isn't what I'm here for. I want a simple answer to a simple question. OK?'

Bannister and his merry men waited silently.

'OK,' said Steve, pinning all three with a cold-eyed glare. 'All I want to know is whether you've seen this woman before. I have reason to believe she's been here. When and why? And who did she come to see? That's all I want to know.'

'She came to see Simon one lunchtime,' conceded Gold Tooth.

Honey adopted jumped in. 'What did she want to see him about? I'd really like to know.' Her look was a world away from Steve's. Her voice was soft too. 'You can tell me,' she said, looking intently into Gold Tooth's eyes. She leaned forward, arms and boobs resting on counter. Her neckline was just about low enough to blink cleavage.

'He didn't say.'

This was disappointing.

'Are you sure? Wasn't Simon your friend? Didn't he tell you things?'

'Ha!'

A laugh. Definitely a laugh.

'Are you kidding? Friend? That nerd!'

The two guys fell to laughter. Bannister shook his head and grinned. 'I've got to agree with them. He wasn't the sort of guy you wanted to get close to — in more ways than one.'

Steve looked nonplussed. 'Tell me.'

Honey butted in. 'BO. Body odour?'

Gold Tooth did a high five with his partner, still laughing.

On her way out Honey chanced one more question.

'Do any of you know a Mr Cameron Wallace?'

'No,' said Bannister, jumping in too quick for comfort.

It was obvious from the looks on the faces of the other two that he wasn't telling the truth.

CHAPTER FORTY-NINE

Loath to arrive back in Bath feeling like an ice lolly, Honey asked Steve to put the hood up on the car. He pulled a face. 'Honey, this is a sport's car, made to travel with the wind in your hair.'

'Please?'

'Cold?'

'Freezing.'

'That's what comes of spending too much time indoors. You should get out more.'

'Out jogging? Sorry, I don't know any blondes.'

'I'm sorry for lying.'

She thought about it. 'I knew you were.'

He looked at her in disbelief. 'Don't believe you.'

'I wasn't scared. You had to be lying.'

'What about the phantom motorcycle?'

She shrugged. 'Just a nut.'

'I'm sorry. I can't say that enough.'

She didn't want to think about it. Whatever he did was up to him. They were hardly an item, just working partners — partners in crime, or at least in solving crime.

She kept her mind busy. 'That stuff they were shredding was from a local development company. Seems they have plans to build houses on an old gas station site.'

'Valuable information for someone.'

Honey frowned. 'Owning a place like this could make you a millionaire.'

'Easily.'

The wind whipped wildly through her hair. 'Glad I don't wear a wig,' she grumbled. She forced herself to think on the matter in hand. At least the fresh air kept her alert.

'I suppose we could go back to his mother's. Perhaps she might know where he's gone, but I doubt it.'

'So we're all in the dark.'

'Seems that way.'

The closer they got to the city, the more taciturn Steve seemed to become. She guessed he was still feeling guilty, but didn't want to go there. If other things hadn't been going on in her mind, she would have been angry with him. But she wasn't.

'Are you listening to me?' she asked, after giving him the low-down on the matter of her mother's shop.

'Sorry. You were saying something about a shop.'

'My mother was threatening to move into the empty hairdressers round the corner. I had to move fast. Wallace has got my mother out from under my feet. Having her just around the corner was a prospect I couldn't cope with. It would have been almost as bad as having her move in with me. Two duchesses in the manor. Seniority would have been an issue.'

'So Wallace chucked her out of the premises in Milsom Street where she sold frocks?'

'Frocks! Don't let her hear you call them that. It's "preworn design couture". Look! There it is.'

Steve slowed the car as they passed her mother's old shop. Honey spotted the new name glowing above the entrance.

'The new people are in.'

'What are they selling?'

'I'm not sure. It's called Teddyitis.'

Honey decided to wreak a little revenge. She'd been pretty lenient so far, but the Warren Price affair was still there in the background.

'I saw the guy on the motorcycle last night. I was closing the window on the top landing and heard a motorcycle. I heard it stop. By the time I stuck my head out of the window it was off again.'

Steve Doherty screwed up his face. 'You're never going to let me forget this, are you?'

'I deserve a little satisfaction.'

'You're needling me.'

'It's your own fault.'

'How's the diet?'

She gave him the evil eye. 'What do you mean by that?'

'Nothing. I was just asking you how the diet was going.'

'You're saying I look fat.'

He shook his head emphatically. 'No! No I'm not.'

'I've lost another two pounds this week.'

'Great.'

'And the jogging?'

'I've given it up. Fallen arches.'

CHAPTER FIFTY

Simon Taylor eyed the brightly coloured brochures lining the travel agent's shelves. An assistant spotted him, smoothed her skirt and put on her best smile.

'Can I help you, sir?'

She smelled of cheap make-up from the two-for-one shelf. Her cheeks were unnaturally peach coloured. She was pretty like a painted doll — not quite real.

He found himself blushing. It wasn't often that pretty women approached him and called him sir.

'That one. And that one.'

Both were for South America. He'd heard that was the place to go if someone — especially the law — was after you.

'Here's my card,' she said with a dazzling smile. 'Once you've perused, do give me a call.'

He said that he would. Actually he had no intention. The brochures could be perused at leisure on a park bench far away, where no one — especially his mother — could see him. He'd done some research online. Getting the hard copy helped set the idea in his mind.

He'd bought a Cornish pasty in Greggs and a latte in Starbucks. Stuff going to work. He'd had enough of work.

Anyway, he thought, smiling at the clear blue sky, he didn't need to work anymore. Not if everything went to plan.

Royal Victoria Park was relatively empty on a weekday. On weekends and school holidays it was packed with parents and kids. He settled on an empty bench, placing the greasy bag and the paper coffee cup beside him.

He couldn't stop smiling. It was amazing how many people smiled back: an old couple, a woman pushing a baby in a pram and a college lecturer type wearing shabby clothes and sporting a grey beard.

He was still smiling when he reached for his phone and redialled.

The silence on the other end thrilled him. It was like going fishing, having a worm wriggling on the end of a hook. He quite liked the feeling for a short while, but then it seemed to go on too long. His smile diminished. A knot of nerves tightened in his stomach. Panic wasn't far away.

'Did you hear me? I said I wanted my cut.' He talked tough. He didn't feel it. Streetwise was just a word to him. Something he'd never quite got his head round.

Again silence, though this time it ended.

'All right. Where?'

They had to meet. He wished they didn't. It was dangerous, but unavoidable. He'd carefully considered the options. A place filled with people was best. Not too public. Somewhere their transaction wouldn't be noticed. Convenient. It had to be convenient, preferably within walking distance. He'd decided on the ideal place.

'There's a matinee at the Theatre Royal this afternoon. Buy two tickets for two seats next to each other. Leave mine at reception. You go on in. I'll join you.'

The line went dead.

Simon heaved a sigh of relief. His smile returned. Pulling back his sleeve, he checked his watch. Ninety minutes to curtain up: plenty of time to compose himself and dream of things to come.

Arranging his biggest project yet had given him an appetite. Settling the brochures on his lap, he got the warm pasty out of the bag and prised the lid from the coffee. Everything was going according to plan.

The time would have dragged if it hadn't been for the brochures. He eyed the name on the card the travel agent had given him. Glenys Watkins. She'd smiled so nicely and smelled real good. He wouldn't go back there, of course. Once he had the money, he would pack the few things he was taking with him and shut the door on his home and mother forever. After that he'd go to the bus station, get the next bus to Heathrow and the next plane to somewhere in South America — anywhere would do. The thought of a new life away from his mother made him tingle. A smirk came to his face. Perhaps he'd ask Glenys to accompany him. After all, he'd be rich. Downright irresistible!

Once it was time to leave, he fed the last crumbs to the pigeons gathered around his feet. Being an eco-friendly guy, he crumpled up the paper bag he'd bought the pasty in. Both bag and coffee cup went into the recycling bin.

Brushing crumbs from his lap to the ground brought a flurry of renewed interest from his feathered friends.

Hands in pockets, like the Jack the Lad he wanted to be, he whistled as he sauntered off, the travel brochures stuffed into his coat pocket.

A bus had stopped outside the theatre. A group of seniors was being helped off and shepherded into the building. He held back, watching the grey-haired biddies and snowy-topped gents with a certain disdain. Some used sticks, a few had walking frames. The sight of them brought a self-satisfied smile to his face. They reminded him of his mother, decrepit and selfish, running his life for him. He would never be like them, herded around like old sheep going to slaughter, lots of yesterdays but few tomorrows.

He had plenty of tomorrows. Even when he was older, he'd be independent because he'd have the money to be so. And he'd be warm. Most of those South American countries had shirtsleeve climates. He imagined himself showing off his torso to Glenys Watkins lookalikes. Oh, yes. He was going places.

He checked his watch. He had no intention of entering the theatre until the lights had gone down and the show was about to begin.

The seniors and the others in the queue shuffled into the foyer — like shuffling into God's waiting room, he thought. At one time he'd wished his mother would snuff it. He would have ended up with the flat and the bank account, such as it was. But not now. Ready cash made more sense. He couldn't wait any longer for her to die.

He waited until the queue had diminished to the last few. His eyes searched for the person he was expecting. Again he checked his watch. No one else appeared. His appointment was either not coming or already inside. He chose to believe the latter. Everything he'd planned depended on it.

Heart pounding and mouth dry as dust, he made his way to the box office. The cashier was just being handed a cup of coffee. Taking money and checking tickets was thirsty work. He wanted to laugh but maintained his smile — a little nervously perhaps.

The cashier put down her cup and asked if she could help him.

'A ticket in the name of Taylor? My friend left it here for me.'

She reached into a small box marked 'reservations'.

'Here you are. All paid for.'

He took the ticket and thanked her. His pounding heart seemed to be somewhere at the top of his throat. He was that excited.

The ticket was for a private box forward of the circle. His sweaty hand squeaked on the brass banister as he climbed the stairs. The light vanished as he pushed open the door and entered the blackness. The show had started, the first performance of a new run of *Hello, Dolly!* He grimaced at the prospect and hoped this wouldn't take too long. He hated musicals. How anyone could bear to watch it beat him. It seemed that plenty of others were of the same opinion. The theatre was half empty, with most attendees seated in the stalls on the ground floor. The circle boasted only a few scattered figures, the few that could manage the stairs. Theirs was the only box in use. A good choice. Just enough darkness and privacy.

The stage was bright, its borrowed light shining on the upturned faces of the audience and the ornate decoration.

His companion was leaning forward, arms resting on the balustrade. Aware of his entering, one hand reached back and indicated an empty seat already unfolded, awaiting his arrival.

Fireworks were exploding in Simon's brain. This was it! This was the moment.

Eyes fixed on the person he'd come to meet, he sat down. He gasped on feeling something sharp nick his flesh. A spring. Nothing but a spring. These seats were old. Time they refurbished, he thought, and relaxed.

What did he care about an old seat and a bit of discomfort? He'd insist on soft cushions and sweet ladies from here on. And besides, he felt no pain, no feeling at all in his buttocks. He tried to shift, but the spring had dug deep and his movement was feeble. He tried to turn to his companion and tell him how it was.

'Something . . .' His tongue refused to obey him. A terrible numbness was creeping upwards. His vision blurred.

Slowly . . . very, very slowly, he raised his hand, meaning to wipe the sweat from his forehead. It flopped into his lap. His other hand was already laid across his beating heart. Its rate had increased, hammering against his ribs.

He heard a voice. 'Hope you don't mind, but I'd prefer to get this over with as quickly as possible. I hate musicals. And it's so hot in here . . .'

A hand came to rest on his shoulder. He felt himself being pressed downwards into his seat. He was skewered on to whatever had pierced his flesh. In his fading thoughts, he knew it could not have been a spring. His hand trembled as he made another swipe at his sweating forehead — and missed. He attempted to rise, but when he tried his legs refused to obey. The theatre itself was a blur of darkness interspersed by light from the stage, by shadows, by ghosts from its past.

The light was obliterated. A figure had arisen between him and the light. His brain had become as numb as his body. The travel brochures fell to the floor. The figure moved away.

'Enjoy the show, old boy.'

A hand gave his shoulder a final pat.

His eyes stared at the dancers on stage, but did not see them. Neither was he aware of the hand finally leaving his shoulder. For Simon Taylor all journeys were at an end.

CHAPTER FIFTY-ONE

'Sausages! We need sausages. Look!' Smudger stood like the Statue of Liberty, a single remaining sausage raised high in his right hand. 'My last one!'

Honey looked. Usually the meaty sausages they used stood upright, stiff in their skins. This one had flopped to one side. Sad. Lonesome.

A full English breakfast was key to a hotel's reputation. The bacon must be lean, the eggs fresh, and last but not least, the sausages had to be low on spice and high on meat content. Hence a day set aside specifically for collecting the sausages.

A whole day shopping usually ensued once the sausage situation was taken care of. This was one of the rare occasions when mother and daughter grabbed some time for themselves. When it came to variety in sausages, Bath had the best — a shop dedicated to nothing but sausages. There was also a fancy fish shop next door. No point in doing things by halves. Following their weekly raid of succulent, shiny sausages and odd fish they'd never tried before, it was tea and scones in the Pump Room.

Honey stood at reception doodling over the handwritten food order. 'I should phone it through, really. There's this murder for a start and I need to visit your grandmother's new shop. She's having it painted, but I'd like a peek before she makes it too spick and span.'

Lindsey stopped her reaching for the phone. 'Take a break. Your little grey cells could do with a day off. A coffee-and-cream cake won't do too much damage to the waistline.'

Just as they were making the decision whether to drive or grab a taxi, Mary Jane breezed in through the front door along with a brisk draught. She looked excited. She was also dressed in strawberry-pink leggings. Strawberries and a pink waistband decorated her tunic top and plastic strawberries hung from her earrings. She looked like a party of excited strawberries on their way to a jam factory. She asked where they were off to. They made the mistake of telling her the truth.

'I insist on giving you a lift. I'm bright as a daisy and the Chick-mobile needs to burn rubber!'

Honey paled. 'It's a Caddy, not a dragster.'

'It's a dragster when Mary Jane's behind the wheel,' muttered Lindsey.

Oblivious to what was said, Mary Jane's eyes glittered with excitement. 'She may be a little long in the tooth, but when my foot hits the floor the old girl can sure still shift her ass!'

The thought of doing thirty let alone sixty down Milsom Street made Honey's legs shake.

'Green Street's no distance,' said Honey. 'I can walk it.'

Mary Jane was adamant. 'I'm not taking no for an answer. You're getting older, girl, and your legs aren't getting any younger.'

'Thanks.'

'The car's outside.' Mary Jane leaned close suddenly, her voice dropping to a whisper. 'There's something I want to tell you. It may shed some light on the murder.'

Honey was none too sure on the validity of the offer, but what the hell.

'I'm coming,' said Lindsey, when Honey said that she needn't.

No one else dared park on the double yellow lines outside the hotel. The regular parking warden — a Sikh gentleman with a white beard and a navy-blue turban — had come back from semi-retirement into his job. He was usually very capable, but Mary Jane scared the pants off him. Honey had seen him hiding in a shop doorway in order to avoid her. One day she'd ask him why. But not today. There were too many other things to worry about. One of them was the shiny pink Cadillac. The other was its driver.

'Hop in!'

Honey took what advantage she could of the situation, diving into the back seat while Lindsey took the front.

'You're braver than me,' Honey said quietly to her daughter.

'And more agile,' Lindsey muttered back. 'I can grab the wheel if I need to.'

Mary Jane blasted off from the kerb like a rocket from Cape Kennedy. Hunched over the wheel, elbows at acute angles, eyes narrowed as though she were taking aim with a high-powered rifle.

Honey gritted her teeth. The city of Bath was passing in a blur of scattered pedestrians and honking car horns. Her eyes were narrowed slits and her teeth were on edge. When it came to white-knuckle rides, Disney World had nothing on Mary Jane.

After the trip to Northend, Honey had worked out that the best course of action when travelling in Mary Jane's car was not to talk. Lindsey had worked that one out too. If any talking was to be done, leave it to Mary Jane. She kept her eyes on the road as long as you didn't ask any questions.

At present everything was fine. Most of the conversation was directed at the traffic. Mary Jane had a lot to say about other people's bad driving habits. She was blind to her own. The same applied to her dress sense.

'Will you look at that cycling get-up? Purple-and-grey Lycra! You can see the guy's credentials! Where the hell d'ya think he's going dressed like that?'

Honey squeezed her eyes tightly shut. 'I don't care. I just want to get to the sausage shop in one piece.'

Lindsey's shoulders began to shake with laughter.

Gritting her teeth, fingers clinging to the back of Lindsey's seat, Honey leaned forward.

It was something of a relief to make it to the car park safely.

'Was there somewhere special you had to go?' Honey asked Mary Jane once she'd stopped the car.

'No. I just enjoy driving. It makes me feel so invigorated. So alive!'

Honey and Lindsey exchanged glances, but remained silent.

Mary Jane added that she was quite happy to give them a hand with their shopping. 'And then I'm going to buy you coffee and doughnuts. Or giant teacakes in Sally Lunn's tea shop.'

Lindsey smiled weakly. 'Today's unwind day. We do the Pump Rooms on sausage day.'

From the car park to Green Street was a short walk. The three of them strolled along, looking in shop windows. Honey remained thoughtful.

They waited outside a needlework shop while Mary Jane went in to browse through a rack of pink silks.

Lindsey noticed her silence. 'Something bugging you?'

Honey breathed a deep sigh. Should she tell or shouldn't she? Yes. She had to.

'I think I'm being stalked.'

'Who by?'

'I don't know.'

Now, how about the rest? Should she tell her daughter she'd been stupid enough to accept a lift from the guy she thought was stalking her? Or was she imagining things about the phantom motorcyclist, thanks to Doherty and the Warren Price debacle?

They moved aside to let a mechanical road sweeper through, then like the Red Sea, merged again. In that short space of time, Honey had come to a decision.

First she told Lindsey about Doherty, the jogging, the blonde and his lie about being stalked by Warren Price.

Lindsey nodded sagely. 'Men are *so* touchy about keeping in shape. Far more so than women.'

'Correct.'

'So if it was a lie, how come you still think you're being stalked?'

This was the difficult bit. How often had she told her daughter in childhood not to accept anything from strangers? And here she was the wrong side of forty and what had she done? Exactly that.

'Look. I know what you're going to say, but I have to tell you this . . .'

She confessed about accepting the lift, about his silence, and of course, about the wellington boots.

'There. Now, go on. Tell me I was stupid. I know. I deserve it.'

Nothing!

Lindsey stood there gaping. Her cheeks were turning pink.

Honey frowned. Never mind little grey cells, straightforward female instinct was kicking in here.

'You're going to tell me that you know a guy who wears wellington boots?'

Lindsey bit her bottom lip. 'Well, actually . . .'

Mary Jane came to a standstill in front of them, her attention on a market stall selling fabrics. 'Hey! Just look at this. A remnant for a knock-down price. Isn't it pretty?'

'It'll have to wait,' said Lindsey, exchanging a secretive look with her mother. 'I'll tell you later.'

CHAPTER FIFTY-TWO

The shops in Green Street still displayed unwrapped wares. A lot of products were still made on the premises without preservatives or additives. Most still boasted the original facades, and there was barely room between the pavements for a car to squeeze through.

The sausage shop was easy to find merely by following the delicious aromas escaping from within.

Sausages and goggle-eyed fish were bought and delivery arranged.

'Juice,' gasped Lindsey. 'I need juice.'

'Coffee!' Honey's feet were already heading towards Bath Abbey.

Mary Jane added her preference. 'I'd love a cup of Earl Grey.'

'And peaceful surroundings,' added Honey.

'Period surroundings. Let's have tea in the Pump Room,' suggested Mary Jane. 'It's my treat.'

The Pump Room was close to the Abbey and part of the famous Roman Baths. Tables were spread with white linen cloths, the cups and saucers were white porcelain, the chairs were Chippendale.

A huge grandfather clock dominated an alcove, and at the far end a trio dressed in period costume were playing Mozart.

Mary Jane narrowed her eyes. 'I can almost imagine a few Gainsborough-type ladies seated at these tables.'

Honey and Lindsey exchanged a knowing look. Mary Jane was having one of her crossover periods. This was when she swore she could see ghosts from the past. It wasn't so much a trance as a blurring of the edges between reality and imagination.

Honey saw nothing. As it was, the tourists were at odds with the elegance of their surroundings. They had a determined look about them, preparing to tramp the streets and soak up the sights.

'Nice trainers,' said Lindsey, nodding at the Reeboks on a pair of feet beneath the next table.

Mary Jane's eyes began closing and she started to make one of her 'crossover' noises. 'Hmmmmmm.'

Mother and daughter exchanged another swift and more anxious glance.

'Well!' Honey slapped her palms together, producing a thunder-like clap. 'So what was it you wanted to tell me, Mary Jane?'

At the clap, Mary Jane opened one eye. Once the question had sunk in she opened both.

'I was worrying about this poor woman that got murdered. And on our ghost walk!'

Mary Jane rolled her eyes upwards until the whites showed, another eerie state she drifted into now and again.

Lindsey gave her a nudge. 'Mary Jane?'

Mary Jane came back to earth, her eyes flashing wide and as normal as they were ever likely to be. 'I enrolled for another walk. I didn't like that one we went on, Honey. It was too wet.'

'I thought you said that ghosts and spirits didn't mind the rain,' said Honey.

'They don't, but I didn't feel anybody on that walk was there to see ghosts. No chance of spirits or ghosts coming through to a mind that isn't in tune with them and their feelings.'

Honey nodded as though Mary Jane was merely talking about her poor mobile phone reception.

Lindsey looked confused. 'Wait a moment. Aren't ghosts and spirits the same thing?'

Mary Jane shook her head adamantly. 'No, no, no! Ghosts are still suffering from the method of their death. Violent death, if you like. Call it post-traumatic stress disorder. Spirits just live in a parallel world. They're all around us. It's just that you can't see them, but they can get in touch now and again.'

Of course.

Their order arrived, and Mary Jane took a swig of Earl Grey with lemon followed by a deep breath. 'So, as I was saying, I arranged to go on another ghost walk. I presented myself at eight fifteen, the time the walk started. As I paid my fee I mentioned about how wet the previous walk had been and what a disappointment it was. The guy was real surprised. He asked me what day and date that was. I told him, explained it was raining heavily and blowing a gale and that the streets were deserted. There was only one night that bad. He remembered. Boy, was I surprised when he told me they'd called off the walk that night. He was amazed that anyone had turned up. He said he'd put a notice on the pub door. Either the wind blew it away or someone removed it.'

'*It was a dark and stormy night*,' Lindsey mused. 'Like the start of a bad book.'

Honey tapped her spoon against her saucer as she thought this through. 'Or our dear little Pamela took it down. So the people who did turn up, were they genuine ghost walkers or were they there by arrangement — for something else?'

Lindsey put her tumbler of juice back down on the table. 'That is a possibility — far-fetched, but nonetheless, a possibility.'

'Except for one or two diehards,' Lindsey added.

'Yours truly and friend,' said Honey. 'Plus a couple of Australian women who had several spirits of their own.' She frowned. 'There was one more. He said little and I never saw his face. Not that I cared. All I really wanted was to get in out of the rain and go to bed.'

Honey stopped herself from piling a third teaspoon of sugar into her coffee. She didn't take sugar. The characters on the ghost walk drifted in and out of her mind. A whole group of people there by arrangement?

'So was Pamela Windsor a genuine ghost-walk guide? Was she known to the organiser?'

'Well, we'll soon find out.'

Mary Jane got her phone out and phoned him.

'No,' she said after a short conversation. 'He doesn't know her.' She shook her head, her long fingers tapping along the edge of the table. 'She wasn't genuine. I should have known it when she left us to our own devices. Left us standing there in the pouring rain.'

Honey jerked round to face her. 'You didn't tell me that.'

Mary Jane shrugged. 'Nobody asked me anything about the ghost walk. Is it significant?'

'You bet. At what point did she wander off by herself?'

Mary Jane explained. 'She disappeared just before we turned down past Great Western Antiques. Came back saying she thought she'd felt a ghostly energy field and had gone off to investigate. Hell, if anyone was going to feel an energy field, it was me. Not her!'

'And you felt nothing.'

'No. Because there was nothing.'

It was unusual to see Mary Jane snarling, but there it was, a definite snarl.

Although Mary Jane was showing definite signs of professional jealousy, Honey felt a sense of misgiving. Pamela had disappeared in the vicinity of Great Western Antiques, a stone's throw from where Lady Templeton-Jones's body was found.

Pieces of the puzzle began slotting together in her brain. Keeping the brain active was, so she'd heard, the secret of living to a ripe old age. If that were so, then the position of crime liaison officer was doing her the world of good. Initially she'd been hesitant when offered the job. Now she was finding that a mind used to juggling guests' requests, chefs' tantrums and a complex laundry list suited the gathering and sifting of clues.

On the night of the ghost walk, Pamela Windsor had come across as a timid, plain little thing. At Bradford on Avon she'd turned into sex on legs! Was it possible she was also a murderer?

A sudden movement, the arrival of two people at the next table, took her attention. A Kashmir jacket in a soft lemon shade was the first thing she noticed: expensive, pastel and eminently Casper St John Gervais. To her surprise he was accompanied by Alistair McDonald from the auction rooms.

Casper gave her a nod of acknowledgement. Alistair waved, got up and came over while Casper turned his attention to the wine list.

Honey smiled. 'I didn't know you two were close.'

The big Scotsman's face remained its impassive self. 'Don't let your imagination run away with you. This is business. I keep him informed.'

He meant with regard to what was coming into the salerooms. In the stock exchange they call it insider trading and it's illegal. In the world of antiques, it's not.

'You'd better get back. He's giving me the evil eye,' said Honey. 'And I'd better be going before he grills me on what's happening about our murdered lady.'

'That's what I wanted to speak to you about.'

The legs of a chair scraped over the floor then creaked beneath Alistair's weight as he sat down. 'If you remember rightly, hen, you asked me about that catalogue and the gaps beside the numbers.'

Honey leaned forward, interested. Mary Jane rested her chin on a bony hand and listened intently. Lindsey sipped at her tea. Her eyes never left Alistair's face.

Honey urged Alistair to go on.

'Sebastian Gaunt, one of the newest additions to our illustrious house, was clearing out his desk.'

'Fired?' Honey raised her eyebrows.

'Double-barrelled. Eton educated, but a bungalow if ever I met one.'

Mary Jane opened her mouth to ask the obvious question.

Lindsey enlightened her. 'Nothing upstairs.'

Big as he was, Alistair had a gently courteous way of explaining things. 'He was a non-event, hen. A disaster with excellent connections. I found this among the rubbish he left behind.'

He reached into his pocket and pulled out a roughly printed list of about four A4-size pages. 'It's the prelim — the rough list of items scheduled for auction. This one's for the auction of marine collectables. It's a special. Once a year only. Quite a feather in the cap for a provincial auction house. Most of that kind of thing only happens in London.'

He pushed the list over and pointed to where she had last seen gaps. Three items were listed. *Film Reel 1, Film Reel 2, Film Reel 3.* But it was the heading for the three that caught her eye. *Taken on board . . . RMS* Titanic*!*

Honey's head jerked up. Her eyes locked with those of Alistair.

He nodded, his thumb stroking his plush red beard. 'Highly sought after.'

'But they never turned up.' Her voice sounded a mile away.

'No. The auction's come and gone.'

Their eyes held again. Honey voiced what was going through her mind. 'And they'd be worth a small fortune.'

Alistair nodded. 'True, hen. Absolutely true!'

Honey scanned the auction lists. 'Lucky he got the boot from the firm.'

'Luckier still that he kept these,' said Alistair, flicking a finger at the papers. 'We're eco-friendly, so most of our old paperwork goes for shredding before its recycled. These listings were scrapped and dumped straightaway. Lucky for you that we employed a numpty who couldn't tell his Hobart from a horse's rear end.'

Honey scanned the sheets. The name Lord A. Bridgewater leaped out at her. Her heart beat faster. That creep! That slimeball! He was the one who'd put them in the sale.

The teacups rattled as Alistair raised his big frame from the table.

Honey looked up into his red beard. 'So why were they withdrawn?'

'Something legal, from what I can gather. They weren't entirely his to sell.'

Casper called across with a request to keep him up to speed on the matter of Lady Templeton-Jones. She told him she'd be in touch. Inside she was doing somersaults. Bridgewater and his cousin Lady Templeton-Jones had been sole beneficiaries of the will.

Outside, the lunchtime crowd bustled around in front of the Abbey and the Pump Room. People were posing beneath the fancy lights outside. A whole coach party were having their smiles saved for posterity using the arched entrance as a backdrop. Honey hardly noticed them. She stopped and took a big breath. 'Wow!'

'Even I know the value of stuff from the *Titanic*,' said Lindsey.

'I've been in touch with a few poor souls who lost their lives,' said Mary Jane. The shape of the blusher applied to her cheeks reflected those on her tunic. 'I wonder if I'd recognise anyone from the film.'

She sounded pretty excited at the prospect.

Honey's mind was whirling. She remembered the old cameras and photographic equipment in the house at Northend.

She got out her phone.

'Who you calling?' asked Lindsey.

'Doherty. I need to look at that . . .'

He sounded dour. She had no time to ask him the reason why. 'I need a lift to Northend. Now! Bridgewater has got a whole lot of photographic memorabilia that has a direct bearing on—'

'Whoa!'

'And it's imperative that I get back—'

'Where are you?'

'I'm outside the Pump Room.'

'Alone?'

'No. I'm with Lindsey and Mary Jane. Mary Jane gave us a lift.' The thought of the inbound journey made her wince. Enduring the same journey back gave her goosebumps.

'Can Mary Jane take you?'

'I'd be fit for nothing by the time I got there.'

Doherty fell to silence.

She knew . . . she knew instinctively that she'd interrupted something.

'Are you kind of indisposed?'

The pregnant silence positively fizzled with potential. 'You could say that. I'm at the Theatre Royal. One of the customers found the show strangely riveting. So riveting, in fact, that he's skewered to his seat.'

'Christ! Anyone I know?'

That pause again. 'Simon Taylor.'

'I'm on my way.'

CHAPTER FIFTY-THREE

'So tell me, Lindsey. Who is that guy in the wellingtons?'

Lindsey turned her head as they marched along. Honey sensed she wasn't going to like this.

'He's a great guy but a little shy. He wanted to introduce himself, but can't quite get up the courage.'

'What are you telling me, that he's your boyfriend?'

'Um . . . yes.'

'So where's the kilt?'

'What?'

For a moment Honey held back the words. Lindsey was becoming more and more evasive about her love life. Perhaps it was an age thing, then told herself an obvious truth.

Let's face it, you don't tell your mother everything.

'You told me he played the bagpipes and wore a kilt.'

Lindsey's hair was blowing over her face so it was difficult to read her expression. She was slow answering.

'Well?'

'It's a very delicate situation.'

How delicate could a man in wellies be?

The area around the Theatre Royal was cordoned off. Scene-of-crime tape fluttered in the breeze. Curious tourists — fed up with Jane Austen, John Wood, Beau Nash and the sulphurous waters of the Roman Baths — aimed their cameras.

Honey eyed them ruefully. Never mind genteel, give them gore every time.

Lindsey had opted to come with her. Mary Jane had fallen in with a crowd of people from Manitoba to whom she was giving an outline of her ancestry.

Doherty waved to her from the other side of the tape.

'I can't let you through until we've sucked the SOC dry.'

'Scene of crime,' Honey said to Lindsey by way of explanation.

Lindsey tutted and pulled a long-suffering-teenager-type face. 'I know he didn't mean sock or something to do with his laundry. Not that kind of sock.' She pointed at her foot.

'So when I rang you just now,' Honey said to Doherty, 'there was a reason . . .'

She told him about the film reels. 'They're worth a fortune. Bridgewater had to withdraw them from the auction. I presume his co-heir was not keen to sell them.'

'Money's always a good motive for murder,' said Doherty, nodding.

'So how does Simon Taylor fit into this?'

He shrugged and held his head to one side. 'I'm not sure. At first glance it seems like it has something to do with the title Wanda Carpenter bought, but maybe it doesn't.'

Honey shook her head. Like the city around her, her brain was working in overdrive. There was so much stuff rattling around in there.

'As for Mr Taylor . . .' She shivered. 'What a nasty way to go.'

'Agreed,' said Steve. 'Examination of the body was pretty specific. Our friend Mr Taylor took it in the arse — that is, a needle punctured his posterior. He was a big lad and must have sat down heavily. The needle went straight in. Some kind of quick-acting poison. Probably potassium cyanide. Nasty. Easily obtainable, thanks to the internet.'

'Ouch!'

Honey gulped and immediately ran her hands over her behind. Never again would she sit down in the Theatre Royal — or any other theatre for that matter — without checking her seat.

'What was he doing here?'

Doherty rubbed at his stubble in thought. His brow furrowed. 'He was meeting someone. But for what?' He shrugged. 'I can only guess.'

'Blackmail?'

'That was one of my guesses.'

'It figures.'

'Why? What makes you say that?'

'He was involved in this Noble Present scam and he might have found something out about somebody . . .' She stopped. Steve was shaking his head in a negative manner.

'It wasn't a scam. Not on his part, anyway. It was a scam on the part of our friend Mr George. He was flogging rubbish. Simon Taylor was flogging the real McCoy.'

Honey frowned. 'How do you know that? Who was he buying them from?'

'I've had another word with Mr George.'

'Was Pammy there? The girlfriend,' she added in response to his questioning look.

'Yes. They both went green around the gills when they heard how Simon Taylor had met his end. She ran to the bathroom to be sick and then she came back and urged Mr Hamilton George to spill the beans. And he did.'

'In detail?'

'Yep. I can tell by your face that you're curious.'

'I am.'

'OK.' Doherty flipped open his notebook. 'Mr Cameron Wallace. Apparently the family inherited a load of titles. He's actually Lord Cameron Wallace, an old Hebridean title, and apparently holds a host of others. But he prefers to use Mr Wallace. Reckons titles can put people off in business.'

In the last hour or so she'd been bombarded with information. First there was this business of film reels allegedly from the *Titanic*. Then there was this revelation about the titles Simon Taylor had been dealing with being genuine, whereas those sold by Hamilton George were not. Added to that a dead Simon Taylor — killed in a most bizarre manner.

So why had Lady Templeton-Jones gone to see Simon Taylor? What were they talking about in the Garrick's Head before she'd been murdered?

Doherty read her mind. 'We could have done with another word with Mr Taylor.'

'Lordy, lordy,' Lindsey murmured. 'What now?'

Honey whipped round in time to see two police constables bursting into action, their radios squawking.

'Hello,' said Steve, eyes narrowing as the two constables broke into a run. 'A street incident.'

He caught the grin of a nearby bobby who'd also picked up the message. Steve told him to wipe the smile off his face. 'We're on the scene of a murder here. What's so bloody funny?'

The constable's jaw jiggled as he tried not to laugh. 'There's a riot at a teddy bear shop on Milsom Street. Some woman is threatening the manager for kicking her out of her shop. Apparently she's fetched him a fair clout around the ear with a teddy bear!'

Honey grabbed Lindsey's wrist. 'Come on.'

'Grandma can get quite bloody-minded when she's roused!' Lindsey exclaimed as they ran.

Honey scowled. 'Forget about her mind being bloody. It's the shop manager's head I'm worried about.'

'Catch up later?' Doherty called after her. She bristled, imagining the amused look on his face. No doubt he'd guessed why she was off at a gallop. He knew Gloria Cross could be a little unorthodox when the mood took her.

Her phone rang. She managed to speak as she ran. That's what losing weight does for you. Casper was in full cry.

'This is too bad! One of the most beautiful, the most treasured theatres in the country. How dare this man die there! How did it happen?'

'Got stabbed in the arse,' Honey said breathlessly. 'Can't talk now. Speak later.'

She could imagine Casper's indignation. Normally she wouldn't dare to cut him off. But this was a family matter.

Happily she was wearing her shopping shoes. They were scuffed, lace-up and ugly, but boy, she could run in them. Jeans were also good for running and looked good with her black polo neck sweater and green corduroy jacket. The jacket helped offset the scuffed look of the shoes, which were of the same bottle green. Co-ordination was good. No one noticed scuffed shoes if you were co-ordinated.

A crowd had gathered outside Teddyitis. Honey recognised Neville, Casper's receptionist. He was in off-duty mode — pink jeans, lime-green sweater and pink silk scarf. He was being as nosy as the rest of them.

'My, my,' he said, on seeing Honey. 'I've never seen anyone do that with a teddy bear before!'

Honey ducked her head and pushed through the crowd. She ignored the titters of amusement.

Lindsey followed beaming with a teenager's quirky pride. 'Grandma's drawn quite a crowd.'

'Let's hope she hasn't drawn blood.'

The floor was littered with assorted sizes and colours of teddy bears. There were bears wearing gingham dresses, bears in leather, bears in pale green and smelling of apples, bears wearing artists smocks and floppy berets.

Her attention was grabbed by an assortment of banners draped from the ceiling and along the shelves.

Teddy bears for all occasions!

Cuddle up to Dudley.

You are never alone with a teddy.

Take me to bed. Love me.

Well, she thought, if an inanimate teddy bear is all you have . . . Perhaps they came with batteries nowadays.

Far from being arrested, her mother was sitting on a chair, head back, eyes closed. A shop assistant wearing teddy bear ears, a black plastic nose and a red gingham dress — a full-size match to the one worn by the teddies — was fanning her with a newspaper.

It appeared the employees of Teddyitis were required to immerse themselves in teddy memorabilia. Honey grimaced, thankful the shop wasn't in the erotic underwear and toy market. Teddies were soft and couldn't do much harm. Rubber dildos were an entirely different matter.

Honey homed in on the most senior police officer. She adopted an apologetic tone and tried a bit of eye-fluttering. 'I'm so sorry. I came when I could. I understand my mother had a bit of a turn.'

He was suitably sympathetic. 'She most certainly has. Does she suffer from some kind of dementia?'

'Yes. The wilful kind.'

The false eyelashes on the woman sprawled in the chair fluttered over rouged cheeks by Lancôme. Honey wasn't fooled. Neither was Lindsey, whose right hand was clamped tight against her mouth. If she eased the pressure she'd burst out laughing.

A short, fat man looking a lot like a teddy bear himself was sitting on a second chair holding a handkerchief to his nose.

Lindsey asked him if he was all right.

'I've goth a thinus throblem,' he said. 'The theddy bear sthumped me.'

Not without my mother's help, thought Honey, wincing.

Smiling and adopting the long-suffering daughter approach, she asked the policeman if she could take her dear old ma home and put her to bed.

His eyes twinkled. 'The manager isn't pressing charges — so long as it doesn't happen again.'

No. She could see that. He was too busy pressing a damp compress against his nose to spend time filling out forms down at the police station.

'She's at a funny age,' said Honey. 'If she gets any worse I'll have no alternative but to put her away.'

She saw her mother's jaw twitch. If there was one thing Gloria Cross certainly was not, it was senile. Not only that, but she lived her life no differently than she'd ever done. She still loved shopping for clothes, still wore stockings and waspie girdles and still had an eye for a good-looking man. Honey blamed the HRT for the latter. Putting her in an old folks' home would be tantamount to being buried alive.

Recovery was instantaneous. The groaning and opening of one eye was pure theatre. 'Where am I?' she asked. Her voice was weak and watery.

'You're in teddy bear heaven,' Honey growled. 'Come on. Straight to bed with a cup of hot chocolate and a sleeping pill — or two!'

Gloria Cross was only seven pounds over the weight she'd been at twenty. It was easy to get her to her feet. A path was cleared through the onlookers.

Neville was still there, grinning from ear to ear. 'This was better than gunfight at the O.K. Corral. I take it your mother is being let off?'

'The manager isn't pressing charges.'

'Never mind him. How about the teddy bear?'

CHAPTER FIFTY-FOUR

It was definitely time for an evening out with Steve Doherty. When he suggested it and she'd leaped at the idea.

'Royal Crescent? Nice meal out?'

He'd shaken his head. 'Zodiac Club. I need to unwind.'

'I'm fine with that.'

Bath is a city of one-way systems. Sometimes it made sense to skirt the maze of old streets and shopping arcades rather than drive through it. Sometimes it was best to walk. Walking allowed time to peer into old windows and wonder at elegant architecture.

Besides the fact that getting a taxi to her destination was a waste of time, Honey enjoyed the balmy June air. Plus, soaking up the atmosphere brought the added advantage of keeping the pounds off; a luscious curve could so easily become a lumpy bump.

The Zodiac Club, that underground haunt of everyone in the catering and hospitality trade, had a blue-black atmosphere courtesy of the dimmed lighting and the smoke rising from the steak grill.

It was ten thirty and Honey had got away early. She'd ordered drinks. A Jack Daniel's for Steve, a vodka and tonic — slimline, of course — for herself.

He came in looking dishevelled, even more unshaven than usual and a tired look around his eyes. His smile was warm but seemed to require effort.

'It's been a long day,' he said, rubbing his face as though he were washing it with a flannel. He gulped the drink in one.

'How did Taylor's mother take it?'

'Stunned. We couldn't give her any explanation as to why anyone would want to murder her lovely boy,' he said with a smidgen of sarcasm. 'Not yet, at least. It was the method that unhinged her, I think.'

'But have you made progress?' Honey ordered him another drink. He didn't seem to notice until she handed it to him. Doherty was in deduction mode, a faraway look in his eyes, a Jack Daniel's down his throat.

'Nasty way to die . . .'

'Don't!' She did the halt sign with her hand. 'Don't go there. I'll have nightmares.'

'I could come and help you keep them at bay?'

Quite frankly it was a tempting proposition. But she'd left her laundry trailed all over the bedroom floor — assuming they got that far.

'Lindsey's having a friend sleeping over.'

'Girlfriend?'

'Of course.'

He took a big swig then eyed her more seriously over the top of his glass. 'The trail keeps leading back to Associated Security Shredding.'

'I think I know why.'

'You do?'

She told him about what Alistair had said about the auction rooms and their commitment to the environment. 'Those reels were detailed on paperwork that was superseded because the seller pulled out. All scrap material went to be shredded so those details never made it into the catalogue.'

'Because the seller was dead?'

'Possibly.'

They looked at each other. 'But Simon knew.'

'So who was it?'

Steve drained his glass and put it down, turning it round and round as he thought things through. 'There was one name on there that flew out at us.'

'Bridgewater!'

He nodded. 'I think he talked to Wanda — Her Ladyship — and she told him of whatever it was she intended bidding on. Perhaps she asked him to find out who had put the items up for sale. I imagine Simon Taylor did some research and was successful in find out what was at stake. Wanda had told him what it was that was so valuable.'

Forgetting that it was Doherty's round, Honey ordered more drinks. She was on a roll. The pieces in this odd puzzle were beginning to fall into place.

'And what was it? What was so valuable about a load of old film reels?'

He shrugged. 'I haven't a clue.'

She raised a quizzical eyebrow.

'So what about Bridgewater?' said Honey. 'Do you think he could have done it?'

'You're biased. You don't like him.'

'I hate people who phone me and try to sell me stuff I don't want.'

'So he killed his cousin over the film reels?'

'Without Wanda around, Bridgewater gets the lot.'

'What about Taylor?'

'Taylor was the spanner in the works. He had to be dealt with.'

'So let's have a word with Bridgewater.' He unfolded from the chair, sending the legs squealing across the flagstone floor.

'Now?'

'Why not?' Placing a hand either side of her seat, he pushed her stool back. She couldn't help but stand. 'People are at their most malleable when they've just been woken up.'

She threw him a piercing look. 'And their most vulnerable. You wouldn't want to get done for police harassment, would you?'

'I've got an excuse.'

'What does that mean?'

'His cousin's handbag. It's down at the station. Bridgewater's been on my back for ages to return it.'

'I thought you had.'

'It was as close as I could get to police brutality. Must admit I enjoyed torturing the slimy toad.'

* * *

It was a quarter to midnight by the time they'd walked to the station, collected the bag and returned to Doherty's car.

They drove with the hood up, for which Honey was grateful. Steve had consumed three Jack Daniel's. He shouldn't be driving, but the air would clear his head. He assured her he'd be OK.

She sat with the bag on her lap. She loved big bags herself, so she understood where the deceased woman was coming from.

Was it big enough to have a secret compartment? Doherty might not be too pleased if she opened it and took a look. Her fingers drummed on the soft leather . . .

Doherty interrupted her thoughts. 'I'm reading your mind, Honey Driver. You're tempted to do something. Right?'

On this occasion she couldn't lie. 'I was trying to remember the stuff that was in here. I remember you listing it.'

'I've got the list with me.'

'No secret compartments?'

He took his eyes off the road and glanced her way. 'It's a big monster of a bag, but no. No secret compartments.'

Honey bit her lip. She was disappointed. 'So what's the biggest item listed?'

'Let me think. Yeah! Yeah! I know. The contact lenses! A month's supply in a green box. Unopened.'

His eyes left the road again. They met hers.

Without another word from him, she undid the single buckle holding the flap shut. Then she slid the zipper.

The box containing the contact lenses was still there: untouched, unopened. Honey jerked it out, tore at the packaging. There was not the normal battle of wills as there is with some modern-day packaging. It opened easily.

'It's already been opened once and resealed,' said Honey.

Too involved in what she was doing to drive, Doherty pulled over.

'Go careful with that. It's evidence.'

Honey took a breath and tipped the box on end.

'Bingo!'

They both stared, taking in exactly what they were looking at.

The tin was round and in good condition, considering its age. He gave it a good shake. Something rattled.

They exchanged wry looks. Film reels didn't rattle.

Doherty took it and prised off the lid. Inside was a USB stick.

They both stared at the unexpected. 'Probably didn't come from the *Titanic*,' Honey remarked.

'So where are the original reels?'

Doherty frowned at the road ahead.

Honey wondered what he was thinking. 'So what gives?'

Sighing and straightening at the same time, he rubbed the back of his neck.

'Leave Bridgewater till morning?' suggested Honey.

'No.' He turned the ignition key. 'Let's get the bastard out of bed.'

* * *

The village of Northend was in near darkness. Doherty rapped the knocker of Bridgewater's three-storey cottage.

The sound echoed between the other cottages and the wall opposite.

'Come on, come on,' he muttered.

He rapped again. This time harder.

Honey cringed. It was late. It was dark. Would she open the door at this hour?

A window opened from the cottage next door. A head popped out.

'It's gone twelve. Stop that bloody racket,' a man shouted from above.

'It's the police.' Doherty flashed his warrant card.

'I don't give a stuff whether you're God Almighty. Sod off and let a working man sleep!'

'Sorry to disturb you, but do you know where Mr Bridgewater is?' Honey shouted up.

The casement, by now half closed, paused.

'No. Ain't been there for days.'

The window slammed shut.

Honey looked at the door.

Doherty did the same.

'Do you think . . . ?' began Honey.

'Possibly,' returned Doherty.

'Shall we kick down the door?'

'I'm Avon and Somerset Police not bloody Miami Vice.'

They went back to the car and sat deep in thought.

'I feel another visit to Trowbridge coming on,' said Doherty. 'It all started at Associated Security Shredding.'

Cogs and wheels were whirling in Honey's head. 'No,' she said suddenly. 'The ghost walk. That's where it started.'

CHAPTER FIFTY-FIVE

Ashwell Bridgewater's neighbour was wrong. He was in but about to go out. What he had to do must be done at night.

Flattened against the wall beside the window he'd listened to what was said. He'd recognised who they were. The cop who didn't own a shaver and the broad with the boobs. No way did he want to speak to them.

Craning his neck so he could see out, he watched the car's brake lights come on at the end of the narrow lane. Then they were gone, the small car heading towards the city.

He resisted the temptation to switch on one of his many alabaster table lamps. A street light gave him enough light to see by. He phoned the person he'd planned to meet.

'I'm leaving now. Give me half an hour.'

The reply was terse. The connection was swiftly severed.

Bridgewater was careful about closing the door. Old doors were buggers to close, swollen in wet weather, shrunken in dry. One hand pulling the knocker and one using the key, he managed it as best he could. His neighbour had given him an alibi and he intended to keep it.

* * *

One o'clock in the morning. Reflections of a sleeping city played on the empty shop windows. A damp mist coming up from the river had turned the cobbles shiny and slippery. Bridgewater turned up his collar. His throat was dry. Both palms — the one holding on to the package and the one thrust into his pocket — were moist.

His footsteps echoed between the buildings. He stopped to catch his breath and listen to the silence. His footsteps were replaced by the hammering of his pulse within his skull.

Come on, he told himself. *This is no different to negotiating a deal with a telephone client.* Much as he tried to convince himself of this, deep down he knew it wasn't true. This transaction was far more important. Far more lucrative.

As arranged, the door was unlocked. He entered the dim interior and shuddered. It was similar to next door, though not so neglected.

'Hello?'

His voice echoed in the emptiness.

'Up here.'

A sharp voice. A selfish voice.

Never mind. Keep going.

He did just that, taking the stairs quickly despite the darkness. On reaching the first landing, he stopped and looked round. A rectangle of light fell in from outside through a single window. The rest of the landing was in darkness.

He looked up the next flight of stairs. A figure stood outlined against the skylight. For one heart-stopping moment he thought it was her: Wanda, his cousin.

You know better than that, he told himself. Wanda's dead. You know she's dead.

'Have you got them?'

He was surprised at how calmly she asked. Did the woman never lose her cool?

'Yes.'

'Bring them up.'

The stairs creaked beneath his feet. He saw her move away from the balustrade. Rotten with age, it moved as she did so.

A candle burned on a table.

'A bit primitive,' he said, and chanced a smile. He didn't know whether she smiled back. Her face remained in shadow, but he could see the thrust of her breasts above a neat waist.

'Hand me the reels.'

'Certainly.' He took the reels with both hands. 'And the money?'

'Here.'

He stared at the envelope she was handing him. Was she for real?

'What is this?' he said without taking it. There was a hint of amusement in his voice, though he wasn't feeling amused — far from it!

'A banker's draft. It's quite safe.'

Bridgewater felt his throat tighten. 'That isn't what we agreed. I want cash. I stipulated cash.'

'Impossible. Unless you want to wait a week or so . . . Now give me the reels.'

She reached to take them.

He took a sideways step. For the first time since their negotiations had started she sounded anxious.

'A banker's draft is as good as money.'

'I don't care. I want cash.'

'You stupid sod! All this money. Imagine what you could do with it.'

'I want cash.'

He didn't want to be traced. Didn't want to have to explain how his cousin had died — and why.

'No.' He began shaking his head and walking backwards.

He saw her step forward. The lower part of her face entered the light. Her lips were pink, plush and slightly ajar as though suddenly surprised.

She cried out, arms flailing. It was as if she were fading away from him, hanging there, unbalanced, waiting to fall.

Blood-red fingernails clawed at the handrail. The glue was weak, the wood brittle with age. The whole thing splintered away from its mooring. She was gone, part of the stairwell falling with her.

CHAPTER FIFTY-SIX

Alistair from the auction room happened to know a retired projectionist who still dabbled with old film.

'Sly Ellis is a wee bit eccentric, but knows his stuff. He'll be able to tell you if it's genuine.'

'It's on a USB stick. It appears Her Ladyship had a copy made of the original reels.'

'But you don't know the whereabouts of the originals?'

'No. But we'd like to take a look at the footage — me and Doherty, that is.'

After reporting to Casper, his name was added to the viewers. Lindsey also expressed an interest.

* * *

Sly Ellis had a shed in his back garden in Marshfield, a stone-built village some miles out of the city and uphill all the way. The shed was in the deluxe bracket of sheds; it was insulated, had double-glazed windows and was big enough to fit several chairs set out in rows.

OK, the screen wasn't exactly up there with Leicester Square or Broadway, but it was big enough.

Their host was happy to be in the driving seat and interesting to meet. His costume was pure Hollywood glory days:

worsted cap worn back to front, checked pullover, striped shirt and tie and all coupled with a pair of tawny-coloured plus-fours, long socks and golf shoes.

Doherty assumed the same as Honey had.

'There was no need to turn out in costume for our benefit,' he said.

'I didn't. Take your seats!'

Casper had come along with Alistair.

'I've brought popcorn,' said her mother. She loved an afternoon matinee. She proceeded to hand around a large bucket. Most declined. Honey's eyebrows rose halfway to her hairline when Casper peered curiously into the bucket and extracted a sticky mass of the stuff.

'You could have looked at this on an ordinary computer,' said Sly, 'though you can't beat seeing old film on a big screen.'

'That's what we thought,' said Doherty.

The inside of Sly's shed was done out like a small movie theatre. The screen was a decent size and so was the plush seating. It looked authentic, taken out from some long-demolished Odeon.

All eyes fixed on the screen. The picture was grainy black and white, the figures promenading in double-quick time.

Alistair whistled through his teeth.

Casper's jaw stopped chomping and dropped onto his silk cravat. 'The dead walk again.'

Honey leaned forward so she could see past Casper. She addressed Alistair.

'Is there any doubt?'

He shook his head, his eyes fixed on a pair of able seamen smiling from the flickering screen. Their Guernsey sweaters said it all: RMS *Titanic*.

Ely made a few adjustments and all flickering stopped and the black-and-white film was pure and fresh.

There was absolute silence once the film had finished. The truth hit them all. Without exception, those people strolling or lounging on the decks were all dead. So many people had died on that ill-fated voyage. The whole world knew the great tragedy of the 'unsinkable' ship.

Honey was the first to find her voice. 'How much is it worth?'

The question was purely academic, but Honey couldn't help asking.

Casper put forward the absolute truth. 'However much someone's willing to pay for it.'

Alistair burrowed his fingers into his beard, sending the stiff hairs into upright tufts. Then he smoothed them down. He did this a few times, his eyes lowered as he spoke in a dark, thoughtful voice. 'A while back a ticket for the launch of the ship fetched around thirty thousand pounds at auction. In London or New York, I think. A copy might have some value, but the film reels would be priceless.'

Honey felt a tightness in her chest. Priceless they may be, but so far they had cost two lives.

She recalled a conversation she'd had with Lindsey earlier that day. Her daughter had remarked that Honey and Doherty were like ships in the night with no lights on. They kept missing each other. Slightly miffed, Honey had answered, 'Better than ending up on the rocks, I suppose — or hitting an iceberg.'

Well, here was the real McCoy.

Doherty had stayed silent but shifted position. He was leaning forward, elbows resting on knees, eyes narrowed.

Honey did the same. Her eyes remained thoughtfully fixed on the screen. 'I wonder who the cameraman was.'

'No point in wondering,' said Casper. 'We know where to find him — many fathoms beneath the North Atlantic.'

Gloria Cross slammed the lid back onto the popcorn bucket. 'That wasn't exactly a full-length feature.'

Honey rolled her eyes. 'It wasn't meant to be.'

Lindsey had been totally engrossed in the film. Now she was frowning thoughtfully. 'Whoever converted those reels into a video file has to have the correct equipment. Right?'

Everyone agreed.

'You'd need a computer plus a film scanner to do the job, but it's not hard to do.' She patted her mother's shoulder. 'I'll take Grandma home now before she asks for her money back.'

Doherty ran his fingers through his hair, flattening it back from his forehead. 'Methinks another visit to "Lord" Ashley Bridgewater is in order.'

'I'll come with you.'

'You're welcome — and you're frowning. Problem?'

Honey smacked her forehead with the palm of her hand. 'Must stop doing that. More frowns, more furrows. Wrinkles,' she said in response to his puzzled blink.

'I'd totally forgotten that Bridgewater had endowed himself with a title.'

'And you're thinking he bought it from the same source as Lady Templeton-Jones?'

'Simon Taylor.'

She pulled the door of the low-sprung car shut behind her. 'Simon worked at Associated Security Shredding. They also run a "copying" service. I'd presumed copying meant photocopying . . .'

'But it might not.'

Doherty's expression said it all. Like the bits in a kaleidoscope all the chips of glass were forming a pattern. It might not be the end pattern, but it was pleasing nonetheless.

'He'll be at work,' said Honey as Doherty turned the car towards Cold Ashton and the narrow B-road leading down to Northend.

Stone chips flew skywards as Doherty did a U-turn back to the main road.

'So where does he work?' Honey asked him.

He looked blankly over the steering wheel. 'Hold on.' He fetched out his cell phone.

'Can you go into the Lady Templeton-Jones file and give me the work address of Ashley Bridgewater?'

The person on the other end did as ordered. Eventually they came back.

'Oh. That's interesting.'

Honey looked at him. 'So?'

He grinned. 'The company he works for is part of the Wallace and Gates group. Same building. Second floor.'

Honey sat back. So APW Marketing and Associated Security Shredding were all part of the same group?

* * *

'I'm beginning to get this,' said Honey as she slid her bottom on to the bucket style seat.

Doherty started the engine. 'And?'

'Wanda Carpenter came over to claim her part of the inheritance and immediately realised the value of the three reels of film. Her cousin Ashley had entered them in an auction. Why would Wanda withdraw them? Sentimental value?' She shook her head. 'Maybe she'd had an offer she couldn't refuse?'

Doherty nodded. 'That's logical. But from whom?'

Honey stared ahead at the long road leading down into Bath. 'She was on the ghost walk to meet the person in question. I'm presuming that for security reasons cousin Ashley first had the reels copied to disc. So they didn't entirely trust whoever had made them an offer. But Wanda decided to be extra careful. She never took her bag with her but left it in the care of Adrian Harris.'

'For what reason, Miss Marple?'

'Don't call me that. It makes me feel frumpy.'

'You'll never be that.'

She wasn't listening. Something else had come to her. 'She arrived by taxi.'

Doherty caught her drift. 'And went straight off on the walk.'

'So where was she between leaving the bag and arriving on the walk? Did she meet someone else? Someone who perhaps changed her mind about selling them at all?'

'And presumed she had the reels on her.'

'Which she did not.'

As it turned out, there was no joy at APW Marketing, a modern glass-and-plastic building on a modern trading estate surrounded by trees and manicured lawns.

Doherty pressed the intercom button and voiced the reason for being there.

'Police. I want to speak to Ashley Bridgewater.'

There was a buzzing as the door clicked open.

The day outside was warm. Inside it was as cool as you wished it to be.

Doherty approached the reception desk. The receptionist, a plump blonde wearing false eyelashes and thick eyebrows explained that Baron Bridgewater hadn't turned up for work.

'You can try him at home, but I don't think he's there. I did give him a ring earlier. No reply though.'

CHAPTER FIFTY-SEVEN

Honey tilted her head back and eyed the building all the way up to the guttering. 'Disappearing is getting to be a habit around here.'

Doherty gave Ashley Bridgewater's front door another firm hammering. A strong wind was blowing down through the narrow gap between the terraced cottages and the building opposite. The effect was to mute the harsh racket, at least to Honey's ears.

Inching along into the flower bed, she peered in through the ground-floor window. The window was divided in three, with iron casements and a stone mullion frame.

The scene inside the cottage was little changed to what it was before — though perhaps a little untidier — as though someone had been packing.

Shielding her eyes with her hands, she peered again. There was no dead body. She wasn't quite sure whether to be grateful or disappointed. Cold-calling salesmen were such a damned nuisance.

'No sign of life,' she said, shaking the dirt from her heels as she stepped back onto the path.

Doherty made a murmuring noise — his thinking noise — a bit like a DVD player when it's on standby.

'He's done a runner.'

'You don't know that for sure.'

'Took the money and headed for the Costa Brava.'

'Uh uh,' she said. 'He didn't seem the Costa Brava type.'

'So where do you think he would go?'

'Thailand. He's the sort that buys sex but never gets it for free.'

Doherty raised his eyebrows. 'You think?'

'Trust me. He hides dark secrets.'

'Do you?'

Honey thought about it. 'I have been known to wander around with Queen Victoria's knickers in my handbag.'

Doherty smirked and leaned closer. 'Or wearing Brunhilde's bra on your head,' he said, referring to the last case they'd worked on when they'd worn the cups of a huge bra on their head to keep them warm while trapped in a deep freeze.

'Down, boy! You'll trip over your tongue.'

Northend was a non-starter. Doherty radioed through for an alert to be put out at airports, ferry and bus terminals. 'And get hold of his car registration details from Swansea.'

The wide wheels rumbled back down the slope and onto the main road. The traffic was sparse as far as the lights at the bottom. A bulk carrier joined them at the junction, 'Wallace and Gates Transport Services' emblazoned across its rear end.

On its way to a landfill site?

It was reasonable to suppose that Wallace and Gates owned that too. Doherty reflected her thoughts.

'Spreads it wide, our Mr Cameron.'

'I take it that Associated Security Shredding is part of the same group.'

'Yup.'

'And the copying facility next door to it?'

'Yup. Got it checked out.'

Of course it was. Ashley Bridgewater and Simon Taylor both worked for a division of Wallace and Gates. The shop where Wanda Carpenter had been found murdered was owned by them, as was the shop next door to it.

'Wallace and Gates owned everything connected with this.'

'And employed the prime movers.'

'And now the murder scene's been re-let to my mother.'

'The murder doesn't worry her?'

'Nah!' said Honey, shaking her head. 'But she's going to have Mary Jane do a little sagebrush burning around the place. It's a kind of spiritualist version of feng shui.'

Doherty laughed. 'A lot of bother to go through. She'd have been better off renting the shop next door now it's empty . . . Holy sh . . . !' Doherty's voice trailed away. Honey sensed he was having a road to Damascus moment — though in this case it was a road into Bath and not half as spiritual. 'The shop next door sold marine artefacts. I looked in the window. There was a load of old marine bits and pieces in the window.'

'But not now?'

He shook his head.

'And the proprietor?'

'Gone abroad. So I'm told.'

Honey ran her tongue over her lips. 'I could do with a drink.'

CHAPTER FIFTY-EIGHT

'Honey Driver, you've taken leave of your senses. Now either sort yourself out or get out of my bloody kitchen!'

Honey considered telling Smudger to sod off, but thought the better of it. Anyway, she was making a mess of things this morning, having just filled a jug with mayonnaise instead of cream.

She was preoccupied. Where were the film reels? That was all she wanted to know. Still, that was no excuse for the state she was in.

'Sorry, Chef,' she muttered, rubbing her iron-hard neck. 'Too much tension.'

'Then get out of my kitchen and find someone to give you a massage.'

'You offering?'

'Out!' He pointed at the door.

She scurried away, thinking that she needed more than a neck massage to sort things out. Her whole body was stiff as a fence post. Unfortunately she was filling in for an absent waitress tonight and being courteous and professional was taking its toll. It wouldn't be long before she lashed out at somebody.

* * *

'Didn't you hear me? I said there's a greenfly on my salad.'

Honey turned to the man with the speckled skin and ginger hair. 'I'm sorry. I didn't hear you.'

'Look,' he said, pointing a square-ended finger at the tiny intruder. 'I didn't order protein with my salad.'

'I'll get you a fresh one.'

'No need. You can deduct the cost from the bill. That's four salads . . .'

'You've been served four salads with greenfly?'

'No, just mine, but my friends have all had salad . . .'

Honey eyed the three empty plates. 'And ate them.'

'That's beside the point . . . And that coffee looks stewed.'

Honey glanced to where the coffee jug was gurgling away on its stand. She made a last effort to be polite. 'I can assure you the coffee is fresh. It empties every few minutes so we *have* to make it fresh.'

'OK, but what about these salads?'

'Leave it with me.'

Two of her regular waitresses had phoned in sick. Lindsey was doing her bit to help out, as was Dumpy Doris. Doris was built like a bulldozer with black hair and piercing black eyes. And she knew everybody. Honey could never figure out how come she knew so many people. She was hardly the Ivana Trump of Bath's social whirl. Sometimes such information came in useful — like now.

Doris's doughy face was twitching as though she'd just stuck her finger into an electric plug. She resembled a wonky automaton. Her eyes narrowed to prune stone roundness and focused on the greenfly grumbler. 'That's Edgar Seymour and his pals. Bleeding typical. They'll find something wrong with the main course as well, and the dessert, and the char and coffee. They do it in every restaurant they go in. I knows 'em. Common as muck. 'E thinks 'e's Lord Bleeding Muck, and she's all fur coat and no knickers!'

'And the greenfly?'

'Old Harry there grows roses. Say no more.'

A speckled ginger man appeared at her elbow, brimming with confidence.

'So what about those salads?'

Honey folded her arms over her chest. 'You planted the evidence, didn't you?'

The man frowned. 'How dare you!'

The day's events had left Honey in no mood for composure. 'Get out of my hotel you downmarket upstart!' She clenched her fists but controlled the urge to fetch him a good one on the nose.

The rest of his party looked horrified.

A woman wearing black polyester trousers and a black-and-red-flowered top got to her feet. Tossing her head high she sniffed like a dowager duchess. 'We've never been treated like this before!'

'Well, that isn't what I've heard!'

She felt Doris's heavy presence behind her, and then heard her voice. 'All right, Maureen? Still buying yer old man's underpants from jumble sales?'

The colour drained from Maureen's face. She was standing half out of her chair, as though not sure whether to sit back down or run for the exit.

'Ed,' she said softly, tugging at his sleeve.

Ed was obviously short-sighted or overly adventurous. He stood swaying slightly.

'And another thing . . .' He was pointing a sausage-like finger.

Doris elbowed forward. 'Sod off, Edgar.'

He looked at her, his jaw and slack lips moving in slow motion.

Doris braced her fists on her hips and edged closer. 'You heard me. Sod off.'

The couple accompanying them, cowed up until now, suddenly jerked to their feet.

'I'm sorry about this.' He sounded downright embarrassed. 'Here's what we owe. Or as near as dammit.'

Honey took the money. She kept a straight face. Inside she was bubbling with laughter.

Doris showed the foursome to the door and flung their coats out after them. 'And don't come back.'

The rest of the clientele seemed to have appreciated the floor show. Most clapped.

Honey concentrated on clearing the table. It occurred to her that Doris was taking her time. She craned her neck and sidestepped so she could see better. Doris was standing very still, watching something on the other side of the door.

'Your mother's here,' she said over her shoulder. 'And she's not alone.'

Doris stood aside as Gloria Cross's head poked through the door. 'I've got Mary Jane out here. She's ready to perform the cleansing on my shop. Margaret gets the willies about the place.'

Honey thought on her feet. 'I'd like to come as well.'

This had nothing to do with Mary Jane and her mumbo-jumbo. It was all about murder and the sinking of the *Titanic*.

She cast an experienced gaze over the restaurant. It was gone ten o'clock. Things were winding down.

'OK. Give me a minute. I need to speak to Chef.'

She peered cagily around the door. 'Smudger, I need to go out. You OK till I get back?'

'I'm not a total idiot, you know!' A meat cleaver came down at the same time, dividing a lamb chop from the main carcase.

Lindsey was waiting with her coat on. 'I'm coming with you. Grandma said I could.'

She looked defiant. Honey was in no mood to argue. In fact she was feeling quite excited.

'I'll get my coat. That place is bound to be chilly at this time of night — unless Mary Jane sets it alight.'

Dumpy Doris and Anna in reception were happy to clear up if she and Lindsey weren't back at the end of the shift.

Mary Jane, an ephemeral vision in pink chiffon, floated towards the door. 'I've got the car outside.'

The right foot that Honey had so firmly put forward now hovered above the rough sisal of the welcome mat. Her mother's hand swiftly cupped her elbow.

'Did I tell you about this interesting guy I met? He's a widower and owns a number of businesses nationwide. Now, don't get uppity if I tell you that he's looking for a wife of about your age . . .'

Her foot went into instant reflexive action. A death-defying adventure in Mary Jane's car was preferable to hearing her mother wax lyrical about a new suitor.

Pedestrians parted as she scuttled to the pale-pink coupe, opened the door to the front passenger seat and shot in.

Mary Jane was already seated. She looked at Honey with some surprise. 'My, but aren't you the keen one? You don't usually like to travel up front.'

'Can't wait,' she said, clipping on her seat belt.

If she thought she was getting away with it that easily, she was very much mistaken. Gloria leaned forward from the back seat next to Lindsey. 'He's got a chain of retirement homes all over England.'

'Great.' Honey just about managed not to puke. Retirement homes! Was her mother thinking of her own long-term future?

As they pulled away Honey wondered whether her will was up to date. A motorcycle swerved, barely avoiding the front wing. A taxi squealed to a stop. Cruising the rest of Great Pulteney Street was fine. In a build-up of traffic at the end, Mary Jane squeezed the Caddy between a hot dog trailer and a bus.

Honey drew herself up as they squeezed through with only a layer of paint to spare.

Mary Jane looked over her shoulder. 'Is someone shouting at me?'

'Eyes front, Mary Jane.'

'That man's smeared in mustard and onions,' Gloria observed.

A few more death-defying manoeuvres and they pulled in.

Honey pointed out the fact that they were parked on double yellows.

'It'll be OK,' said Mary Jane. 'Just think positive and nothing negative will happen. Let's move!'

She swooped on her bag of tricks and sprang from the car. The rest followed her like a clutch of baby ducks.

'Does she know where she's going?' Lindsey sounded as though all this was one big joke.

Gloria shrugged.

'Do you know where you're going?' Honey asked Mary Jane.

'Instinct,' said Mary Jane. 'I can find it purely by instinct.'

CHAPTER FIFTY-NINE

Mary Jane stopped by the right one. 'Looks real good,' she said, eyeing the shop window. 'More colour would be good. Pink especially.'

'It's not in vogue,' said Gloria.

Mary Jane stated the obvious. 'It is with me.'

Mary Jane began untying her bag. It was made of canvas, had wooden handles and a large drawstring holding it shut. It was pink, of course — with psychedelic swirls in pistachio green.

Gloria's gold bracelet, earrings and necklace jangled and flashed with brilliance as she wrestled with the ancient lock.

'Let me.' Lindsey took over. Placing her ear against the door, she fingered the key with a surgeon's light, dextrous skill.

The door opened.

Not for the first time, Honey Driver wondered about her daughter's hidden talents. Where had they come from?

Mary Jane swooped in first and stood twirling in the centre of the shop.

'Strong smell,' she said, sniffing the air like a true-blue bloodhound.

'Paint,' said Gloria. 'I had to freshen it up a bit — or rather I had a guy freshen it up for me. He came cheap.'

Honey smelled more than paint. It was faint, but definite. 'I smell perfume.'

'Mine. Chanel No.5. Marilyn Monroe wore it to bed. No nightwear. Just the perfume.' Trust her mother to wear only the best.

'The only perfume we want in here is from this little beauty,' said Mary Jane. She took a bunch of sagebrush from her bag and waved it. 'Anyone got a light?'

Gloria, Honey and Lindsey looked at each other. Nobody smoked.

'I know!' Gloria's clicking heels made for the back of the shop. 'We have a gas cooker. It isn't exactly space-age technology, but it fires up OK.'

She turned a dial and pressed the ignition. A circle of blue flame sprang into life around a cast-iron ring.

'Great!'

Mary Jane's eyes sparkled by gaslight as she dipped the sagebrush into the flame. The dry leaves sparkled red. The embers changed swiftly to smoke.

Mary Jane began pacing up and down.

Gloria frowned, caught the door between kitchen and shop and slammed it shut.

'I prefer you didn't go wafting that stuff around in the shop. The clothes will take up the smell. Smoked salmon is very nice, but nobody wants to go around smelling like it.'

It was agreed that the top landing was the best place to start. Mary Jane led the way, sagebrush held aloft.

The stairs were dimly lit by candle bulbs in wrought-iron sconces. The top landing was much darker. The ceiling receded into the rafters of an enormous mansard roof. Sloping walls and oak trusses created shadows where none should exist.

Being scared is for screaming teens in silly movies, Honey told herself. She carefully avoided looking at the more suspect shadows.

Mary Jane began doing her thing, waving the sagebrush around. At the same time she chanted something in a language no one could understand. Trance-like, she wandered around barely missing falling down the stairs.

Lindsey grabbed a trailing sleeve and hooked her back. 'Steady on.'

Mary Jane insisted on 'cleansing' each landing.

Honey reconnoitred behind her. There was little to see. The stars were out, and it was easy to see through the overhead skylight. A sheet of tarpaulin had obliterated the view on the night of the murder. It would have been much darker here when Wanda Carpenter died.

Honey felt an immediate sadness and a sense of foreboding. She wasn't prone to premonitions; she left that sort of stuff to Mary Jane. Still, she had to mention it.

'I've got butterflies.'

'Of course you do,' said Mary Jane in a matter-of-fact manner. 'This is an old building full of old ghosts.' To her, such stuff was as normal as breathing.

'And old doors,' Honey added. She noticed an area of the wall was inside an architrave, where a door once would have been. 'I think this place used to be part of the building next door. They were one big building, now divided into two.'

On a whim, gave the wall a push. It opened easily.

'Someone's been through here!' Honey was convinced of it.

Lindsey was a mine of historical information covering a wide spectrum of interest. Old buildings were no exception. 'When one building got separated into two, they didn't necessarily bother with the attic rooms. They didn't close up the door properly, just papered over it.'

'That's it,' said Honey. 'That's it!'

Everyone shushed her.

'Sorry.'

Her mind continued to tick. She remembered the candle burning in a shop window. The one next door to Marine Heritage! The empty one. Looking at the shops from the outside it was difficult to know where one began and the other ended. The candle had acted like a lighthouse on a dark night. The killer had lured Wanda in like a siren onto the rocks, then escaped through the building next door.

They stepped over the threshold. Honey fingered the wall and found a light switch. There was a clunk, then darkness.

'Drat. Fuse blown.'

'Keep your voice down.'

'I am keeping my voice down, Mother.'

'Shouldn't we all keep our voices down?' Lindsey added in a warning whisper.

'Seeing as we're trespassing the shop next door, yes is the answer to that,' Honey whispered back.

The one thing Honey could count on with her family was their capacity for declaring the obvious and going ahead with breaking the law. She vaguely remembered some ancestor her mother insisted had sailed with Blackbeard the Pirate and stocked up a huge treasure. He liked gold. Lots of gold. She could well believe it, if her mother was anything to go by.

The darkness smelled musty.

With only the feeble light of her mobile to guide her, Honey felt her way along a makeshift workbench. Her hand knocked against something metallic that wobbled. *A torch!*

'Stop!'

Mary Jane had been leading the descent. She stopped so quickly it was like hitting the proverbial brick wall. Everyone collided.

'Flash that light, Honey.'

Honey flashed.

Lindsey called the police.

CHAPTER SIXTY

Ashley Bridgewater was the happiest he'd been in his life. He'd done the deal and was driving back to his little terraced cottage in Northend. *No more Mr Nice Guy*, he thought to himself. Using his syrupy voice over the telephone was a thing of the past. He patted the small brown leather case sitting in the passenger seat. Faraway places with strange-sounding names beckoned him. Red sunsets, exotic maidens and plum-coloured cocktails would be *de rigueur* in the future he'd planned for himself.

Daydreaming is never a good idea when driving. Worse still when overtaking. The bus coming the other way, full of seniors on a trip from Germany, had no chance to swerve, and hit the car head on. There were two tour guides on board. Their first duty was to the party of tourists in their care.

'Just cuts and bruises,' said one to the other. They looked out of the big front windscreen to where the bus driver stood, running his hands through his hair.

The car was squashed, a single arm trailing out of the driver-side window.

CHAPTER SIXTY-ONE

Cameron Wallace poured himself a drink, downed it in one then poured himself another. He swiped at the sweat on his forehead. He hated sweating. Other people sweated and stunk. Never him. Until now. Where the bloody hell was she?

The sudden sound of the desk phone sent him striding across the floor. Just as he picked up the phone, his office door sprang open.

'You can't go in!'

The sound of his receptionist's voice was echoed on the telephone receiver.

'Yes, I can.'

The voice had authority. He recognised the policeman. He recognised the woman with him.

Without thinking, Cameron Wallace blurted out the uppermost question in his mind.

'You've found her?'

Doherty weighed him up. There were a few reasons for him disliking the man. Money was one. Secondly he didn't like the over-groomed facade. This was likely a man who spent more time looking at his reflection than looking at women.

'If you mean a Ms Lisette Fraser, then yes, we have found her.'

Wallace looked troubled. 'Tell me the rest. Is she dead?'

'Very. Do you know anything about it?'

Wallace shook his head. 'No! She didn't turn up for work this morning. It's unlike her.'

'Didn't exactly send out a search party,' said Honey.

Doherty shot her a warning look. She'd promised not to poke her oar in. Difficult that. She was really keen on oar poking.

She left Doherty to it. The open bar area to the side of the big glass mural looked interesting.

Doherty was in agreement with Honey. Wallace was nervous. His gut feeling told him the man had something to hide. What was he not saying?

'I don't believe you,' said Doherty. 'Now let's have the truth.'

Faced with Doherty's accusing look, Cameron sunk onto a corner of his glass and stainless-steel desk. He looked disconcerted, even frightened. 'Did he kill her?'

Honey paused, her head just about to peer behind the mural.

Doherty congratulated himself. 'Who would kill her?'

Wallace swiped nervous fingers over his face. 'Jan Stevensen. Tall, skinny chap . . .'

Doherty looked blank.

Honey remembered a tall skinny chap from the ghost walk — but he'd been named Kowalski. Were they the same person?

A good cop didn't betray his ignorance. 'Go on. What's he been up to?'

'Lisette went to see him on my behalf.'

'With regard to the film reels.'

'That's right. The reels are absolutely authentic, a unique record of the *Titanic*'s maiden voyage right up until the ship began to sink. The cameraman had perfected a sure-fire filming system he intended patenting and selling in America. Then the famous sinking. Somehow, I don't quite know how, the reels were passed to a passenger from first class — they had better access to the lifeboats. I think the cameraman must have been in steerage.'

'An immigrant,' said Doherty.

Honey stood holding on with both hands to the edge of the coloured glass, fascinated by the chain of events.

Wallace nodded. 'He wanted money for them. A lot of money.'

'Where did he get them from?'

Cameron Wallace shrugged broad shoulders beneath a pure cotton shirt. 'I've no idea. I didn't care. All I wanted was the film reels.' He looked down at the floor and cleared his throat, a picture of embarrassment. 'The *Titanic* is an obsession of mine, as are all things nautical, but the *Titanic* most of all.'

Honey took a step forward. 'That shop was yours, wasn't it? Marine Heritage.'

One look at his expression and she knew she'd hit the jackpot.

Doherty had been about to tell her to butt out, but clocked that look and remembered. He clicked his fingers. 'Got it! You came out of that shop on the day of the murder. Why the disguise?'

Wallace shrugged. 'It was my secret world away from all this.' He indicated the sumptuous office with a wave of his arms. 'There's no law against it.'

Doherty's jaw stiffened. 'Disguises make me suspicious. They're used by people with something to hide.'

'I did not kill Lisette!' Wallace thundered.

Doherty shook his head. He thought of the young woman lying with her neck broken. She might have fallen. She might have been pushed. He was obliged to tell Wallace this.

'Nothing's been confirmed. We await reports. If it wasn't an accident I'll have some questions to ask.'

Wallace had turned defiant. 'I had nothing to do with it. I told you, she went to meet Stevensen.'

'I heard you the first time. Where can I find him?'

Wallace shrugged. 'I don't know. He found us.'

CHAPTER SIXTY-TWO

At Doherty's insistence, they took the glass-enclosed panoramic lift back down. 'Helps me think,' he said in response to Honey's amused expression. 'Gives me a wider perspective.'

'Only of the city. Tell the truth. You're a big kid at heart. You like fairground rides too.'

'What was so interesting behind that picture?'

Honey recognised a parry when she heard one. OK. She'd oblige.

'It was like a shrine to the *Titanic*. That's what he collects. I couldn't even begin to imagine how much a collection like that is worth. There must be hundreds if not thousands of collectors who . . .'

The elevator doors opened. So did Honey's mouth. She gulped.

'That's it!' She bunny hopped out of the elevator. 'That's it! That's it!'

The glass doors huffed shut behind them. The sun was out. The alloy wheels on Doherty's sports car gleamed like small suns.

'Elucidate!' Doherty leaned on the black cloth roof, feeling pleased with himself for using such a grown-up word that early in the day.

Honey stood with her arms stiff at her side, eyes wide, face lit up with excitement.

'I was right. Everything goes back to the ghost walk. Mary Jane was told that it had been cancelled. The organisers hadn't expected anyone to turn up in that weather, but they did.'

Doherty couldn't resist a jibe. 'And let's face it, anyone who did turn out had to be nuts or there for a purpose . . .' Then it clicked. 'They were all there to bid for the big one.'

Honey nodded, almost too excited to breathe. 'Except for Mary Jane and yours truly . . .'

'Who are known to be nuts . . .'

'Thank you. And the Australian women who were just out to have a good time.'

'None of you were invited. It was a filthy night and the walk was invitation only. Simon Taylor, Wanda the would-be titled lady, Pamela, Hamilton George . . . and the fourth person whose face you didn't see. It's too much to ask for other names. A pound to a penny that the travel guides don't keep records of names, and in this case, no chance.'

Doherty fast-tracked. He got out his phone and issued orders that each of those interviewed were specifically asked about an internet auction. Honey phoned Lindsey and got her to look something up. She wasn't long coming back. Honey flipped the control to loudspeaker so Doherty could listen in.

'Yep! I searched through a few maritime collectors' forums online, and there were a few references to a closed auction, subject to a twenty-thousand-dollar registration fee. The dice were rolled and just six people were selected.'

Doherty's jaw dropped. 'Hells bells! How many people registered?'

'Thousands I should think.'

'Who instigated the auction?'

'Someone calling himself Sir Prancelot of the Cake.'

Doherty arched quizzical eyebrows. 'Hamilton George?'

Honey shook her head. 'Someone pudgier — and a total nerd. Simon Taylor.'

Doherty was miles away, his fingers drumming on the car's soft top. 'Simon Taylor was employed by Associated Security Shredding, which is owned by Cameron Wallace, an avid collector of anything to do with the *Titanic*.' He looked up at the office frontage, his gaze focusing on the penthouse suite. He slapped the soft top. 'That bastard!'

'Simon was also working for Hamilton George and, as his late departed wife explained, there was nothing her husband didn't know about computers.'

Doherty gunned the engine into life. 'Where to first?' he pondered. The decision was made for him. His phone rang.

Honey watched his expression change as he listened. 'Keep him there,' he said, and put the phone down. 'Stevensen's at the station,' he told Honey. 'He heard about Ms Fraser. He knows something about it.'

CHAPTER SIXTY-THREE

The moment she saw him, she recognised him. 'You said you were Polish!'

Jan grinned sheepishly. 'We thought it best to do so.'

'You're Swedish, like the other couple.' Doherty glanced down at his list.

'We are related. A number of us joined the online auction to retrieve what is rightfully ours. The reels belong to my great-great-grandfather, Lorne Stevensen. He was a passenger in steerage on the *Titanic*. Like most of those passengers, he could not get into a lifeboat, so he gave it to someone who could.'

'Wanda Carpenter's great-grandfather.'

He nodded. 'The reels rightly belong to my family.'

'Have you got them?' asked Doherty.

'No. Wanda's cousin offered the film to me. My family had raised a certain amount, but Bridgewater wanted more. Wanda had promised me that film. She thought it only right that it should be back with the family of the man who had taken the footage. She was a very fair person. I began following Bridgewater. He was casting his net for a buyer. I thought I would approach whoever was offering and see if they would consider donating the film to a museum. Cameron Wallace was one of the last two players. I asked him. He refused. I also went to see Mr George at his hotel but didn't get to see him. His wife died there. I knew Bridgewater would do a deal shortly and followed. I was sure he was meeting Wallace, but he wasn't. Wallace didn't turn up, but the girl did.' He shook his head vehemently.

Doherty screwed up his face as though he were sucking on something sour. 'Excuse me for being a moron, but how come you didn't declare that the reels were yours anyway? Why go through this charade, this online auction thing?'

Honey jumped in. 'Because if a legitimate claim turned up the reels would have instantly disappeared, whisked out of the country and sold on to an overseas interest. They'd never be seen again and become the stuff of legend. Did they exist or didn't they?'

Doherty nodded. 'I get you. I figure Wanda wouldn't let go but kept on bidding — unless she had something else in mind.' He glanced at Stevenson. 'Like handing them over to you.'

Honey frowned as she thought things through. Wanda hadn't seemed a bad sort; determined, yes, but not bad. Perhaps she'd had another motive. People who found buried treasure sold or bequeathed it to a museum. Perhaps she had had that in mind if she got her hands on the reels.

'She might have voiced it to someone she thought she could trust, then that someone, or someone they'd told, lured her into the empty shop. There's one other thing — those reels might be viewed as a national treasure. They'd have to have clearance before being allowed out of the country. It happens to paintings and stuff, so the same would apply to them.'

'That's correct,' said Stevenson, his long legs stretched out beneath the interview table. 'My family would have been willing to loan the film for, say, six months at a time. That would be only fair.'

Doherty shook his head. 'It appears Her Ladyship tried to play fair but got killed for it. She'd decided to swap hotels for her own safety and she was looking to find a safe haven for the reels once she'd got her hands on them. She must have known where they were by then.'

'The shop,' Honey exclaimed. 'She was told to come to the shop where they would be handed over in exchange for a very large sum of money.'

'An eye-watering amount,' said Doherty.

Stevensen listened carefully, his calm grey eyes fixed on them. 'She said she would get them for me. She said it was only right and was glad she'd come over to ensure they were returned to the rightful owner. We met up before she went on the ghost walk. That's when she made up her mind to do this. Her great-grandfather had survived the sinking, but other family members had not. She felt it a fitting memorial to their memory.'

Honey frowned. 'Her great-grandfather came back from America sometime in the twenties and bequeathed the film to his son, Bridgewater's grandfather. He died a short while ago, that's why she came over. She kept it pretty secret. Why was that?'

'She didn't want to draw attention. Rumours about why she was here could have caused problems.'

Honey recalled the list of possessions she'd inherited from her own husband when he died, some stuff she never knew he had. Wanda would have been surprised to learn of the reels. Perhaps she already had an inkling about them from something her great-grandfather said.

'But you didn't step forward when she was murdered.'

'I was booked to fly back the next day. My grandmother was dying. I had to be there. When I got back I found out what was happening. I thought it better to keep a low profile.'

'So why go to see Simon Taylor?' asked Doherty.

'Because it was him that connected with her online. They exchanged interests. That's what I think anyway. It all began with his site and from there it was downhill all the way. Simon was naive enough to share the information with Bridgewater. Simon was into ancestry. Before selling titles, it wasn't beyond him to do a little research on the person buying a title. He must have discovered Wanda's connection with Bridgewater. The reels were among Bridgewater's grandfather's possessions. Bridgewater. That snake!'

Doherty stopped her from dashing off to do serious injury to a guy she'd disliked on sight. The look on Doherty's face told her this was not a good idea. At this point they were interrupted by Doherty's phone.

'Our professional cold-caller is as flat as a pancake.' He gave her the rest of the details. 'He was on his way along the A4 from the direction of Bradford on Avon.'

The looks they exchanged said it all. Once Doherty had ordered backup, they hit the ground running.

CHAPTER SIXTY-FOUR

Hamilton George answered the door. He looked knocked off balance to see them. Behind him sat a clutch of baggage labelled with Virgin Atlantic tags. Convinced this was the man who had the original reels from that fateful night in April 1912, Doherty pushed his way in waving a warrant. 'Baggage first,' he said to the team tumbling in behind.

Honey's hands were itching to join in, but Doherty had reminded her that she was only here to observe. But, hey, a girl could push her luck just a little, couldn't she?

'Where's Pammy?'

She said it with a smile, as though she was on intimate terms.

Hamilton George smirked.

'She's out.' He turned to Doherty. 'Look, officer, you'll find nothing of interest to you in my luggage.'

'Might I ask where you're going, sir?'

'Home! Where the hell else? And I sure as hell won't be coming back. My wife died here, for Christ's sake!'

Honey couldn't resist. 'Is Pammy going with you?'

At first it seemed she'd thrown him, but he quickly regained his posture. 'What's it to you?'

'Caught you on the rebound, did she?'

His hands balled into fists. Doherty sent him a warning scowl, but Mr George was not easily intimidated.

'I'm going to make an official complaint,' he snarled. 'I'm a bereaved husband. Can you have some consideration? Is that too much to ask?'

'We've found Bridgewater.'

Doherty's sudden declaration made Honey turn her head. He wasn't saying Bridgewater was dead. He was hinting that Bridgewater had talked.

The pale, round face flexed for a minute like stretched rubber. 'I want a lawyer.'

'Famous last words,' Doherty muttered.

'Where's Pammy?' Honey asked again.

Hamilton George frowned at her. 'She's gone to sort out a few personal things.'

'Where are the film reels?'

He grinned. 'What does it matter? I bought them legitimately.'

Doherty nodded. 'OK. You're probably right, but I still want to ask you some questions about the death of Wanda Carpenter and Simon Taylor.'

George's laugh was as loud as a baying hyena. 'Not me, pal. Certainly not me! All I've done is outbid another *Titanic* enthusiast.'

'Have you got clearance to take the film out of the country?'

It was clear from his expression that he did not. His look turned from surly to nasty. 'The film's mine. I paid for it. I'll do with it as I please!'

Honey watched as Doherty's look turned cast iron.

Once he was read his rights, Hamilton George was bundled into the back seat of a squad car. He still maintained the same smug expression. Honey could tell that Doherty was uneasy.

'He's right about the reels. He paid for them.' His eyes stayed fixed on the car until it moved away.

'But is he the killer?'

Doherty shrugged. 'Your guess is as good as mine.'

CHAPTER SIXTY-FIVE

Twenty-four hours later Pamela Windsor made her entrance at Manvers Street.

George had called in some high-powered solicitors, and having made an official complaint about harassment was in the process of being released, checking his stuff out from the desk sergeant. He looked rather happy with himself, which was more than could be said for Pamela.

'Let's celebrate,' he said to her. 'Champagne and cream scones at the Pump Room.'

Doherty noted that she didn't look too happy at the prospect.

Once they'd left, he phoned Honey, telling her they'd found nothing in his luggage. If he did have the reels of film, they were well hidden.

'That figures. He wouldn't want to be detained any longer than necessary. Claims take a long time to sort out and the films would have been held in a treasury vault until it was all settled.'

'Now he's on his way to celebrate at the Pump Rooms. Champagne and cakes.'

'Fancy that. I'm already there with Mary Jane.'

'You've got that quivery tone to your voice. Did she drive you again?'

'We walked. By the way, guess who else is taking a mid-morning break. Cameron Wallace. I'm not sure, but I think he's following me.'

Doherty paused. 'I might see my way to joining the scene. Save me a cream slice.'

* * *

As he entered the Pump Room Hamilton George was sporting a smile wide enough to crack his face in half. Pamela looked a little out of sync with his good humour. She was well groomed, and her face *Vogue* perfect, but something was wrong.

George had the cheek to nod in Honey's direction.

Between talking with Lindsey, she watched the pair order and be given their champagne. George urged Pamela to take a sip. Pamela snatched the glass he offered and downed the lot in one.

George poured her another. 'Sure,' he drawled. 'Why not swallow it whole? The world's our oyster. You and me'll settle real well once the old girl's safely planted and we've finalised our little business in New York. Everything settled on that score? We're all going home; you, me and my late departed wife.'

Two tables away, Cameron Wallace was staring at the pair with a look in his eyes that Honey couldn't quite understand. He appeared to be burning a whole into the back of the American's head.

Doherty arrived just as Pamela Windsor sprang to her feet. The table went crashing over. Champagne, glass and cream cake spattered those sitting closest. Pamela ran towards the toilets bawling her head off.

'Pammy!'

Hamilton George staggered to his feet, apologising to the manager as two waitresses bent to clear up the mess.

Honey got to Pamela before she disappeared and did her best to comfort her.

Doherty was next, closely followed by a shell-shocked Hamilton George.

'What the hell is this, Pammy?'

Honey hugged the girl. 'There, there. Let it out. Nothing can be that bad.'

But it was.

Pink cheeked, Pamela Windsor seemed to wince and smile both at the same time. She gazed beseechingly at the man who had taken over her life. 'I'm sorry, Hamilton. It wasn't my fault. The funeral parlour made a mistake. They cremated the wrong coffin.'

Honey gasped.

Cameron Wallace had been loitering in the doorway. His face turned red with fury. 'You bastard! You stupid bastard!'

Doherty called for backup.

Hamilton George tried to make a run for it. Wallace stopped him with a rugby tackle a quarterback could only dream of. Both men went down. Chairs and tables went flying; people still clasping their cream buns got out of the way.

Wallace had his hands around George's throat, squeezing the life out of him.

A woman clutching a teapot looked on in alarm. 'Is someone going to stop them?'

Doherty stopped the Pump Room manager from attempting to do any such thing. 'Let them tire themselves out. The cavalry are on their way.'

The manager looked relieved.

Hamilton George broke away and recovered his smug expression. 'Couldn't raise the cash, old boy?'

Cameron tried to fly at him again but was restrained by two uniformed police.

'I outbid you, you bastard! That film was rightfully mine. I lay everything on the line for it. Everything!'

Hamilton George laughed. 'Well, it ain't yours now, *old boy*! Ashes. That's all they are now. The film and my wife are nothing but ashes.'

'I killed for that film!'

The room went silent.

Honey made a clicking sound at the side of her mouth. 'It figures. He owns the shops. He also owns a whole range of businesses, including photocopying. Potassium cyanide is used in some forms of printing. Wallace can lay his hands on anything he wants.'

'Including you?'

'Nah!' She shook her head. 'Too smooth for my liking.'

Doherty grinned. He looked scruffy. He spoke rough. But hell, he was all man. And who wanted to go to bed with a perfume bottle, anyway?

'Yeah. Some blokes are like that — obsessive about their appearance.' He shrugged his shoulders inside his leather coat. The leather was scuffed around the cuffs. Like Doherty it had seen better days, but both were built for comfort.

'So what swung it in favour of Cameron Wallace?'

'He had one great passion besides making money. *Titanic*.'

Honey's face saddened. 'It's a shame that people are still losing their lives over it. Enough were killed at the time.'

'Just ghosts now.'

'Just ghosts.'

CHAPTER SIXTY-SIX

Back at the Green River, Honey treated her mother and daughter to hot chocolate. Honey tipped a little brandy into hers. Lindsey made toast that she dipped into the frothy surface. Gloria added a large blob of clotted cream and two spoonfuls of sugar.

Lindsey looked thoughtful. Honey sensed that some kind of confession was brewing.

'Something up, kiddo?'

Lindsey took one of those deep, purposeful breaths that people take when they've come to a sudden decision. 'I've got something to tell you,' she said, looking at her mother.

Honey looked up at her from over the rim of her mug.

'You're not pregnant?'

'The angel Gabriel would have to break that news.'

Honey felt a great sense of relief. 'Point taken. Like the Virgin Mary,' she said to her own mother, just in case she hadn't cottoned on.

'I'm not senile, Hannah!'

Lindsey waited for a suitable pause. 'As I said, I've got a new boyfriend, but he's very shy. He wants to introduce himself but chickens out easily. And he doesn't play bagpipes or wear a kilt.'

Honey and Gloria stared in disbelief.

Lindsey looked away as though deciding whether to continue. With a big sigh she faced front again.

'Mum, I think he may have put the wind up you, though from what I can gather, you threw your leg over the pillion seat pretty fast.'

Honey swallowed. 'You could have told me that all he wanted to do was to introduce himself to me. I thought I was being abducted.'

Lindsey sat with her hands cupped around her phone. When she took on that old look, Honey braced herself for what was coming.

'I knew that a guy in a kilt would get your juices going. A guy in wellington boots would be a big no-no. Especially a pig farmer. Right?'

Gloria was not impressed. 'A pig farmer!'

'Ah!' said Honey. She had to admit she would have turned up her nose if she'd known her daughter's latest was a pig farmer. Who wouldn't? A brawny bloke with a few yards of tartan swinging round his thighs was a different matter. Wellington boots around the shins didn't do much for her.

Her daughter shrugged and retreated behind her phone, leaving her mother feeling strangely adrift. OK, Lindsey did most of the things other teenagers did, but she came with extras.

After seeing her mother into a taxi, Honey retreated into her room, slipped off her shoes and lay down on the bed. Her big toe wiggled at her through a hole in her tights. Like a friendly face it seemed to smile at her.

Lindsey knocked and came in bearing a second mug of hot chocolate.

'Am I dim or what?' Honey wiggled her toe. 'Fancy thinking your boyfriend was abducting me.'

'Can we change the subject, Mum?'

'Sure?'

'I get the impression you had it in for the wicked cousin.'

Honey ground her teeth. 'Obnoxious.'

'You're biased.'

'Of course I am. I *wanted* Bridgewater to be the murderer. But he wasn't.'

'So what about the guy in the black patent shoes and evening cape?'

Honey felt her jaw go slack. So what about the guy in the black patent shoes and evening cape? 'I think it was Bridgewater keeping an eye on things.'

'Mary Jane will be disappointed. She was sure you'd seen a ghost.'

Honey shrugged. She couldn't admit to the truth now, could she? Or was it the truth? She wasn't sure herself. The eyes played tricks, especially on dark and stormy nights.

There was still one query she had. Those patent shoes had been stone dry. Perhaps because he was walking six inches above the ground?

'Nah!' she said to herself later on as she lay back in bed. 'Of course he wasn't.'

THE END

ALSO BY JEAN G. GOODHIND

HONEY DRIVER MYSTERY SERIES
Book 1: MURDER, BED & BREAKFAST
Book 2: MENU FOR MURDER
Book 3: WALKING WITH MURDER

Thank you for reading this book.

If you enjoyed it please leave feedback on Amazon or Goodreads, and if there is anything we missed or you have a question about, then please get in touch. We appreciate you choosing our book.

Founded in 2014 in Shoreditch, London, we at Joffe Books pride ourselves on our history of innovative publishing. We were thrilled to be shortlisted for Independent Publisher of the Year at the British Book Awards.

www.joffebooks.com

We're very grateful to eagle-eyed readers who take the time to contact us. Please send any errors you find to corrections@joffebooks.com. We'll get them fixed ASAP.

Printed in Great Britain
by Amazon

11354855R00166